PAYBACK

Gary Hazlewood

Published by Acorn Independent Press Ltd, 2015.

ISBN 978-1-911079-53-8

Acorn Independent Press

PROLOGUE

The blue van snaked rapidly along the dark, twisting tarmac, its red lights blinking furiously at every bend. The early morning ice had retreated to the hedge-line, leaving a muddy, brown sludge at the edges of the road. At every turn, the van's wheels splashed through the sludge, coating the wheel arches in even more dirt. The driver fought tirelessly with the steering wheel, keeping the van moving swiftly forward on the winding road.

Up ahead, the trees bordering the country road arched together, forming a tunnel of autumnal foliage. As the van rounded a sharp bend, the driver steered into the tunnel on the wrong side of the road. The blinking red lights disappeared into the darkness.

Inside the back of the van, Lewis' eyelids slowly opened as he stirred from his state of unconsciousness. He could make out an unknown man staring down at him. Lewis felt groggy; his eyes slowly adapted to the darkness and refocused on the inside of the van. The shape of the seated man gradually adjusted, and then the images from the last hour swamped his mind.

Lewis recalled the gunfight in the kitchen, wincing as he did from a sharp, burning pain in his shoulder – a savage reminder of the wound he'd sustained. The faces of the two men in that kitchen came flooding back to him, but neither of them was that of the man he wanted. The image of a bright orange flame erupting from the muzzle of the shotgun was the last thing Lewis remembered seeing. He now wondered how he had ended up in the back of a van, and who the mystery figure sat over him was.

The van swerved violently as the driver negotiated a sweeping left-hand bend. As Lewis slid across the van floor, reaching out a hand to steady himself, the seated figure launched a foot into his ribcage. Lewis instinctively brought his arm back for protection. The figure stamped down hard on Lewis' upper arm, causing a painful deadening of the limb. He tried to protect his arm with his free hand, but the awkward positioning of his body and the pain from his shoulder prevented him from doing so. He gritted his teeth and hoped the discomfort would soon be over.

Lewis tried concentrating on the images flooding his mind; he tried desperately to make sense of them.

As the smoke from the explosion cleared, Lewis checked himself for injuries then looked around at his team. The third man in the patrol indicated that the lead scout was dead and his best friend, Tony Jackson, also looked in a bad way – a piece of glass about the size of a matchbox had lodged itself just above his scapula. His face was already losing colour and the front of his combat jacket was soaked in blood.

Lewis stared blankly at the roof of the van; his body swayed as the driver negotiated the twisting road.

Jackson's eyes flickered rapidly as he struggled to draw breath. "Adam, Adam," he wheezed. "I don't feel too good . . ."

Lewis quickly removed another dressing from his tactical vest. He noted the amount of blood on his hands. "Hang in there, mate, I've nearly stopped the bleeding."

Lewis unwrapped the dressing.

Jackson's vision dimmed so he tried turning his head towards the sound of Lewis' voice. "Adam . . ."

"Save your breath, Tony, I almost have it."

"Adam, don't give up on Hannah . . ."

Lewis looked at his best friend. "I won't, mate, now stop talking, please."

He fumbled inside a pouch and retrieved a third dressing.

A single shot rang out and startled Lewis.

The van bumped across a series of potholes, shaking Lewis from the realisation that his best friend had been killed. But Tony had mentioned Hannah – what had happened to his daughter? Lewis concentrated on the images until he found himself standing in an office.

The army chaplain looked Lewis straight in the eyes. "I'm very sorry, Adam, but your daughter . . ."

Lewis closed his eyes. On opening them, he was now stood in a cemetery.

Hesitantly, Lewis approached the headstone.

He crouched down beside it and traced the epitaph with his fingers. He mouthed the words silently to himself.

"She will be deeply missed by all the people whose lives she touched. Sleep soundly my little angel, now you have found your peace eternal."

Lewis could barely control his emotions. He rose to his feet and drew in a huge breath before screaming towards the heavens.

He yelled until he felt a burning pain under his ribcage; a rancorous sound reverberated around the huge, empty cemetery, silencing the nesting birds.

Lewis looked down to read the wording again. He dropped to his knees and raised his hands to his face, sobbing uncontrollably. A garbled apology could just be heard above his crying. His shoulders heaved as his crying continued.

Overhead, the skies darkened. The first droplets of rain splattered against the shiny, marble surface of Hannah Lewis' headstone.

The sides of Lewis' mouth knotted as he fought the urge to cry. He breathed rapidly as he focused on other images. Lewis had struggled hard putting his daughter's death to rest, but with the pain and stress he was now suffering, these memories were being dragged kicking and screaming from the recesses of his mind. Lewis had to focus all his physical and emotional strength on his current situation, and right now, that meant he needed to know how he had ended up in the back of this van. The images of his daughter faded.

As the van hurtled erratically down the country lane, Lewis once again trawled his memories of his recent past trying to piece together some semblance of an explanation for his situation.

Lewis put the barrel of his pistol up against the bulge in the rear of the driver's seat and pulled the trigger three times. The muzzle flashes illuminated the interior of the car. The driver screamed out in pain. Lewis then poked the pistol over the top of the seat and fired a further three shots; blood splattered across the dashboard. The driver twisted in his seat as he fought, pointlessly, with death. Lewis pulled himself from the recess and then opened the rear passenger door. Climbing out of the car, he walked around to the driver's door. He looked in through the window and saw no movement. He fired one shot that partly shattered the window, and then he cleared the rest of the glass until he had a clear view of the driver. The figure was still. Lewis fired the remaining rounds into the motionless shape, to make the killing look as violent as any other IRA informant's execution.

More memories were returning. Lewis clung to the image of a tall, grey-haired MI5 agent, Colin Fullerton. He raced through his thoughts, trying to piece together his last few days.

Lewis walked to the passenger side of the car, stopped and rested his elbows on the blue roof. He stared straight at Fullerton.

Lewis clenched his fists and banged them down hard on the roof of the Mondeo.

"Don't take the piss out of me!" he spat. "You set me up and now I'm here to collect in person."

"Wait a minute, what if I can give you something more than a few pieces of paper saying where Boyle may or may not be?" Fullerton offered.

"What can you offer me? Because of you and your pals, I've also lost my job. Now you tell me how you're going to get me my fucking information."

Fullerton leaned across the roof of the Mondeo and said, "What if I can give you something more? What if I can give you the man who killed your daughter?"

Lewis tensed his body, swallowing hard, trying to dislodge an invisible lump stuck in his throat.

"What if I can give you Sean Boyle in person?"

Lewis remembered the name, Sean Boyle, the man responsible for the deaths of his daughter and best friend. The man he had tried to kill on a covert operation, which cost him his job with the SAS.

"Here, I've circled the place."

Lewis took the atlas; he turned on the interior light and looked for a circle. He found one about two inches to the right of Lough Allen.

"Altnakereen?"

"Yes, there's an isolated farmhouse three miles from the village . . ."

One more image formed in Lewis' mind; he was finally making sense of his situation.

Lewis reached into his jacket pocket for his mobile phone.

"Hello? Jesus, Adam, it's not even half-past seven. Okay, I'll call them off. You better stay out of sight for half an hour whilst they pack up. Call me when you're done."

Fullerton had set him up.

ONE

Colin Fullerton checked his watch: 12:26p.m.

The MI5 section chief had just finished a meeting with his small department of agents. Earlier that morning, Fullerton had received a call from London, explaining that his department was finally being closed down. The majority of what was once Ebrington Barracks had, over a drawn-out period of time, been handed back to Derry City Council. Although Fullerton's compound had remained in a secure location, it was now due to be handed back.

Fullerton, a 53-year-old agent, was finally coming back into the fold. He had spent over 20 years working in Northern Ireland, mainly because he was very good at what he does, but also because of a number of unproven allegations about the way he went about his job. His bosses had previously decided this was the best place for him, but now, after his success at foiling a renegade group of terrorists' plots to set up a drug-dealing business and murder ex-servicemen, they had to rethink their position. Fullerton had been offered a new job back in London.

Fullerton left his desk and picked up his coat, which was hanging on a vintage coat stand beside his office door. He reached into a pocket and removed a packet of cigars. Grabbing a cigar and lighter, he left his office and headed for the small shelter at the rear of the building. Behind a closed door, he heard a telephone ringing.

Across the River Foyle, the afternoon sun reflected in the many shop and office windows. Fullerton drew heavily on his cigar and puffed out a thick cloud of smoke. The overhead canopy offered little shelter from the cold. He regretted not putting his coat on.

Fullerton removed a small key from his trouser pocket and stared at it. It had been over four hours since Lewis had called, asking for the fictitious agents to be removed from the over watch positions at the farmhouse in Altnakereen. Although this worried him a little, as he was uncertain as to the ex-soldier's fate, he thought that no news could only mean that Lewis had been dealt with and that he wouldn't be hearing any more from him.

Now, Fullerton had his future to think about. Although he wasn't a family man, he still had plans to retire early, and now that he was coming back home, planning for his retirement would be a lot easier.

Fullerton's mobile phone started ringing.

TWO

". . . And in five weeks, this is what we know of Luay Abass, his movements, and his associates?" asked James Strong.

"That's right, James. He lives above an electronics shop with his family and so far this week, as usual, he has only left the shop four times; three times to attend his computer games programing course and the other to go to prayers. Unfortunately, today, I was blocked in by a delivery van and couldn't get away to follow him. He hasn't given us much to go on," replied Hassan Falah.

James Strong headed a section of agents responsible for recruiting and monitoring people deemed suitable for gathering information on radical Muslim groups. He had been working in this department since November 2001, and during his time, had thwarted dozens of threats to the nation's security. Not only was he an accomplished field agent, fluent in Arabic and French, but he was a happily married family man with two young daughters. And at 45, he still prided himself on his athleticism. Only the previous year, he had completed the New York Marathon during a family holiday.

"We have been watching four men for five weeks and Abass still stands out as the likeliest candidate, doesn't he?" Strong picked up the latest pictures, walked around his desk, and stood in front of a board with a number of photos with name tags underneath. He looked at Falah. "Apart from the limited amount of photos, we do have a half decent pattern of life, don't we?"

Hassan Falah had worked in Strong's section for three years. He was 28 years old, 5' 6" with a slim build and short, well-groomed, jet-black hair. Falah had been born in London of Iraqi parents; his family had fled Iraq in 1982 after his father had deserted the Iraqi National Army during the Iran-Iraq War. He never knew the full reasons for his family fleeing Iraq, but he knew it had something to do with what his father had seen during his service, as the old man still had nightmares nearly 30 years on. Falah had started his service with MI5 in an electronic surveillance department before transferring to Strong's team.

"Since he came to our attention after his fight with one of Mustafa al Dulhaimi's bodyguards outside the mosque in Whitechapel, all that we know is on those two sheets of paper. He's 23. He lives at home with his parents and two sisters above the family's electrical goods shop in Ealing, which is 14 plus miles from where we want to insert him, in Whitechapel. His family moved down from Manchester a year ago, so are still relatively new to their community. These two factors should help give him some anonymity. They visit the family mosque in Acton every Friday, and leave by car from the alleyway at the rear of the shop.

"Abass has been active within a Muslim group with the main aim of disrupting the activities of the more radical factions, especially the ones demonstrating at parades with British troops in attendance. He has been arrested and cautioned, once, for his involvement in one such confrontation in Watford. We think he's possibly looking to his father as a role model; Mushtaq Abass once had a similar involvement with a group of protestors in Saudi Arabia. His father spent four years as a political prisoner, back in the early seventies." Falah paused momentarily as he gave thought to his own father. "Resulting in Amnesty International campaigning for his release and successfully relocating him and his wife to Manchester. Although Abass is an active member, he doesn't hold any position of authority, which helps keeping him off any watch lists.

Falah turned the sheet of paper over. "We have the family's vehicles' details and have done the usual background checks; nothing untoward was flagged up. The rest you have in my report," answered Falah.

Strong sifted through the photographs before taking and fastening the clearest facial shot to the board.

"It does show that he has potential and we are, once again, under pressure with this task. I think we need to move in now and make contact with Abass. Despite the lack of intelligence on the four men we have earmarked, to me, he still seems to be the most likely candidate. The only real opportunity to approach him is during his computer course."

Falah looked edgy. "Do you not think we are rushing this, James?"

"I don't think we can leave it much longer. The anonymous caller said al Dulhaimi was plotting something for December," said Strong, glancing up at the digital clock above the main operations board. Its bright green digits displayed the time as 11:08, with November 6 glowing defiantly beneath the numbers as a stark reminder of the timescale pressure his section were working strenuously under. "So, we potentially have less than a month to get someone into his prayer group and find out what is happening."

Falah nodded in agreement.

"Well, if you'll excuse me, Hassan, I have a call to make."

Falah turned to leave the office, retrieving a folder from Strong's desk as he left.

Strong looked deep into the eyes of Abass' photograph, cupping a finger and thumb around his mouth. He desperately needed this to work, as hundreds, possibly thousands of innocent lives depended on it.

THREE

Colin Fullerton stared at his phone, vibrating in his hand. The screen displayed the message "caller unknown". He took his cigar from his lips and dropped it on the ground before crushing it beneath the heel of his Oxford brogue and extinguishing the glowing red tip. His eyes narrowed and his brow furrowed as he tried to project an image of the caller onto his phone's screen.

Fullerton was reluctant to accept the call, as it was his own personal mobile, not the one supplied by his department. The list of people that had this number was very short, six, maybe seven at a push, as his family was limited to his parents and a sister, who lived in South Africa. And the number in his circle of friends was only slightly bigger.

The mobile still vibrated.

"Shit!" Fullerton muttered. It can't be Lewis, he thought.

No way, Billy Boyle and his men should have finished him off. Fullerton was certain that the tip-off he had given Billy would have been enough to convince him to go to Altnakereen and take on Lewis, finally ridding him of the "pain in the arse" Lewis was fast becoming.

Fullerton's thumb hovered over the call accept symbol; his mind raced. Lewis had managed to escape from captivity in the back of a van once before – maybe he had gotten away again. Fullerton worked through his thoughts: no, not this time, his men were unarmed. Surely, Billy and his men would have guns, pistols at the very least, or maybe an Uzi or AK-47. They wouldn't be unarmed. Lewis would not have stood a chance.

Fullerton had to make a decision soon, as the vibrating would stop and the call would be lost. He swiped the red phone symbol and cut off the caller; whoever it was would have to leave a message now.

He waited and watched the silent mobile, wondering if someone was now speaking to the answer machine. The seconds ticked by. Suddenly, the chill didn't bother Fullerton, as he was too busy focusing his full attention on the slim, rectangular object in his right hand.

It vibrated. The screen displayed a red telephone symbol for missed call and a small picture of an envelope. Fullerton had an answerphone message.

He tentatively went through the series of actions to retrieve the message then raised the handset to his ear, and waited for the message to play out.

"*Hi Colin, its James, James Strong. I thought I'd give you a courtesy call to speak to you about joining the team. I guess you're busy, no problem. If you can call me back at your earliest convenience. My number is 078 . . .*"

Fullerton exhaled. He had not realised that he had been holding his breath whilst listening to the message. He breathed a huge sigh of relief as he pocketed the mobile phone.

Once again, he felt the cold wrapping itself around his large frame. He shivered involuntary. It was time that he headed back inside.

FOUR

The blue van carrying Adam Lewis slid to a halt on the damp ground. Billy Boyle switched off the engine and climbed down from the driver's seat.

"Ginty, grab that bastard and follow me."

Ginty prodded Lewis with the end of the shotgun. "On ye feet and out the back, and no funny business."

Lewis used his one good arm to push himself up onto his knees and then to his feet. His right shoulder still throbbed with a sharp, burning pain. He felt blood slowly running over the back of his hand and dripping from his fingers. His head was spinning from blood loss, but he did feel like the wound was congealing and the flow was stemming. Perhaps his captors would dress the wound.

"Get moving!" Ginty spat out the words as he jabbed Lewis sharply in the ribs with both barrels of the shotgun.

Lewis squinted his eyes to block the glare from the sunlight, as he climbed down from the gloom of the rear of the van. He refocused on his surroundings and saw one of his captors, who was now holding Lewis' pistol, standing by the door of a rundown barn. Turning his head slowly, all he could see were fields, bordered with hedges and stone walls. Lewis was in the middle of nowhere with two very pissed-off terrorists.

I've had better days, he thought.

Boyle had been driving around the Irish countryside for over two hours, looking for the perfect place to stop. He wanted somewhere sheltered and out of the way. Boyle had seen the barn as they had coasted over the crest of a hill; finding the track that led to it was the problem. He had driven slowly alongside the treeline that separated the woods. The barn was partly hidden from the road. After driving progressively slower along the same stretch of road, for a third time, Boyle finally spotted the cluster of fallen branches, hiding the track that led to this isolated place. The woods were about half a mile from the sparsely surrounded barn, offering up good cover from the road and shelter for the van.

Boyle pointed the pistol at Lewis. The temptation to pull the trigger was overwhelming, but he needed to know who this man was, what he was doing at the farmhouse, and what he knew about his plans. But more importantly, who was responsible for his brother Sean's death.

Before the questioning could really begin, Boyle needed to stock up and prepare the barn for his needs.

"Hurry up and get in here," said Boyle. As Lewis passed by him, entering the barn, Boyle cracked him on the back of the head with the pistol butt. Lewis stumbled forward.

"Get over there, right to the back, and sit the fuck down," ordered Boyle.

Lewis dragged his feet through the dirt towards the rear of the barn, as he had been told to. He turned and slumped down at the base of one of the four support posts that held the roof in place. The posts were positioned, one in each corner. In one corner, towards the barn door, the roof beams had rotted away, leaving a gaping hole, through which Lewis could see the afternoon sky. The whole place was no bigger than an average-sized garage, and from the smell and the mess across the floor, Lewis guessed that the barn had once been used to store animal feed.

Once Lewis was seated, Boyle handed Ginty a length of cord. "Here, tie his hands behind his back while I cover you."

Ginty took the cord and crossed over to Lewis. He grabbed his hands and pulled them around behind his back. Lewis tried offering resistance at first, but Ginty just kneed him hard in the back. He wrapped the cord around one wrist and then the other, finishing off by wrapping it three times around both wrists and then tying it off with a series of knots. Once finished, he slapped Lewis hard on the shoulder, pushing him off balance. Lewis fell sideways onto the dirty floor. Ginty walked back to Boyle.

Boyle pulled Ginty closer so he could quietly give him his instructions. "Take the van and drive back to the junction we turned around at. I saw a sign pointing to a town about 10 miles away, I think." Boyle paused and took out his wallet. "Take this and see if you can find a shop. I need a large knife, a hammer, something stronger to tie this fucker's hands with, also a chain and padlocks, in fact, two chains and some heavy-duty bin-bags." Boyle looked at Ginty and then at Lewis, shuffling in the dirt. "I tell you what, see if you can get a camping stove or firelighters, something to make a fire with and also, look for somewhere for us to stay."

Ginty rolled his eyes and went over the shopping list in his head. He had a fair idea what Boyle had wanted the items for, and was glad he wasn't in Lewis' shoes right now.

"When you come back, hide the van in the woods and walk up to here. Shout when you get close, I don't want to shoot you by mistake," laughed Boyle.

Ginty took the keys from Boyle then set off back to the van. He climbed in, switched on the engine, spun it around, and headed for the road beyond the woods.

"Right then, it's just you and me now. Let's have a fucking chat!" said Boyle, closing the barn door and throwing the inside of the decrepit structure into shadows. Boyle stepped out of the malevolent darkness surrounding the door and, taking short steps, he walked slowly towards Lewis.

FIVE

The clock in Colin Fullerton's office showed it was half-past three.

Fullerton closed the filing cabinet drawer and exhaled a sigh of relief; all the files going to Holywood, County Down were in order. The job hadn't taken as long as he first thought. Then again, his team worked very efficiently, which made his life easier.

Earlier that afternoon, Fullerton had received a call from HQ Northern Ireland, explaining that, under military supervision, all his documentation and computer wares would be collected in five days and taken to Palace Barracks, Holywood. The only things to be left behind were the office furnishings. If Fullerton wanted to retrieve anything then now was the time.

Fullerton opened a small cabinet, situated behind his desk, and removed a brandy decanter and two glasses, which he carefully placed into a cardboard box on top of his desk. He nestled them in snuggly between the few personal possessions he was taking from his office. After taking down a single picture and putting this into the box, he picked up the telephone handset and dialled a number. The call was answered on the second ring.

"Hi James, it's Colin, I'm returning your call."

After listening to what Strong had to say about him not having to rush across the water to join his team, as they were currently in the middle of an operation, Fullerton struggled to think of how he was going to fill his time.

He reached back into the box and removed the decanter and one glass. He poured himself a large measure of brandy and sat back in his chair. Once again, he removed the red-capped key from a pocket and examined it once more. I could always try to find out where this key fits, he thought, swallowing a large mouthful.

No, Fullerton decided on a better idea.

He opened the bottom drawer of his desk, reached inside and removed a metal strong box that was about the same size as a telephone directory. The key for the box was attached to a bunch of keys in his coat pocket; he left his desk to retrieve the keys. Finding the one he needed, he unlocked the box and opened the lid. He removed two objects from the box, carefully placing them down in front of him. Fullerton re-secured the box then placed it inside the large cardboard box, along with his other effects. He lifted the brandy glass and swallowed the last mouthful, savouring both the taste and the warmth.

Fullerton picked up one of the objects from his desk. Carefully turning it around in his right hand, he familiarised himself with its weight and feel. The Browning Hi-Power pistol felt comfortable in his grip. Most of the paint around the rear sight had worn away, exposing polished metal. Most of the chequered pattern on the hard plastic grips had disappeared also. The pistol was over 30 years old; a relic removed from a house search on information received by Fullerton, and agreed by an army operations officer. The weapon ended up with Fullerton as payment for a gambling debt from a desperate Royal Engineers officer. He'd kept the pistol for the occasions he'd needed more than just his service-issued Sig Sauer P226.

Fullerton retrieved the spare magazine from his desk and stood up. He slipped the pistol into his waistband and dropped the magazine into his coat pocket, as he collected it from the stand on leaving his office.

Fullerton rapped gently on Nicholl's office door before letting himself in. "Rob, I'm leaving you in charge for a couple of days. I have something I need to do before we shut up shop completely. Could you oversee the rest of the handover for me? I'll be back before Monday, but if you need me, I'll have both phones with me."

"Okay Colin, is that all you want me to do? Can I help with anything else?" asked Nicholl.

"No thanks, Rob," Fullerton replied. "Oh, and I'll be taking one of the unmarked cars as well. See you on Monday."

Fullerton closed the door behind him and, at a brisk pace, headed for the staircase and the exit, stopping only to collect a set of car keys. He wanted to get away immediately, as he had a long drive to get to Altnakereen.

SIX

Billy Boyle stood over Lewis, staring down at him with hate-filled eyes. He launched a heavy kick into Lewis' exposed midriff, then a second, and finally, a powerful third. Lewis curled into the foetal position, trying to shield himself from the savage blows. Boyle stopped for a second, but then swiftly stamped down hard on Lewis' head. Blood spilled down to his cheek from the small tear. Lewis felt a stinging pain from the fractured bone.

Next, Boyle kicked Lewis hard in the face; his toecap connected with the bridge of Lewis' nose. The force broke the appendage instantly, sending blood and mucus in all directions. Lewis' head jerked violently with the force of the kick. He screwed his eyes up as a dull, throbbing pain left him seeing white. As his eyes refocused, a dancing myriad of red blotches obscured his vision. All he could do was try to bury his face in the dirt, as he drew his knees tighter to his chest in a feeble attempt at defending himself.

Boyle's next attack was four swift, savage heel stamps to Lewis' exposed shoulder wound; this time, Lewis relented, screaming like a wounded animal. His voice echoed around the cramped confines of the derelict barn. Boyle allowed the faintest smile of satisfaction cross his thin lips. Lewis blinked hard and rapidly, concentrating every effort on trying to focus his mind; he needed to take himself away from the brutality of his attacker and to a place of distraction.

Lewis was stood outside a Portakabin; the night air was warm and dry. A small sandstorm had just passed. Lewis found himself in the company of three men: Mo Hurley, a short, well-built man with extraordinarily large hands; Mick Bradshaw, a fit, balding man in his early 50s; and Terry Swain, a tall, athletic man with a broad . . .

Lewis paused briefly; what was that accent? Never mind. He explored the images more.

Hurley was re-telling a tale about foiling an Iraqi ambush and tying the suspects up whilst they waited for the security forces to turn up. Like Lewis, Bradshaw and Hurley had been working in Iraq since the

2003 ceasefire. Bradshaw turned to Lewis and asked if he remembered when he took the fridge padlock and . . .

The dull cracking sound was Lewis' left wrist snapping, the pain growing more and more unbearable with each strike. He gritted his teeth and tried to focus on the group of men he had previously been sharing a drink with. The images blurred and danced around inside his head as the pain intensified. Lewis let out a scream from deep within the pit of his stomach. Dry dust swirls rose and fell as he drew in deep breaths, exhaling heavily. Then he realised Boyle had ceased his assault.

Lewis turned his head slowly, trying to catch a glimpse of his attacker; dirt caked one side of his face. He looked like a dirty, bloodied, grimacing harlequin. Boyle was stood, statuesque, less than three feet away, with one arm extended, pointing accusingly at Lewis. A dark object protruded from Boyle's hand; the very same pistol Fullerton had given him in the car park at New Buildings. Lewis wished to be back in the car park once more, instead of peering up at a man pointing a Glock at him. Unlike most pistols, the Glock didn't have a safety catch. This concerned Lewis because Boyle's finger was on the trigger.

Boyle stared down at Lewis; the pistol wavered slightly in his tight grip, as he focused on keeping the white dot on the front blade sight between the two white dots on the rear sight. Not that it mattered much, from the distance he was standing from Lewis.

Boyle felt the first bead of sweat roll down his cheek; his mouth was suddenly parched. He licked his lips as if savouring the moment he was now in. Lewis would be the first man to be killed by Boyle's own hands. Sure, he'd maimed before. Boyle and his brother had had a very violent reputation to live up to – it came with the territory – but Sean was the killer.

As the seconds ticked by and a blinding red mist clouded his thoughts. Both Boyle's underlying rage with this nobody and his need to satisfy his bloodlust for his brother's death were too strong to ignore. His index finger twitched on the trigger as animalistic urges for revenge overwhelmed all thoughts of questioning Lewis. Boyle's logic and calm disappeared in a swirling maelstrom of hatred.

Boyle prepared himself for the pistol's recoil by bending his arm slightly, and then he slowly closed his left eye. He wanted to be sure with his aim.

Three loud retorts echoed around the barn.

SEVEN

Finally, James Strong's day was winding down. He just needed to shut his computer down and tidy away a couple of files. He returned his coffee cup to a small kitchenette opposite the toilets.

Strong pushed open the door, triggering a sensor, instantly switching the lights on. He stood in front of the nearest urinal and unzipped his fly. The automatic flusher activated as he finished. He turned towards the sink. After placing his hands under the tap, the water cascaded through his fingers. He looked up at his reflection and stared blankly into the mirror.

Outside the car, a strong wind penetrated the exposed gaps between the surrounding trees, the branches swayed like waving arms, causing the leaves to rustle loudly. Strong stared out into the darkness, his eyes straining to penetrate through the gloom. He could just make out the structure of a fence in front of the trees and behind it, shadows danced between the dark trunks. Through his windscreen, in the distance, Strong watched the glow of a single light approaching, and as it drew closer, the light separated into two headlights. The lights dipped from view for a few seconds then reappeared again. The oncoming car pulled into the lay-by behind Strong's car; the driver parked his car then walked towards him.

Strong gripped his pistol as the figure approached his car. The passenger door opened, switching on the interior light, bathing the two men in a soft yellow hue.

"Where the fucking hell have you been? You're nearly 20 minutes late! Get in!" Strong blurted out through clenched teeth.

Strong continued to stare blankly at his reflection. He recalled the short journey with the doomed man; the fake debrief and stilted conversations he had with his passenger. All this happened as the SAS assassin, left behind in the lay-by, climbed into the car, waiting for his return.

Logan climbed out of Strong's car and walked back to his own. Strong observed the scene through his rear-view mirror. Logan pulled his car door shut and then, literally seconds later, the interior was illuminated with a number of flashes, followed by a figure emerging from the rear of the car. The figure stood at the driver's window and fired a pistol continuously at Logan. Before returning to Strong's car, the figure reached in and retrieved something from the rear of Logan's vehicle. The SAS man climbed into Strong's passenger seat, and slammed the door shut.

Strong splashed water onto his face, washing away the memories from his past. He dried himself and then left the toilets. The lights extinguished, casting the room back into darkness.

During his drive home, Strong relived the execution of Gerard Logan another three times. Each time, the gunshots appeared to grow louder. By the time he parked up in his driveway, he noticed the car stereo was almost at maximum volume. He twisted the headlight control off, switched off the stereo, and then turned off the ignition. He sat in darkness for a moment gazing into his interior mirror and then he was bathed in light. Without realising Strong had opened his door. He reached across to the passenger seat and grabbed his briefcase before getting out of the car.

Strong paused briefly at his front door. He could recall the name of the murdered Irishman and the name of the man who ordered his death, Colin Fullerton, but who was the mystery assassin? He pushed his door key into the lock and let himself in, stepping over a doorstep, through the doorway into the sanctuary and welcoming warmth of home.

EIGHT

Ginty eased off the accelerator as he approached the gap in the trees. He checked his mirrors – the road behind him was clear, as was the road in front. He jammed his foot on the brake pedal and swung the van off the road, through the tree break and onto a muddy track. He continued along the track until he found the parking spot he had made before leaving Boyle and heading for the village.

Ginty finished pulling some broken branches around the rear of the van before grabbing his bag. He pushed his way through the last thicket until he could see the old barn. Ginty approached cautiously, taking slow, deliberate steps as he avoided hidden holes and small stones. He stopped short of the barn – silence. Ginty crouched down. Reaching into his bag, he cautiously removed a claw hammer. He called out Boyle's name in a low voice and waited for a response.

Nothing.

"Billy?" Ginty hissed. Still, he got no reply.

Ginty tightened his grip on the hammer, drew in a deep breath and, taking tentative steps, moved forward. "Billy?" he hissed once more, only louder and through clenched teeth.

Still no reply.

Ginty was now an arm's length away from the barn door. He turned his head slightly so his ear was facing the building, and opened his mouth to listen. He'd picked up this tip from some survival programme with a bloke that drank juice from elephant shit. That was one thing Ginty wouldn't try.

He felt the cold biting at his exposed face and now, the tips of his teeth began to tingle. Ginty heard nothing. The night was still. He stepped closer to the door, raising the hammer above his head. Taking hold of the handle, Ginty yanked it open with all his strength, jumping back, allowing himself space to strike out with the weapon.

No one rushed out to attack him, no one discharged a weapon. The door squealed under the force used to drag it open, before the night, once again, descended into silence. Ginty stared into the dark abyss.

"Billy?" Ginty again forced out the name through clenched teeth.

"What?" came the single world reply.

Ginty stepped into the barn. "Jesus, Billy, ye shit me up. I've been calling ye for ages."

Boyle moved out of the shadows and looked towards his friend. "What were ye going to do, smash me brains in?" he asked, casting a glance at the hammer.

Ginty realised he still had his arm raised. "This was for my protection but I should be bashing ye bleeding brains in, just fer shitting me up like that."

"Aye, well aren't I the lucky one? Did ye get the stuff I asked for?"

"Yeah, I did, and I sorted out a room for us. Where's the Brit?"

Boyle nodded his head towards a still, face-down figure. Ginty stared at the lifeless form. "Jesus Billy, I thought we were gonna get information from him, about your Sean . . ."

Boyle cut in. "I couldn't . . . I just needed . . . Ginty, I don't know what happened. I kicked the bastard like a dirty hound, but then I just couldn't stop myself."

Ginty brushed passed Boyle as he slowly approached the curled-up figure of Lewis. The corner of the barn grew darker as the light from the open door rescinded. The prone man still didn't move.

Boyle continued. "I hurt the bastard, I heard his bones crack but couldn't stop. Then I took a hold of my gun. It was so easy. I had the bastard in my sights."

Ginty stood over the prostrate figure and struck out with a hefty kick.

"I've never killed anyone before, but when I had this bastard there in front of me, all I could see was him and the white dots. Those bleeding dots, they pointed at him, begging me to pull the trigger. And then I did . . ."

Ginty's boot struck Lewis right between his shoulder blades; he let out a sharp moan in protest. Ginty turned to face Boyle and as he did, his eyes caught sight of three holes in the wooden, slated wall behind Lewis. Moonlight pierced through the damaged structure.

“I bottled it, Ginty, I just couldn’t do it.”

“Don’t be worrying about it, Billy, I’ll tie the bastard up and then we’ll leave him till tomorrow.”

Ginty strode purposefully to retrieve his bag from outside. He returned and removed two padlocks and a chain from the large bag. He moved in on Lewis, quickly looping the chain around the support beam close to the hunched figure. Ginty swiftly applied one of the padlocks and then proceeded to do the same with one of Lewis’ legs.

Lewis put up little resistance as one of his legs was chained to the beam; he was cold and tired, and still hurting from his earlier beating. He tried to imagine how much blood had been lost from the shotgun wound, enough to make him weak and lethargic, but not enough to end his suffering. One of the farmers had stemmed the blood flow with a makeshift bandage before he had been bundled away in the back of the van.

“Don’t be trying anything stupid while we’re gone, do ye hear me?” Ginty punched Lewis in the area of his kidneys. “Did ye hear what I said?”

All Lewis could manage was a moan.

Ginty stood up and looked around. He sought what he was looking for and quickly retrieved it. He opened up the sacking cloth before draping it over Lewis.

“Here ye go. See, we’re not totally heartless bastards. Now have a think about why you’re here and what we might want to know from ye, because tomorrow, we will be right fucking bastards. That ye can bet on, fer sure.”

Ginty stuffed the large bag into one corner of the barn. “Have ye still got the pistol, Billy?”

“No, I’ve tucked it away out of sight,” answered Boyle, fully aware of the consequences of being found in possession of a weapon and not wanting to take any risks.

“Right then, let’s go and get some warm food and a few drinks,” replied Ginty.

The two men left the barn and headed for the van.

NINE

James Strong sat in his car, facing his house. The drive home had been uneventful and relatively quick, and now he was home, sat deep in thought. He peered into his interior mirror and caught sight of a neighbour leaving his house across the street and getting into his car. The interior light came on briefly before being extinguished, plunging the car interior into darkness.

The wind outside howled, gently rocking the car. Strong stared intently at the interior mirror. The car parked behind him was in darkness. Suddenly, light flashed inside the vehicle. Strong lost count of the number of flashes, as he now focused on the distinctive sound of gunshots. Each one came a fraction of a second after a flash of light, caused by the gases burning and illuminating from the barrel of the pistol, as the informant was murdered. Suddenly, a figure emerged from the car, stood at the driver's door; once more, he discharged his weapon at the occupant. When all the flashes and bangs had stopped, the assassin walked back towards Strong.

The tapping on the window startled him. The images from the interior mirror faded away fast until all he could see was an empty driveway. Strong turned to face his wife. She opened the car door. "Is everything alright, James, you looked miles away?"

Strong composed himself, "Yeah, I'm fine, Amanda, it's been one of those days. I've got a very tight deadline and things are starting to build up."

"I tell you what, you get yourself out of the car and into the house, and I'll make you a nice cup of tea,"

Amanda Strong knew what her husband's job was, but never pried. She had an idea something was happening at work, as her husband had been keeping erratic hours over the last few weeks. She knew that if he came home earlier than normal, she'd have to cherish the time together, as it was invariably interrupted by a call from the "office". Amanda left her husband to lock up his car and went inside.

Strong watched his wife disappear back inside the house. He checked his interior mirror once more; just an empty driveway. Colin Fullerton had a great deal to answer for. Strong was tiring of the guilt he had carried with him since that shooting in 1995. With the man he had loathed ever since that killing returning to work in his department, Strong wondered if it was now time to speak up about the crime.

Strong had finished putting his daughters to bed. Now, he was on his way back down the stairs to snuggle up with his wife and enjoy an evening, sipping wine and watching television. Amanda had already poured the wine and offered a glass to Strong as he entered the lounge. He gratefully accepted the drink, as he sat down on the corner sofa and reached for the remote.

"Here," said Amanda, as she passed the black control to her husband. "I don't think there's much on tonight, darling."

Strong pointed the remote at the television and depressed two numbers. The channel flicked to a 24-hour news station. "I just want to see what's happening in the world, and then I'll switch it over."

After 10 minutes of death, floods and sport, Strong switched over to a movie channel. A car chase was taking place through the streets of San Francisco; a large Humvee was being pursued by a bright yellow sports car. Sean Connery bounced the large military vehicle off everything in its path.

"We've seen this about half a dozen times," protested Amanda.

Strong switched channels again. This time, builders were trying to drop a large, wooden beam into place – something neutral, thought Strong.

He gulped a large mouthful of wine, swallowed and then spoke. "I've got a small problem in the office." Strong and his wife always referred to his work with MI5 as the "office". To him, it seemed to bring a little normality into their lives. "We have a new guy starting shortly and I have a bit of previous history with him."

Amanda tucked her feet underneath herself and turned to face her husband as Strong continued. "Anyway, to cut out all the gory details, he committed a crime, well not exactly him, he got someone else to do it for him. And now, he's coming to work on my team."

"So, what's the problem?"

"I'm caught in two minds as to whether I do anything about it or just forget it ever happened and move on."

Amanda sipped at her wine. "If it's going to cause problems for you, James, then it may be for the best if you do something about it."

"Maybe I'm being petty?"

"No, not at all," replied Amanda. "If it's bothering you then you probably need to do the right thing, which I think is to report him."

Strong took another large gulp of wine. "Maybe you're right, darling. I'll see how I feel in the morning after a good sleep."

"I'm sure whatever you do will be for the best, James," said Amanda, snuggling closer to her husband.

Strong raised his glass once more. Pausing briefly, his mind wandered back to those flashes and echoing gunshots.

TEN

Colin Fullerton arrived at his destination. He parked his car away from any prying eyes. Once done, he looked out towards the farmhouse; most of the lights were on, but he was yet to see anyone.

He reached into the glove box and removed a pistol; it had been a while since he had last fired a Browning Hi-Power 9mm. It was once a favoured weapon with the British Army; now it was all Glocks and Sig Sauers. Fullerton gripped the top-slide between his thumb and fingers, and in an overhand grip, he drew it back, pausing briefly before allowing it to slam forward. The function extracted the first round from the magazine seated inside the pistol grip, and guided it firmly into the barrel's breach chamber.

One up the spout, as it was commonly known in military terms.

Fullerton climbed out of the car, walking cautiously towards the track that led to the farmhouse. He stood in the entranceway and stared up at the isolated building. Suddenly, a door opened, and what appeared to be an elderly man stood silhouetted inside the frame. From what he knew of the occupiers, this person must be the father; the only other resident was the son. Fullerton couldn't see what the old man was doing, but now he could hear a dog barking.

Fullerton returned to his car.

Satisfied the car was sufficiently hidden from the chance sighting of any passers-by – not that he was expecting many at this late hour and in such an isolated location – he climbed back into the cold vehicle. Although a hotel would have offered more comfort and welcoming warmth, Fullerton wanted to leave as little a trace of his excursion into the Republic of Ireland as possible. After locking himself in, Fullerton began reclining the driver's seat, and for peace of mind, he placed the pistol into his lap. Overhead, the moon cast a chilling glow from behind a cluster of dark clouds. With rods of light piercing the night canvas and reflecting across a fresh dusting of frost, Fullerton was ready for his night-time vigil. He pulled up his coat's collar and settled in for the night as best as he could. He knew that daybreak was his best time to attack. After all, so many of the world's great strategists could not be wrong. It was worth the wait.

Outside, it began raining.

ELEVEN

A crisp, light frost covered the sacking lying across Adam Lewis' battered torso. Blood from his broken nose and dirt from the ground, where he had tried to bury his face during the savage beating, clung to the stubble on his face. Beneath his flattened nose, dried blood cracked and flaked. Lewis could still taste the coppery texture inside his parched mouth; he tried moving his tongue around to produce saliva. As he swallowed, messages of excruciating pain shot through his body. Lewis slowly lifted his head, trying to look towards the shed door. His whole body shook, but he eventually managed it.

Light from the early morning sun filtered through all the gaps in the splintered woodwork. Without being able to see the sun, Lewis had no way of working out what time it was. He'd been on many military exercises and woken up in a variety of countries, in numerous makeshift shelters, and had fairly accurately guessed the time based on the sun's position with the skyline. Although, on those occasions, he'd usually had a watch to confirm his estimates. This time, he had no watch and no clear view of the sun. The only thing he could be sure of was that it was daytime. *No shit, Sherlock.* Lewis managed a thin smile across his cracked, parched lips. The sun was filtering towards him through the dilapidated door and casting long shadows all in his direction; even these were too random to help Lewis judge the time.

After a restless, painful night, Lewis' thoughts were now trying to focus on his two captors – who they were, and what they wanted with him. He had no doubt they were IRA men, and from past knowledge, he knew it would only be a matter of time before they killed him. Lewis had to focus on prolonging his chances of survival, but what for? He was fully aware that no one would be out looking for him; there was no cavalry coming over the hill to his rescue. He was alone, in all aspects of the word.

The first thing Lewis decided he needed to do was to try to escape – well, at least from his shackles. He tried moving his wrists.

Fortunately, the bindings weren't too tightly wound around the joint, so he had some movement. He gritted his teeth, in a bid to block out the pain from his shoulder wound, then tried to twist his hands free. Even though the cord had some slackness to it, his damaged joint offered up too much of an obstacle. And as the pain from his shattered wrist became unbearable, he teetered on the verge of blacking out and gave up. He fought the blackness of unconsciousness, along with every other painfully sensation his body was going through, realising his efforts were futile. Lewis succumbed to the situation; his wrist was too badly damaged to make another attempt at freeing it. He surrendered to the knowledge that the cord had deliberately been tied just tight enough to not cut off his circulation.

Giving up on freeing his wrist bindings, Lewis pushed himself over with his one free leg, moving his body around so that he could examine the chain around his other leg. Again, there was no way he could remove the chain from his ankle without hacking his foot off, and he felt that such desperate measures like that were still a long way off. He couldn't see any cutting tools to hand, and he would probably bleed out before he could get anywhere close to safety.

Lewis examined the support beam he was tethered to, and despite the state of disrepair of the barn, the beam looked solid. He checked for any visual weaknesses, but couldn't see anything. Lewis turned his body again so that this time, he had his free leg in such a position that he could strike out at the beam. He drew his knee towards his chest then launched his foot towards the wooden support. As his kick connected, dust fell from the rafters and dead wood flakes broke from the beam, but the structure remained intact. Lewis tried changing the angle of his assault and lashed out again – the beam stood defiant. Once more, Lewis was showered in wooden debris. Next, he attempted two swift strikes to the same area, and again, he made barely a mark on the beam. Lewis geared up for one final strike before his energy levels subsided. He aligned the heel of his boot with the wooden beam and launched his foot towards the support. Lewis' boot glanced off the corner of the beam; his calf scraped along its rough edge, taking a slither of his skin as it passed by. He screamed in pain and then lashed out at the beam in sheer frustration. He rained blow after blow down on the wooden support until, gradually, the distance and ferocity off the strikes subsided.

Lewis tried to extend his chest to maximise his oxygen intake in an attempt at replenishing his battered and depleted body. His head dropped into the dirt and his short, sharp breaths disturbed the earth around his mouth. He closed his eyes as he concentrated on regulating his breathing. Lewis took slow, deep lungfuls of air in through his nose and exhaled out through his mouth, rasping his lips as he gradually calmed himself down. The stinging sensation around his grazed calf subsided as Lewis regained his composure. He checked the beam once more, hopeful that his aggressive melee had had some impact on the wooden support, but again, he was left disappointed.

Lewis curled into a foetal position and gradually closed his eyes. He was exhausted from lack of food and sleep, and now he was feeling worn out from trying to displace the wooden support beam he was chained to. All he could do now was wait for the two Irishmen to return. Maybe they'll bring me a big mac, he thought, and yes, I would like fries with that!

TWELVE

James Strong finished dabbing away the excess water from his face with a towel while catching brief glimpses of himself staring out from the bathroom mirror. He thought he was due a haircut, as he hung up the towel. He switched the bathroom light off and returned to his bedroom to finish dressing before going down for breakfast.

Amanda greeted her husband with a kiss and a cup of coffee. His daughters were sitting at the kitchen table, tucking into bowls of cereal.

"Morning girls," said Strong, bringing his coffee to the table.

"Hello Daddy," the girls chimed.

Amanda placed a small plate with two slices of lightly-buttered toast down beside Strong's coffee cup.

"There you go, honey," she said, returning to the kitchen.

Strong switched on his tablet and brought up a news feed. He scanned through the headlines before opening one about an attack by extremists in Northern Iraq. Strong speed-read the details before clicking on another headline.

Amanda joined her family at the kitchen table. After sipping from her herbal tea, she looked across at her husband. "Anything interesting?"

"Just the usual; bad people doing bad things. Oh, and Chelsea were beaten again last night," smiled Strong.

"Have you had anymore thoughts on what we talked about?"

"I have, I'm going to see Robert today and discuss my options with him. It just doesn't feel right. I should have said something years ago. I think today should be the day I put things right."

Amanda smiled. "For what it's worth, I think you're doing the right thing, honey."

The two girls finished their cereal and took their bowls through to the kitchen sink.

Strong downed the last dregs of coffee before switching off his tablet and following his daughters to the kitchen with his empty cup.

He rinsed it out and stood it on the drainer. Before the girls went to fetch their coats and school bags, Strong kissed them both goodbye.

"I'm gonna stop off for a haircut on my way home tonight so I may be a little late home," he Strong, as he collected his jacket from the hallway. He checked his car keys were still in one of the pockets before returning to kiss his wife goodbye.

"Good luck," she said, as he headed for the front door. "I'm doing fish tonight."

"Great," shouted Strong from the doorway. "Have a good day, darling."

Strong slammed the door shut behind him and walked around his car to the driver's side. He climbed in and fed the key into the ignition. He switched on the engine, and then took a moment to look into the interior mirror. This time, all he could see was his driveway, leading to the road and the house across the road. He felt a little more at ease, as he selected reverse, that there were no reflected images from his past playing out in the interior mirror.

Accelerating away down the street, Strong joined the steady flow of morning traffic. Hopefully, Robert Macleod will understand, he thought.

THIRTEEN

Colin Fullerton fastened his fly after taking an early morning piss. A plume of steam rose from the sodden grass. He lit a cigarette before climbing back into his car and turning on the ignition. The engine fired into life, spewing out dark fumes into the cold, morning air. The car stereo kicked into life with a radio DJ announcing the next track. Bryan Adams played a guitar riff intro before singing the *Summer of '69*. Fullerton waited until the end of the first line then switched off the stereo.

The dashboard clock displayed 09:06.

Time to go and speak with a farmer, thought Fullerton.

Carefully, he guided the Mondeo up the pot-holed track towards the farmhouse. He stopped a few metres short. Fullerton noticed a curtain in one of the upstairs windows being drawn back, and then a man's face appeared, staring down at him. He held his gaze before getting out of the car and striding towards the front door. Fullerton checked his pistol. He'd already cocked it so it was loaded; now, he removed the safety catch. The pistol was ready for firing. He raised a tightly-clenched fist and hammered on the heavy door.

Fullerton adjusted his coat and stood staring at the peeling paintwork on the large farmhouse door. Anticipating questions from the occupier, he removed a slim, black wallet from an inside pocket. The door opened.

"Can I help you?" asked a broad-shouldered, younger man.

"Good morning, sir," replied Fullerton, holding up the police warrant card. "I'm Detective Sergeant Armitage. Can I come in?"

Fullerton realised attempting an Irish accent would not only have been foolish, but would have drawn unnecessary attention to him, should he slip up. Besides, the warrant card was genuine enough and would stand up to scrutiny, so he was confident that just being himself would get him what he wanted.

The younger man stared at the ID card and then at Fullerton. "What can I do for you, Mr Armitage?"

“I’d rather discuss it inside, if it’s all the same with you, Mr . . . ?” Fullerton paused, leaving a gap for the younger man to fill. Instead, he just stepped to one side, allowing Fullerton entry into the farmhouse.

“The front room is on the right.”

Fullerton stepped past the younger man, stopping short of the living room. “After you, Mr . . .” Again, he prompted the younger man into divulging his name.

“Tommy, Tommy Macleish.”

Fullerton followed Macleish into the front room. He was greeted by a roaring fire, which almost immediately thawed his chill from sleeping in the car.

“We don’t get many peelers in these parts,” said Macleish. “‘Specially no British peelers!”

Fullerton casually strolled to the far corner of the room until he was standing away from the only window and door.

“We rarely venture out this far; tend to leave it to the country boys. As for me, I transferred over from Manchester nearly five years ago.” Fullerton was once again facing Macleish. “Is there anyone else in the house besides your good self, Tommy?”

Macleish’s eyes flickered briefly upwards, unnoticed by Fullerton. “No, just me.”

The words had barely left his lips when, as if on cue, an upstairs toilet flushed. Macleish rolled his eyes. “That’ll be me da,” explained a blushing Macleish. “I thought he was already up and outside.”

“Ask him to come down and join us, Tommy, and then I’ll explain why I’m here.”

Macleish left the front room. Walking to the foot of the stairs, he shouted up to his dad.

“I’ll be down,” was the curt reply.

“He’s on his way,” said Macleish, as he re-entered the front room.

“Good, take a seat please, Tommy.”

Macleish stared at Fullerton, who just raised his eyebrows and gestured with his head towards the settee. Macleish begrudgingly obliged.

“You still haven’t said why you’re here, detective.”

"I'll explain everything once your father joins us, Tommy. Now, how long have you owned this farm?"

"It's been in our family for years," replied Macleish. "My da says it goes way back to his great-granddad. There's been a good few generations of Macleishs farming these fields," Tommy added. "And when he passes, it will be mine."

"And who will you leave it to, Tommy?"

An older man entered the room before Macleish had chance to answer.

"Good morning, Mr Macleish, my name is Detective Sergeant Armitage. If you'll be so kind as to take a seat, I'll explain my reason for this visit."

"It's okay, I'll stand if it's all the same with you, Mr Armitage."

Fullerton placed a hand into a coat pocket, wrapping his fingers around the pistol grip of the weapon stashed inside. He slipped a finger inside the trigger guard and effortlessly drew the pistol.

"Sit down, Mr Macleish, I insist!" Fullerton's words were now more forceful.

Tommy dug his fists into the settee cushions, stiffening his arms in readiness to launch himself from the seat, caught in a quandary of stepping in and protecting his father or going straight for gunman.

Fullerton seized on his movement and fired a shot into the wall, just to the left of Tommy's head. "Sit down, Mr Macleish. I won't ask again."

The father and son were now sitting side by side on the settee, staring up at Fullerton with contempt.

FOURTEEN

Tommy Macleish regarded Fullerton's face for any expression or hint of emotion. Apart from what looked like a strange-shaped scar beside one eye, his face gave nothing away. Tommy had been in enough bare-knuckled fights to know a man with a straight, poker face was a dangerous man to be around.

Tommy wiped plaster dust from his shoulder and glanced at the bullet hole in the wall behind him. It looked like the bullet had missed his head by about 12 inches.

Macleish senior spoke first. "Okay fella, you've got me attention now, so what do ye want with us?"

Fullerton remained standing in the corner of the room; his gaze passed slowly between father and son. "I'm here because I'm looking for a friend of mine."

"We haven't had visitors around here in a long time," answered Macleish senior.

"Now, why would you lie to me, Mr Macleish?"

"I'm not lying to ye, 'tis the truth. We don't get many people coming round here on account of us being miles from anywhere."

Then Tommy added, "And that's the way we like it." He continued, "It's true, detective, what my da is telling ye, we've not had anyone knocking on our door in ages."

Fullerton took one step closer to the seated men. "I wasn't asking for you to contribute anything to the conversation, Tommy."

"I was just saying . . ."

"There you go again, interrupting. Sit still and keep quiet. Your time will come, Tommy."

Tommy clenched his fists in anger. He felt like he was being treated like a naughty schoolboy. His cheeks reddened as the rage and hatred inside him rose. Chewing his bottom lip, he bided his time.

"Right, Mr Macleish, *senior*!" Fullerton emphasised, looking at the older man. "You had a visitor come to your house a couple of days ago. Where did he go after here?"

"We've had no visitors," insisted Macleish senior. "Not yesterday, not the day 'fore that. Not even the week 'fore. We've seen no one here in ages, apart from ye, ye self, today!"

Fullerton stared back at the older man as he continued his questioning. "Look, Mr Macleish, before I ask you again, take a moment to think before you answer."

Tommy lowered his head until he was staring at his boots.

"Think about the question and ask yourself why I am asking it," Fullerton said. "Ask yourself whether there is something you know that you're not telling me."

Macleish senior opened his mouth to speak, but Fullerton continued. "Ask yourself this: 'Does he know something that tells him that I'm lying?' And when you have, give me your answer."

Without dropping his gaze, Fullerton again asked Macleish senior, "What happened to the visitor you had to this farmhouse, two days ago?"

Once again, Macleish senior opened his mouth to speak and once more, Fullerton interjected, "Remember, think first before answering, as I'm only asking because I sent the man to this address!"

Macleish senior closed his mouth. As he did, Tommy raised his head until his eyes stared straight at Fullerton's weathered face. He was greeted by a blank, expressionless look. Tommy had to believe the detective from the Garda, if that's who he was, was not bluffing, as they had indeed received a visitor. But how much of his hand was he showing? Tommy then wondered how far away Boyle had gotten with the stranger; he also thought how stubborn his father would be.

"Well, maybe he got lost. 'Cause, as I keeps telling ye, we've had nobody round these parts, 'cept ye self, detective."

Fullerton gave a disapproving look to the older man. "I'm afraid you leave me with no choice, Mr Macleish," he said, levelling the pistol at Tommy and firing a single shot. The echoed retort around the confines of the room was ear splitting.

Tommy's kneecap split under the force of the round blasting its way through his left leg joint. He let out a growling scream as he clutched at the shattered joint. He felt bone fragments moving, jellylike under his hands, as he pushed down to stem the flow of blood. The harder he pressed, the more searing the pain.

Macleish senior rose from his seat.

"Sit down!" barked Fullerton, as his unemotional mask slipped. "Unless you want me to put another bullet in your son, I suggest you answer my question!"

Tommy groaned, continually rocking to and fro, clutching his shattered kneecap. Both his hands were dark red with blood, which was spilling through his fingers and onto the wooden floor, pooling around his mud-caked boots.

"Okay, okay, whoever ye are," conceded Macleish senior. "We did see someone but he left. He come looking for someone, and I told him he had the wrong house; that's when he left."

Fullerton fired another shot. The round skimmed through Tommy's left arm, burying itself deep inside his thigh. An electrifying pain raced its way around Tommy's nerve system, setting off every pain receptor on the way.

Macleish senior looked nervously between his son and the lunatic with the gun. "Stop shooting my fucking son!" he yelled.

Fullerton lowered the pistol. speaking to the older man again. "I know someone came here and I know he came looking for Sean Boyle." He paused. Macleish senior took his eyes off his wounded son and stared straight into the gunman's dead eyes. "I want to know where he went"

"I don't know where he went! Ye seem to know an awful lot of what went on around here, so ye tell me what the fuck is going on!"

Once again. Fullerton raised the pistol.

"Stop it! Stop it! Look, Billy Boyle came and took him away," blurted Macleish senior.

Tommy reached for a cushion. Holding it tightly in his hand, he pushed it down onto his thigh. The wound throbbed like a massive dead leg, sending twitching spasms down to his toes. He sensed the room was gathering motion, as his head fogged with the pain. A calming numbness enveloped him, as the effects of blood loss began cutting down supply to his body's extremities. His brain was diverting what blood he had remaining to his vital organs and away from those it deemed less needy, relaxing Tommy in the process.

Macleish senior watched as his son's grip on the cushion loosened. He looked up at Fullerton with pleading eyes. "Look sir, I've answered your questions, let me get help fer me boy. Please sir, or he's gonna bleed to death."

"Tell me about Boyle," said Fullerton, ignoring the older man's plea. "Where did he take him? Was he still alive when they left?"

"I've no idea where he took him," answered Macleish senior, with a rising, frustrated tone to his voice. "The man was alive when he left here. He was shot and bleeding, but he was still alive."

"What do you mean shot?" Fullerton asked.

"He was shot, I shot him. Now let me get help fer me son! Take me away if ye have to, but please, let me help me boy before it's too late!" Macleish senior was now fraught with frustration. His eyes darted between the blood-soaked cushion, his son's greying pallor and the pistol in Fullerton's outstretched hand.

"One last question, Mr Macleish. If you don't know where they were headed, what did Boyle take the man away in?"

Macleish senior gritted his teeth as his patience ebbed away. "A van, a blue van. I think it was one of them German ones. And 'fore ye ask, I don't know the registration number, just that it was blue and foreign!"

"Okay, thank you, Mr Macleish. "

Fullerton fired another shot.

The round smashed into the crown of Tommy's bowed head. His skull burst open with a sickening pop as blood, brain tissue and bone fragments exploded across the settee and Macleish senior. Blood and sinew spewed from Tommy's open mouth, soaking his lap and spilling onto the floor.

Macleish senior pushed himself up onto his feet, but unfortunately for him, Fullerton was much quicker and fired four rapid shots into the older man's torso. The force from the close-range volley pulverised the older man's chest and knocked him back onto the settee. His fragile upper ribcage seemed to collapse in on itself as his aged bones shattered under the immense impact of the red-hot rounds. Splintered bone and metal fragments decimated his internal organs, killing Macleish senior instantly.

The two men slumped against each other. Fullerton opened his mouth, rotating his jaw, in an attempt to expel the ringing from inside his ears. Surveying the two bloody figures, Fullerton was content he'd gained most of the information he'd come for. He also knew that at some point, he'd have to follow up on the blue van, although he was confident that a wounded Lewis would be no match for two armed terrorists.

As he left the farmhouse, Fullerton heard the barks from a dog echoing around the yard at the rear of the building. Turning away from the farmhouse and the noise, he pocketed his pistol and headed back to the Mondeo.

After climbing into the car, he swung it around, heading back down towards the main road, driving just as cautiously as he had when arriving, doing his best to avoid the large potholes.

FIFTEEN

The street lighting and neon signs reflected in the late, winter's afternoon puddles of a rain-soaked London.

Inside his father's shop, in the centre of Ealing, Luay Abass handed a customer his change. "Thank you, sir, and don't forget to keep your receipt, as it's also your guarantee."

The customer accepted the paperwork and money with a polite smile.

Abass removed a brightly-coloured waistcoat, with the name of his father's shop embroidered into the breast pocket, and navigated his way through the shelves and displays into the rear of the electronics shop.

"Dad," he shouted, "I'm off to my course. Can you take over the front please?"

"Okay, I'll be right out," came the reply from the storeroom.

Abass hung up his waistcoat and collected a shoulder bag, hanging on the only peg. He opened the flap and gave the contents a cursory glance before refastening the bag and slinging it over his shoulder, allowing it to rest at his side. Abass turned and headed towards the shop door.

"Right, Dad, I'm off now."

He waited momentarily for a reply, but didn't get one. As a new customer entered the shop, he repeated, "Dad!"

The customer crossed over towards a display of MP3 players.

"*Dad*!" called Abass, once more.

An older man of a similar portly build to Abass entered the shop from the rear storeroom. He also sported a goatee beard similar in style to that of his son, Luay Abass.

"Okay Luay, off you go to become the next Bill Gates."

Abass had grown accustomed to his father's favourite joke, but smiled to humour the old man. He turned to see his father, once again chuckling. "See you later, Dad."

Abass passed the customer comparing MP3 players as he left the shop.

"Can I help you, sir?"

Hassan Falah replaced the MP3 players and checked his watch. Half-past one. Abass was leaving on time, as he had done for the previous three weeks.

"No thanks, I'm just looking." Falah paused a moment and then retrieved one of the players. "Maybe you can. If I was buying one of these, which one would be similar to the iPod?"

The shop owner looked at the product held up by the customer. "The red one you have hold of is the better of the two you were comparing, but on the next shelf down is a purple one. It has a 64 GB memory and almost identical features, for about half the price."

"Thanks, thanks for your help," said Falah, as he replaced the red player back onto the shelf. He turned and headed for the exit.

"Masalamah." Out of habit, the shop owner spoke an Arabic goodbye to the departing customer. Falah turned slightly and repeated the gesture before leaving the shop.

SIXTEEN

The mobile phone on James Strong's desk vibrated wildly. He glanced down at the flashing display and read the name filling the small screen.

"Hello Hassan?" Strong picked up a black pen. "Okay, go ahead." He began taking notes on an open pad next to his keyboard. "Right, I've got that. Good luck."

Strong disconnected the call and flipped the notepad closed. He looked up at a wall clock before double-checking the time with his wristwatch. Now was a good a time as any, he thought. Strong stood up from his desk and left his office.

The department head's office was located only a short walk down the corridor. Strong stopped halfway at the coffee percolator, and poured two coffees.

"Come in," boomed the Scottish voice from behind the office door.

Strong opened the door, collected one of the cups from a nearby table and entered the office, closing the door with the heel of his shoe as he passed inside. He approached the desk and extended an arm to the man seated behind the large desk. "Coffee, Robert?"

"Thanks James. Take a seat."

Strong was glad to be relieved of the hot cup. He sat down, nursing a bright red thumb and index finger. Of the five Scottish people that Strong knew in this department, Robert Macleod was the only one who still spoke with a broad accent.

"Just give me a moment, James, and I'll be right with you."

Macleod was in his late 50s. He had a bald, freckled head, partly circled by short, cropped, white hair. He sported a well-kept, droopy, grey moustache that was a remnant from a secondment with the SAS during the early 80s. Most of the squadron he'd served with in Northern Ireland had grown one too. Taking advantage of one opportunity, the whole team had taken a group photograph with them all sporting sombreros. It had helped him to blend in, he had once explained. After the attachment ended, he had decided to keep it, much to his former wife's annoyance, and so, it had remained to this day. And the old group photograph was still hanging with pride of place in his office.

"Right, James," spoke Macleod, as he removed his glasses, "what can I do for you?"

Strong paused, drew a deep breath, and then spoke. "It concerns Colin Fullerton. Before he joins the section, I need to inform you of an incident from our past. I'd like to keep it between you and I but I think it's too serious for that."

"Why don't you explain to me what has happened and let me be the judge of how we proceed," replied Macleod, picking up his coffee.

"Okay Robert, but I also need to tell you why I've not spoken about it before now."

Macleod interrupted. "Tell me what it's about first and then we can start delving into the whys and wherefores at the end."

Strong composed himself then began. "Back in 1995, during October, around the 18th or 19th, I was called into Colin's office. When I arrived, there was already two soldiers in with him."

Macleod clicked the nib out on his gold pen and proceeded to take notes.

"We were all introduced and then after the pleasantries, Colin produced a folder containing the details of an IRA informer."

Macleod rested his pen. "Sorry, James, do you recall the names of these two soldiers, their unit etc . . . ?"

"I remember the name of one of them; he was a captain, Captain Roberts. Unfortunately, I can't recall the other one's name." Strong thought hard for a brief moment. "I don't think I was introduced to the other one. I'm sure Colin knew them; well, the officer at least. They were on pretty familiar terms, if I remember correctly."

Macleod cut in again. "What about their unit, James, do you remember that?"

"They were both with the SAS. I do remember Colin speaking with me a few days earlier and telling me I would be working with a couple of soldiers from the Troop." As the memory flooded back, Strong continued, "Yes, that's it. He'd told me that all I had to do was identify a target for them." Strong reached for his coffee and downed a mouthful. "Anyway, Colin finished with the intros before producing the folder. This contained a photo of Gerard Logan, the IRA informer, and brief notes on basic details about him. I remember that he'd been very useful to us in the past. In fact, the last piece of information he had passed to us resulted in the deaths of a three-man ASU team."

Macleod continued with his note taking, only stopping briefly to drink his coffee.

"Colin had explained that he had information from a reliable source, that Logan was double-dealing with ourselves and another Republican group, and the only safe option was to eliminate him."

Macleod looked up from his notes, resting his pen. "James, I must stop you there a moment." He then pressed an intercom buzzer on a small console seated on his desk. A female's voice echoed from a concealed speaker.

"Jane, can you make sure I'm not disturbed for the next 10 minutes, please."

"Okay, sir," came the monotone, echoed response.

Macleod looked across his desk at Strong. "What I want you to do, James, is take a moment to think. It's clear you have something you want to get off your chest, but the second it is out in the open, it will leave me with very limited options."

Strong nodded his head.

"Whatever it is you want to say may or may not impact on you and Colin in ways that are out of my control. Do you understand this, James?"

Once again, Strong nodded his head. "Yes, I understand, Robert," he answered.

"I'm not trying to put you off, James, I hope you understand that. I'm wanting you to appreciate the fact that if you choose to continue, there is a real chance of serious repercussions for either or both of you." Macleod picked up his pen again. "You see, as far as I'm aware, no officer from MI5 has been implicated or prosecuted in regards to any deaths in Northern Ireland throughout 1995. So, to me, that implies that whatever you know is only privileged information between those involved, and has remained so for a very long time."

Macleod poised the pen over the notepad and, once again, looked across his desk at Strong. "Okay, James, do you wish to continue?"

SEVENTEEN

Hassan Falah followed Abass up the stone steps and into the college, maintaining a gap of a few feet and matching his target stride for stride.

Both men entered a large study hall; Abass with his student ID and Falah with his pre-arranged day pass. It was brightly lit from numerous overhead fluorescent lighting tubes. A maze of desks expanded out across the floor and on each desk was a flat-screen monitor with a keyboard. Abass weaved his way to his usual desk, followed by Falah, who seated himself at the desk immediately behind him.

The student that normally occupied the desk had been, unfortunately, detained at his flat by repair work to a boiler. An operation meticulously planned by Falah's teammates.

Abass removed his notes from the shoulder bag, placed the bag at his feet and arranged his notes before switching on his monitor. The screen lit up as it went through its loading procedures. Once ready, it offered Abass a choice of profiles. He selected his and waited for the login box to appear before entering his user name and password.

A red message appeared above the password box: "incorrect password". Abass retyped his password then depressed the enter key. Again, the red typeset appeared. This time, Abass checked the caps lock key was off and then, one key at a time, methodically retyped his password, and was once again denied access.

Falah reached into his laptop bag and retrieved a memory stick. He manipulated it between his fingers as he watched Abass retype his password. Falah waited patiently for his moment. The system had been locked with a secure program that only Falah could access. The technical work had been carried out the previous evening, after Falah had approached the college head with a specific government request.

Falah leaned across the open space between the two desks. "Excuse me, are you having trouble logging in?"

“Logging in? Yeah, the system won’t accept my password, I can’t get into anything.” Abass turned in his seat until he was facing Falah. “I have a backup copy of my work, but that’s not the point, I can’t access anything and I don’t know what’s the problem.”

“Oh, I see. Do you want a hand?”

Abass depressed the enter key. Once again, the words “incorrect password” flashed up on screen. He turned in his seat once more. “I don’t know what else I can do. As far as I know, the system is fully protected from outside interference, plus, we’re wholly discouraged from tinkering with the system, with the threat of dismissal. I don’t even think there’s a back door to get in!”

Falah rose from his seat, walking around to Abass’ station. “I’m Mushtaq,” he said, offering a hand.

“Luay Abass.” The two men shook hands.

“Right, let’s see what I can do.”

Falah turned the monitor to face him and then slid the keyboard across. His fingers danced across the keys as he typed in a series of words and symbols. He finished by hitting the enter key. Nothing happened. Falah retyped a new sequence of letters and symbols before depressing the enter key. Again, nothing happened.

“Can I sit down, Luay, please?”

Abass vacated his seat. Before sitting, Falah reached into a pocket and removed a flash drive. “Right, let’s give this a try,” he said, inserting the stick into a vacant port.

This time, Falah added numbers to his typing sequence. Abass stood behind him, watching his fingers gliding with expert ease across the keyboard. The voyeur couldn’t make any sense of what was being typed; he just watched on in silence. Once again, Falah finished his input by hitting the enter key. Nothing happened. Falah waited patiently, his fingers hovering above the keyboard. Suddenly, the screen went black. A white cursor flashed in the top left-hand corner of the monitor for a brief moment before the screen flickered between blue and black. Next, the screen burst into life as rows upon rows of commands appeared in identical columns. New columns appeared as fast as the older ones moved off the screen. Then, nothing.

A password box reappeared in the centre of the screen. Falah pushed back on his chair and stood up. "There you go, Luay, try it now."

The two men swapped places and then Abass retyped his login details.

"I'm in!" whooped Abass in amazement. "What did you do?"

"Sorry, Luay, tricks of the trade. I could tell you . . ."

"But then you'd have to kill me?"

"No, you might pinch my idea and make millions," grinned Falah.

"What did you do? I mean, you don't need to go into detail?"

Falah pocketed the flash drive. "It's a program I've been working on. Basically, it allows me to upload a back door into any system with a vacant USB port. I've been fine-tuning it to appear non-threatening to most software security programs, and now I'm working on its power outage to make it virtually undetectable."

Abass looked on in wonder.

"Without explaining the technical jargon, the program also creates a false login, whereby when someone types in their password, once their system is online, it emails me their details. Thereby, allowing me remote access from anywhere I have online access."

"So I didn't need to enter my details?"

"Nope, once you've pressed three or more keys and hit the return key, it allows you access and I have total control of your system."

Abass looked aghast. "What the . . ."

Falah held his hands up in mock surrender. "No, no, no! Sorry, I'm joking about the second part. I'm still working on that," he offered as his defence. "But, I'd still change your password," winked Falah.

Abass looked perplexed. He raised his eyebrows as a rush of thoughts bombarded his brain. He opened his mouth.

Falah spoke first. "I tell you what, Luay, meet me in the café after this session and I'll let you into a little secret," he smiled, giving Abass a telling nod.

"Okay," was all Abass said, before returning to his monitor and commencing his coursework.

EIGHTEEN

James Strong drew in a long, deep breath as he looked first at Macleod's notepad and then straight into the eyes of his department head.

"Well, James, you've had time to gather your thoughts. What do you want to do?"

Briefly, the image of an interior mirror from a car raced through Strong's mind. He could just make out the reflected silhouette of a man standing beside a parked car. The sound of rain drummed in his ears as he strained to see the dark figure, shadowed by the night sky. The man was suddenly illuminated by a succession of flashes as he fired into the side window of the car. Strong's eyes diverted from the mirror and back at Macleod.

"Fullerton gave the order for the soldier and myself to murder an IRA informer."

There, the words were finally out, thought Strong.

"I was to lure him to a secluded spot on the outskirts of Londonderry and the soldier was to shoot him dead." Strong felt his breathing steadily growing more rapid, the palms of his hands were starting to become clammy, and he felt the hairs on the back of his neck rise, as a rush of adrenalin coursed through his body. The relief was, strangely, becoming more of a thrill to Strong.

Macleod made his notes in a bastardised shorthand as Strong narrated. "Okay, James, I need you to pause for a second so we can break down what you can remember."

Strong clenched his sweaty fists before retreating back into the briefing in 1995. In his mind, he ran through events as he recalled them and he then recommenced his account.

"Colin finished the introductions by producing a file containing details of a known intelligence source; his name was Gerard Logan. Colin asked me to arrange a meeting with him before taking the soldier to the rendezvous point."

Macleod paused the recount. "Do you recall where the meeting was to take place, James?"

"Yes, I do. I don't think I've ever really forgotten the place. It was in a lay-by on the outskirts of Londonderry, on the A40, just two miles short of the border checkpoint."

Macleod scribbled down the location before indicating for Strong to continue.

Strong obliged. "I was to get Logan to the lay-by and then take him for a short drive as a distraction, to allow the soldier to get into his car. The plan was to convince him his life was in danger and that he had to be extracted to a safe house." A knock on Macleod's office door interrupted the interview. "Come in," invited Macleod.

"I'm very sorry, sir," apologised his secretary. "I have an urgent request that requires your signature." The secretary offered Macleod a large, sealed envelope and an electronic signature pad. Macleod accepted the envelope and pad, placed the envelope into a tray of paperwork, and signed the pad with the attached stylus. He returned the apparatus back to his secretary, who immediately turned and left the office.

"Thanks Jane." Macleod's tone was softer than usual. His secretary gently closed the door behind her, leaving the two men staring at each other across the desk.

"Okay, James, continue."

Strong finished his coffee, composed himself then continued his account.

"After meeting with the informer and returning him back to the lay-by, I asked him to get back in his car and go collect his wife. The plan was for the two of them to meet me at the police station on Strand Road, where I would be waiting to take them away to their new life."

"It all sounds like an elaborate plan."

"It had to be; this was my first and only meeting with Logan and I needed him to trust me for Colin's plan to work."

"So, tell me about the killing, James."

"The soldier was now hiding in the other car. I watched as Logan walked back to his car and climbed back in. Next came the flashes from inside the car as he was executed." Strong paused momentarily, realising how parched his mouth was. "The soldier got out of the car and fired more shots through the driver's window. Once he was finished, he returned to my car and we drove back to camp."

Macleod finished his notes then raised his head, looking up at Strong. "Did you and the soldier talk about anything whilst you drove back?"

"No, we drove back in complete silence. Once we arrived back, I parked up the car and returned to my office; I think the soldier reported back to Colin."

"Why didn't you go back to Fullerton's office with the soldier?"

"I just needed a moment to think about what had happened and also to regain my composure; the whole event really shook me up." Strong stared straight at Macleod. "I've fired guns at targets before and I'd seen the videos of the death and destruction conflict brings during my N.I. training, but that was the first time I'd been so close to an actual killing." Strong swallowed hard. "One moment I'd been talking with Logan and the next . . ." He paused, again, trying to think of the right words. They didn't immediately come to him.

"Being so close to death really affects you. It's not something you can prepare yourself for," added Strong eventually.

Strong noticed that Macleod had stopped writing. "I understand fully, James, and it's very hard to take the emotion out of a situation involving the taking of another human life."

For a brief moment, Macleod appeared to drift. Strong wondered what thoughts his boss was toying with; he chose not to ask.

"Okay, James, you've done really well. Do you think you've missed anything out?" Macleod waited, pen poised over the notebook.

"No, sir, I think that is everything. I'm just sorry I can't recall the name of the other soldier, as I know how much more of a help it will be."

"Do you remember anything at all about him?" asked Macleod.

Strong delved into the deep recesses of his mind. His eyes rolled upwards, flicking quickly from left to right. Slowly, a frown creased his face as he shook his head.

"I'm sorry. I could say he was about my height with dark hair, but I wouldn't be confident that it's correct," said Strong.

Looking disappointed, Macleod took this opportunity to read through his notes for the benefit of Strong. "Does that cover your account of the events, James? At this moment, is there anything you'd like to add or, indeed, alter or be omitted? "

Strong shook his head. "No, that's everything," he repeated. "What happens next?"

"First thing is, I'll appoint someone to look into your statement and ask them if there's anything you've said that can be supported with corroborating evidence. That will be followed by the taking of a statement from Fullerton."

Strong nodded.

"I've someone in mind, so I'll get them onto this matter immediately. As soon as something comes up, if at all anything does, I'll get you back in here and we'll see where we stand."

Again, Strong nodded. "What about Fullerton?"

Macleod closed his notebook. "He'll still join your section as previously discussed. It's not that I doubt what you're saying, it's more in following procedure. And until we have something tangible backing up your statement, Fullerton has to be treated fairly."

"Okay," replied Strong, as his shoulders dropped.

"Let's do some digging first, James, and see what we can uncover." Macleod retrieved the telephone handset. "Get back to your operation, I'm sure I'll be speaking with you again soon enough."

Macleod pressed a sequence of numbers on the dialling pad and waited for the call to connect. Strong collected his coffee mug before leaving the office. Outside the door, he breathed a huge sigh of relief. Briefly closing his eyes, he recalled the image of a soldier firing through the driver's side window and the car's interior lighting up with each blast. He shook the vision from his mind as he headed back to his office.

"Hello, Ms Scott?" asked Macleod. "Great. Tracey, I have an assignment for you. Can you drop by later today please?"

Macleod thanked the woman on the phone before hanging up. He tapped the computer mouse on his desk and the dark screen reopened, asking for his password. As he typed, his thoughts became preoccupied with visions of Colin Fullerton; he'd known the man for almost 25 years. Fullerton was transferred to Northern Ireland under a dark cloud. The man with the questionable work ethics. The man with the Teflon exterior and nasty reputation that nothing seemed to stick to. The man who'd slept with Macleod's first wife!

Now it is time you got what is due to you, thought Macleod, now it is time for payback.

NINETEEN

Colin Fullerton paused briefly, looking up at the sign above the entrance: "Garda". There was also a golden harp painted either side of the Irish word for police. He pushed one of the double doors open before stepping through and into the warmth of the reception area.

Fullerton crossed the tiled floor towards the duty officer's desk. He glanced around for any signs of life, noting on a wall to his right. Just above the crime prevention and general information posters was a single, fixed security camera. A small red light below the lens indicated that the camera was on. It was too late to hide his face now; he just made sure he kept his exposure to the watchful eye of the camera down to a bare minimum.

A door behind the desk and off to the left opened, and a middle-aged Garda officer, sporting a well-groomed beard, walked through into the reception room. He carried a large red mug with a Liverpool FC crest on it. The officer placed the mug down onto a flattened, worn-out coaster.

"Good afternoon, sir," said the officer, as he checked the time on the clock above the entrance doors. Three o'clock; three hours until shift change. "How can I help you, sir?"

"I want to report a missing person," replied Fullerton.

"I see, and how long has this person been missing?"

"A couple of days . . . that I'm aware of."

The officer reached below the counter to retrieve a large pad of forms. Before opening the pad, he fished out a pen from a shirt pocket. He pressed out the nib.

"Okay, sir, I'm going to be needing some details from ye," he said, adding the date to the top sheet. "Right then, we'll start with your name first."

Fullerton gave one of his cover names and started relaying his telephone number. The officer stopped writing for a moment and began scribbling on a pad of Post-it notes until he got the ink flowing. "Okay, can you spell that again fer me, sir?"

Fullerton rolled his eyes then spelt out his name.

"Right, now, ye friend. Ye say he's been missing for a couple of days? When was the last time you saw him?" The officer paused momentarily. "I'm sorry, what's your friend's name?"

"Adam Lewis," replied Fullerton, almost through gritted teeth. "We were supposed to be meeting up for a spot of fishing, but he failed to turn up, and now no one can get hold of him."

The officer wrote Lewis' name into one of the boxes on the form. "Okay, sir, and the last time you'd seen him was when?"

"It would have been Friday morning. Well, I hadn't seen him, but I had spoken with him. I'd booked us into the White Horse hotel in town. He was running late and said he'd meet up with me so we could go fishing as planned," explained Fullerton.

"So, Friday morning was the last time ye'd heard from him," the officer muttered to himself. "And was that morning, the last time you spoke to him?"

"It was. I've left messages on his voicemail, but he's not returned any of my calls." Fullerton paused. "He's not returned anyone's calls, and now we're getting worried."

"Is he the sort of man to just go off on his own? I mean, would he just change his mind and not bother turning up?"

Fullerton thought for a moment. He was aware he was taking a huge risk by involving the police, especially asking them to look for Lewis, but he needed to know Lewis was out of reach of everyone, and that included the authorities. Fullerton had used one of Boyle's own men to plant the seeds of doubt about Lewis, and so was in no position to just call up the Irishman and ask if Lewis had been dealt with. He hoped that the ex-SAS soldier was now dead and buried in an unmarked grave, deep in the southern Irish countryside. Fullerton wasn't prepared to take the risk that Lewis could possibly turn up at a hospital, ferry port, airport, or even police station, and drop him right up to his neck in shit!

Fullerton believed he was taking a calculated risk. He saw this more as reassurance that Lewis was indeed dead and buried, and he meant it quite literally.

"Sorry, where was I? No, Adam was, I mean is, the sort of person who is always punctual. If he says he'll be at a certain place at a certain time then he'll be there."

The officer nodded as if agreeing with Fullerton. His pen poised over the section headed description.

TWENTY

Adam Lewis noticed that the light outside the barn was fading.

The shadows around the inside walls grew, spreading their dark tendrils out towards the centre of the barn, swallowing everything up in a creeping, silent blackness. Lewis had an idea it was late afternoon, only because darkness descended earlier during the winter months. What he didn't understand was why the two Irishmen hadn't returned. In his mind, it just didn't make sense. So far, all they had done was beat him up. Maybe they weren't the torturing kind; maybe after having time to think, they've realised how hard it is to beat someone up for information. It would be especially hard if, as Lewis knew, he had no information to give out. All he could tell them is why he was at the farmhouse, and that was something he had to hold onto for as long as he physically could, because once it was out, the countdown to his death would begin.

A noise outside the barn startled Lewis. All the sinews through his body tensed, pulling tightly around his curled-up form. As his eyes grew accustomed to the darkness, the shadows retreated, until he could see the barn door. His breathing dissipated into shallow rasps as he waited for the door to open. He stared intently, willing the wooden structure to allow him to see beyond its confines. It never happened. His breathing was now a soft, slow, steady rhythm; he could almost feel his blood pulsing around his body. The only noise was the rustling outside the barn door. Lewis held his breath. Someone made contact with the bottom of the door, and an involuntary shiver passed through Lewis' whole body.

He waited.

Nothing happened.

Whoever was outside, and Lewis had a good idea who, had decided not to enter. He heard movement down one side of the barn; it was slow and deliberate, and steadily getting closer to Lewis, chained up at the bottom end of the barn, directly opposite the doors, where it had first originated. Lewis followed the noise with his eyes until it was behind him. He was now restricted from following the sound by his restraints. He waited.

As the noise from the crunching of foliage moved along the outside of the back wall, Lewis craned his head, searching for cracks or breaks in the wall, looking for somewhere he could see through to the outside. The noise stopped before whoever was outside backtracked towards Lewis. Once again, the noise stopped. Only the wooden wall and a gap of five feet stood between the unknown entity outside and the chained-up ex-soldier. Lewis held his breath, as whoever was out there was now level with his head. *What are they up to?* They knew he was inside, chained to a post! How in the hell did they think he could escape?

The movement started again, continuing at the same deliberate, slow pace. A shadow passed by a gap, about a foot from the ground. Whoever it was was now walking along the other side wall, back towards the doors.

Lewis wondered why he could only hear one person outside. Had the other guy waited at the door, or had only one of them returned to the barn? He'd also not heard a single voice. Was this their idea of playing with his mind? Were they trying to psych him out with, what appeared to be, very basic mind games? Lewis fought hard to remain composed. He wouldn't let the unknown get the better of him. He was much stronger than that.

The outsider was now back at the barn door.

Once again, Lewis braced himself, ready for whatever they had planned for him. Like a bolt of lightning, a sudden thought flashed through his mind. His eyes widened as he heard a noise at the door: what if they intended just to kill him? What if that was one of them, checking no one was nearby, before coming inside to finish him off? He'd assumed he'd be questioned and tortured. But Lewis had realised earlier that he didn't have much information to give them. Lewis' mind raced, as he fought to overcome the rising feelings of panic.

Maybe subconsciously, he'd buried thoughts about them just wanting to kill him deep inside his head. But now, as clouds covered the sun, sucking away what little light there was inside of the barn, and with his captor only the length of the barn and the thickness of a door away, Lewis realised these could well be his last moments alive.

During his army career, he had never seriously thought about dying or being killed. He'd always believed in his own abilities to keep him safe. But here he was, shackled to a post, with no way of defending himself. *Is it too late to pray?*

Lewis was hardly a church-goer. If he was honest, religion had rarely touched his life. Apart from the odd church service that he was compelled to attend during his military career, Lewis had never set foot into any sort of religious building. Still, he did remember the *Lord's Prayer. Is now the time to recite it?*

He murmured the first few words: "*Our Father, who art in heaven . . .*" Lewis paused for a moment. The noise outside was suddenly becoming a more familiar sound. Lewis could hear an animal scratching at the bottom of the barn door.

He breathed a huge sigh of relief and screamed at the top of his voice. The animal stopped scratching and ran off.

The thought that the two men would, at some point, return was pushed back into the dark shadows of his mind. For now, Lewis had a stay of execution.

However, he continued with the prayer.

TWENTY-ONE

Luay Abass and Hassan Falah finished their coursework and started packing away their equipment. "Do you still want that coffee?" asked Falah.

"Yeah, sure, why not? And then maybe you can explain how your magic device works."

After tidying their workstations, both men left the IT department and went for a short stroll to the cafeteria on the first floor. Once there, Falah bought two coffees whilst Abass found a vacant table. Falah joined his new friend and handed over a mug of coffee. Once he'd taken his seat, he retrieved a handful of sugar packets and cream pots from a jacket pocket, which he piled neatly in the centre of the table. Abass collected three sugar packets and a single cream pot. Falah left his black and sugarless.

"Sweet enough, eh?" joked Abass, immediately regretting opening his mouth and uttering what sounded like a corny chat-up line.

"Sorry, Luay, that wasn't even funny," said Falah, before cracking a weak smile. "Anyway, the reason I wanted to have a quiet drink with you . . ."

Abass looked across the table with an expression of puzzlement. "I thought you were going to tell me about your magic password device, weren't you?"

Falah bent down and retrieved his laptop from the satchel, resting against the table leg. He opened it and proceeded to log in; this was all done in a hushed silence. Once the screen opened up, he selected a media player icon then turned the laptop around so that Abass could see the screen.

"I haven't been completely honest with you, but bear with me please," said Falah, clicking play.

Abass was still unsure about his new friend's motives but, for the time being, decided to indulge him. He moved closer to the screen as an image came into view.

The video clip started with a bearded, young man reading from a sheet of paper. Even with the volume down low, Abass soon recognised them as words from a passage in the Qur'an. He also stared at the green and white banner behind the man. It was daubed with black, painted Arabic writing. Abass could read "Brotherhood of the . . ." Unfortunately, the last words were obscured by the bearded man's head. The following half-dozen silent clips were of various explosions; two of them appeared to be images caught by CCTV cameras from inside a building. The last lot of clips were attacks on an assortment of military vehicles. The low sound returned once more, finishing with another man dressed in white robes and brandishing a large machine gun, threatening all Western governments with more violence if they failed to remove themselves from all Middle Eastern countries. Then the screen went blank.

Abass looked shocked. His mouth was dry and opened slightly. He lifted his head slowly. Taking a quick look around the cafeteria and seeing that the other students hadn't heard anything, and were oblivious to what he had just seen, Abass addressed Falah. "I'm very sorry but I'm not joining any group; none of *that* is for me." He pushed his chair back, making a move to stand. Falah reached across the table and grabbed Abass' forearm. "Please get off me, I want to leave now!"

"Don't go, Luay, it's not what you think." Falah released his grip. "Please, sit back down and listen to what I have to say. I'll explain everything if you give me the chance. You'll understand, once you hear me out. It's the complete opposite of what you're thinking."

Halfway between sitting and standing, Abass looked first at the blank laptop screen then at Falah's face; his eyes pleaded for him to sit. He sat back down.

"Thanks, Luay. Thank you for staying."

"Okay, but . . ."

"Let me explain," interrupted Falah. "I work for a government department. The video clips you have just seen all have one thing in common." Falah depressed the enter button and a series of faces flashed up on the screen. As they did, Abass suddenly realised that he recognised one of the faces. Surely not, he thought. His next thought was, why would someone from his prayer group be blowing up army vehicles?

"All the young men you have just seen were responsible for each of the attacks in the short clip. They all attended one particular mosque in the Whitechapel area. In fact, I believe at least one of them once attended the same mosque as you, Luay."

Abass stared back in disbelief. Maybe he did recognise one of the photos after all.

"Luay, all those young men have been radicalised not too far from here, and by one cleric in particular, Mustafa al Dulhaimi. He preaches in a mosque less than 15 miles from where we're sitting right now. As a matter of fact, you have already met him."

Abass' disbelief turned swiftly to faux outrage. "No! No, I have not!" he asserted, through gritted teeth. "I only go to one mosque and it certainly isn't his!" At the back of his mind, Abass had a nagging feeling that this stranger knew about his involvement with the group of young Muslims set on fighting against people like al Dulhaimi.

"Now that's not quite true, Luay." Before the now worried student had chance to speak again, Falah continued with his explanation. "Don't worry, you probably weren't even aware that you'd even met with al Dulhaimi. Cast your mind back about two months ago."

Abass mellowed slightly, as a look of puzzlement washed over his face. He couldn't quite work out this man's game.

"You went to attend evening prayers, but there was a group congregating outside the mosque. An imam was preaching to the crowd about the ethics and motivation into the West's involvement in Syria. Things got a little heated between those wanting to enter the mosque and those gathered outside." Luay was beginning to remember the occasion. "You were one of three men who physically removed al Dulhaimi from the premises."

"That was hardly a meeting," responded Abass. "He was taking the Qur'an completely out of context to suit his own twisted beliefs. We just wanted to get into our mosque, and besides, the police did nothing to intervene, so we had to take matters into our own hands. It was hardly . . ."

Falah interrupted. "See, you do remember."

"But, what has that got to do with me?"

"Al Dulhaimi takes a select group of young men for prayers at his mosque, and we think you would be the right person, for us, to penetrate that group."

"On the back of one little scuffle?" asked a perplexed Abass.

"No, not one little scuffle. We've been watching you for a while. We know of your involvement with the group of 20 other likeminded young Muslims standing up against these radical groups. We also know of your arrest and caution. These are some of the reasons we believe you have the required values to help us."

Abass gripped the sides of the table. "Wait a minute, you've been following me?"

"It's standard procedure . . ."

"I don't care about your rules and procedures. What gives you the right?" demanded an incensed Abass.

"In other circumstances, we would have approached this differently, Luay, but this time, things are against us – we are working to a very tight schedule."

"What do you mean by that?"

"I can't go into too much detail until you agree to work with us."

"And if I don't?"

"If you don't, Luay, then all I ask is that you don't mention this meeting to anyone," explained Falah.

"Okay, if I agree, then what?"

"You need to agree first," said Falah bluntly.

"I don't know . . ."

"You have to trust me, Luay; it's a simple yes or no!"

Abass realised he was still gripping the sides of the table; his knuckles were bulging and white due to the tightness of his grip. He released the table and sat back in his chair. "What do you want me to do?"

"We have recent intelligence, suggesting al Dulhaimi is planning an attack in London, sometime in the next few weeks. We need you to help us find out if there is a target and if so, when and where the attack will take place."

"How will I do that, I'm not a spy?"

"We can prepare you, Luay, we can give you all the help and support you'll need, but you will have to get into that private room on your own and find out what's happening."

"You make it sound so easy," answered Abass. "As if I can just walk into his mosque and ask to be accepted into his private prayer room."

"We know it won't be easy. We will give you as much help as we can in such a short space of time." Falah's mobile vibrated in his trouser pocket. "We need to get into that room and you're the best option." Falah removed the phone and sent the call to voice mail. "You have experience of the routine, so we just need to help you hone a new skill set to be accepted by al Dulhaimi."

"Again, it sounds so simple," answered Abass.

"Look, Luay, we don't have the resources to follow every member of that mosque to get answers, so we need a viable alternative, and we believe that's you."

"Okay then, what happens next?" asked Abass.

"I need you to leave your family for a short time and come with me to a safe house where I'll rehearse you with your cover story and prepare you to work undercover."

"A cover story? And what about my family, what if they get suspicious? What do I tell them? They need me in the shop."

"Don't worry, we have that covered. We understand you are studying computer game design. Well, we have an offer of a placement with one of the biggest companies in England."

"It sounds plausible," said Abass.

"It gives you a reason to be away from home for the next few weeks or so," replied Falah. "And, once this is over, by way of a thank you, we will endeavour to get you an actual placement."

Abass thought briefly about Falah's offer. "It sounds very tempting, that's a very tasty carrot, but I do have some concerns."

Falah had suspected throughout his conversation that Abass was still a little apprehensive, but he knew that he had to show some give and take just to get Abass on-board. A little understanding was possibly the difference that could make or break this.

"It's understandable that you will have doubts, Luay, and I'm sure most will be put to bed once we begin preparing for your insertion. But if there's anything I can help you with now, I'll do my best. What concerns do you have?"

A rush of thoughts clouded Abass' mind. He took a brief moment and a deep breath to compose himself. "I know the mosque you want me to attend is nearly 20 miles from where I live, but I'm sure I recognised one of the faces in the video clip. What happens if someone recognises me at the new mosque?" Abass paused. "In fact, not just me, but my family."

"I can't go into too much detail here, Luay, and that's only because it would be easier to show you the steps we will put in place. Apart from reporting to me every day, you will have equipment with you that will trigger an immediate response to wherever you are." A thin smile appeared on Falah's lips. "Your own on-call personal security team."

Abass shared Falah's attempt at humour. "And do my family get the same?"

Knowing the risk of potentially putting doubt back into Abass' mind, Falah decided to answer with the negative aspect first. "Unfortunately, we can't afford the same level of protection for your family, but as you know, we don't want them involved." Falah watched the look of doubt fall across Abass' face. "However, they won't be left on their own. We will have a small team monitor your family as we do have a duty to ensure their safety. And if at any time, you feel their safety is at all in doubt, we will act." Falah took a moment to allow Abass to digest his response before continuing. "I appreciate the situation we are potentially putting you into, and managed correctly, it will not impact on your family in any way, but as a last resort, we do have the option of relocating you all somewhere safer. But that's a bridge we should only cross in the highly unlikely event that we have to." Falah hoped he was offering some peace of mind to Abass.

As the enormity of the task he was taking on weighed on his conscience, with Falah's answers echoing inside his mind, Abass' thoughts were drawn to his father. He recalled the first time he was told of the time he spent in prison, the reason he was there, and the conditions he had endured. His father had pulled through it all and Abass had so much respect for the man he had become. He'd survived through appalling conditions and treatment, this humble man epitomised. In many ways, his father was what Abass was striving to achieve within his group of activists. Maybe this was his chance to show what he could do, and maybe, one day, he would be able to talk to his father about the part he played in the "War on terror".

With a renewed vigour, Abass addressed Falah. "As long as you do everything possible to protect my family, should it come to it, then I'm happy to help you."

Falah felt more at ease now that he had a definitive answer, but before he could say anything, Abass spoke up once more. "From what you say, it seems you have most things covered. What if I had said 'no'? Had you had that covered?"

"Luay, I'll be straight with you, we have others we can approach, and with a little tweaking, the plans could be rearranged to fit them, but with you, we feel we have more chance of success."

Abass felt a swell of pride.

"You understand the situation we're in at the moment, and all al Dulhaimi is doing is manipulating people's beliefs to suit his own twisted agenda."

The two men looked straight at each other, Falah felt that he had won Abass over. "Islam may have its faults, but the general peaceful message is being distorted and abused to justify terrible acts of violence."

Abass nodded. "I agree. The vast majority of Muslims are peaceful, along with our religion. It's people like this al Dulhaimi who are giving the rest a very bad name, and if I can help then I will."

Falah closed his laptop.

TWENTY-TWO

James Strong was finishing the process of logging out of his desktop when his mobile phone rang.

He picked it up and glanced at the caller ID, before swiping his thumb across the green answer symbol. "Hello Hassan, how did it go?"

Strong continued packing his briefcase as he chatted with Falah. Before ending the call, he collected his coffee cup from a coaster besides a family picture, walked across to a display of photographs and notes attached to a mobile noticeboard, and cast his eyes over the images. He scanned them until his eyes rested on a picture of Mustafa al Dulhaimi. "Great, Hassan, let's get him in for a briefing."

Strong pocketed his phone. Raising his coffee cup towards the picture of al Dulhaimi, he gave the image a mock "cheers".

Before leaving the building and heading for his car, Strong visited Macleod to inform him that Operation Vagrant was now officially on.

TWENTY-THREE

Adam Lewis was half awake from another cold, restless night when the barn door swung open. Through bleary eyes, he watched as two figures entered the wooden structure and appeared to glide across the ground towards him.

Lewis was suddenly aware of a soft pounding sound that seemed to be growing. As his breathing turned to short pants that did little to fill his lungs, he was now aware that the rhythmic pounding was his heart. As the two apparitions closed in on him, Lewis realised he had to contain his panic, he needed a distraction.

Lewis had tried keeping track of the time of day in order to best guess how long he'd been held captive. As he came to his senses and managed to take slower, deeper breaths, Lewis craned his neck until he caught sight of sunlight cutting through the gaps in the roof. He estimated that it was somewhere around midday, and this was his third day of captivity. He set himself the task of trying to steal a glance at one of his captors' watches to satisfy his guesswork.

Billy Boyle spoke first. "Wakey-wakey!"

He kicked out at Lewis as he shouted the words. The force from the blow sent throbbing spasms across Lewis' thigh, as the excruciating pain from the dead leg spread.

Boyle removed the Glock from his waistband and fired one round into the dirt, just above Lewis' head. He felt small particles of earth bouncing across his face and hair. Lewis resisted the urge to shake the dirt free.

"Time we talked, ye Brit bastard!" snarled Boyle.

Ginty dropped a heavy bag onto the ground in the centre of the barn. With his right hand, he reached inside and fished out a craft knife, of which he then extended the retractable blade. He crossed over to Lewis and proceeded to manhandle him onto his side before cutting through the plastic cable ties securing his wrists together. Lewis felt relief as the numbness dissipated from his fingers from the sudden release of pressure, allowing more blood to flow up his arms.

The stiffness in his joints eased as the unhindered blood flow rapidly returned. He flexed his fingers and slowly rotated his shoulders, until Ginty balled a fist and struck Lewis on the side of the head. "Don't be making ye sel' comfy! Just sit there and don't move," he warned.

Lewis eased himself into a sitting position as best he could, with the restriction of a chain securing his ankle.

"Right, listen up, this is how it's gonna be. I'll ask ye some questions and ye gonna give me some answers." Boyle crossed his arms while still holding the pistol. He then took slow, deliberate steps towards Lewis. "You *will* answer my questions and you *will* tell me the truth. If I think ye lying to me, I *will* hurt you!" Boyle emphasised each "will" by nonchalantly tapping the pistol against his arm.

Lewis raised his head slightly and looked up at Boyle, who was now standing directly in front of him. "Do we have an understanding, fella?"

Lewis nodded.

Boyle kicked out. Lewis fell backwards, gasping for air. "I didn't hear ye?"

"I understand," he managed to reply, between sharp breaths.

Ginty left Boyle and Lewis in the barn and went outside to look for a rock or log. He needed something large enough to support a hand. Luckily, his searching didn't take too long and he soon came across a large log, resting in the foliage of a clump of trees at the rear of the barn. Ginty twisted and turned the log until he had it in a position he could manhandle back to the barn. Exhausted, he finally dragged the log inside. Lewis was still seated on the floor with Boyle standing menacingly over him, only this time, Lewis had a bloody nose.

"What happened, Billy?"

"Nothing much, I'm trying to get his name but the fucker keeps refusing to answer me."

Ginty half-dragged and rolled the log closer towards the two men. After one last roll, he toppled it over beside Lewis. Dust and earth splashed up, sticking to the congealed blood around Lewis' nostrils. He coughed, expelling particles of grit from his mouth.

Ginty turned and fetched a hammer from the large canvas bag. Holding it up, he asked, "Do you want it, Billy, or shall I do it?"

On seeing the log and then the hammer, the colour drained from Lewis' face. During his SAS selection course, one phase consisted of escape and evasion from an enemy force, which always ended with the recruit being captured. For some, what came next was a major breaking point, and for Lewis, it pushed him to the very brink of quitting. But he managed to cling on till the very end, using every last ounce of determination and energy. The tactical questioning phase, or torture, as it was in basic terms, resulted in the recruits being deprived of food and sleep, disoriented through constant noise, and having a stinking sack fastened over their head, and finally, being bullied and humiliated by trained interrogators. The whole phase was designed to push the recruit's mind and body to its very limits. But there were boundaries to how far the directing staff could go, and smashing a recruit's hand with a hammer was not permitted, despite being the IRA's favoured method of extracting information from a prisoner.

Boyle tucked the Glock into his waistband, behind his back, before taking the hammer from Ginty. He passed it from one hand to the other, getting a feel for its weight, then let it slide through his fingers until he gripped its head. Boyle pointed the shaft towards Lewis. "Right then, Mr Fucking Hero, I'll ask again. What's ye fucking name?"

In a single fluid move, Boyle knelt down, grabbing Lewis' right hand, and stretched it across the log. Lewis wrestled his arm back from the Irishman's strong grip. He strained with every ounce of strength he could muster, and the two men played tug-of-war with the hand, heaving it across the log. Splinters broke the skin around Lewis' wrist, sending a sharp pain up his arm, but he still resisted. His resolve was eating away at his depleted energy reserves. He knew at some point, the two men would get the better of him, but Lewis wasn't going to make it easy for them. He gritted his teeth and fought hard to keep his hand off the log. In a swift change of tack, Ginty dropped down behind Lewis, forcing a knee into his back. Lewis arched as the pressure from behind threatened to snap his spine. His switch in focus allowed Boyle to pull his hand back onto the log and, with the help from Ginty, the two men secured the limb. Boyle raised the hammer. "What's ye name, big man?"

Lewis relaxed his body as he prepared for the strike. Boyle shouted the question once more, spittle from his mouth flecking across Lewis' face, but still, he kept quiet. Boyle swung his arm and brought the hammer down heavily towards Lewis' outstretched hand. Lewis collapsed to his left, taking Ginty with him; the hammer struck the log ,sending a powerful shockwave up Boyle's arm.

"Fuck!" he raged.

Ginty pushed himself back onto his feet and once standing, kicked out at Lewis. Once again, Lewis was left struggling for breath as he slumped forward. Ginty reached into a trouser pocket and removed the craft knife. He bundled Lewis back upright again. Then he got down behind him and grabbed him around the neck in a stranglehold. Ginty held the blade against Lewis' throat. "Grab his fucking hand!" he snapped.

Boyle reached for Lewis' hand, and once again, Lewis resisted. "Give him ye fucking hand!" Ginty spoke softly into Lewis' ear. Despite the menacing undertone, Lewis still withheld his hand. Each time Boyle struggled to pull his hand forward, Lewis, somehow, through sheer desperation, mustered the strength to drag it back again. Ginty pushed the blade into the side of Lewis' dirt-covered face. The tip broke the soft flesh; a drop of blood formed over the tiny wound. "Give him ye fucking hand, big man!" Ginty spat out the order.

Lewis still refused to comply.

Ginty looked up at Boyle and motioned, with his eyes, for his friend to pull the hand again. Only this time, Ginty stabbed the blade into the side of Lewis' face and sliced open the skin. A bloody line about three inches long stung Lewis' face, and distracted him long enough for Boyle to grab his flaccid hand, pull it back to the centre of the log, and drive the hammer down onto it. The steel head smashed hard onto Lewis' trigger finger. The joint nearest the knuckle separated and split, spilling blood onto the log. Lewis yelled out in agony, his pain filled every corner of the barn.

"Ye fucking name!" demanded Boyle.

Lewis clenched his mouth shut, stifling his cries of pain, as Ginty, once again, pressed the blade into his flesh. He drew the blade across Lewis' forehead, slicing another bloody, stinging wound to his head, and again, Boyle grabbed his weakened wrist and slammed the hammer down once more. This time, it connected with the knuckle of his middle finger. The bone shattered and the metacarpal and phalanges either side of the knuckle splintered under the force from the blow. Bone fragments from the damaged digit split the skin and released more blood onto the log. Small rivulets trickled down towards the dirt, gathering in miniature pools at the base of the log. Lewis felt himself on the threshold of unconsciousness.

Boyle slapped Lewis hard across the face. His palm split open, the first wound exposing pink flesh. Lewis snapped back into the moment, hearing Boyle barking out his question once more. "Give me ye fucking name!"

Lewis parted his parched lips, the fight in him waned. "Burrows," he whispered. "Pete Burrows."

"I can't hear you," answered Boyle.

"My name is Pete Burrows," said Lewis.

Whatever energy Lewis had left was expelled as he slumped backwards against Ginty. A vision of a rugby match filled his mind before being clouded over into darkness, Lewis had grabbed the name from one of the players on the field, someone he'd been teammates with during his early military career. A large brick shithouse of a man from somewhere in Yorkshire.

Despite the energy-sapping tug-of-war, Lewis still felt like he had won a small victory. If he was to find a way out of this situation, he needed these two thugs to think it was in their best interests to keep him alive. And deep down, Lewis was aware that the only way he could do this was to put up as much resistance as he could, no matter how hard they beat, broke or cut his body. His very survival had never relied so much on his fight to overcome such impossible odds at any point in his life as it did now.

"Right, Pete, now we know ye name, ye can now explain what ye were doing at the farmhouse."

Lewis drew in as deep a breath as he could manage. A mental image of a bell played out inside his head.

Ding, ding. Round two.

TWENTY-FOUR

Colin Fullerton arrived into work as the last covert car was being loaded onto the transporter truck. Once it was secured with loading straps, a blue tarpaulin sheet was used to cover the car over.

Fullerton parked his car before heading inside the compound. Rob Nicholl, his deputy section head, met him. "That's just about everything done, Colin," he explained. "The only thing left is to secure all the doors, that is, after you collect the two boxes from your office."

"How did the documents transfer go?"

"Without a hitch, everything is now secured away in Thiepval Barracks. Do you want me to help you with your boxes?"

"If you don't mind, Rob. I don't suppose there's a kettle left out, is there?"

The two men entered the large, white building for the last time, Nicholl holding the door open for Fullerton. "I'm afraid not. 'Everything must go', as the phrase goes."

They climbed the staircase to the first-floor office; their shoes echoed around the empty shell of the once busy intelligence hub. They entered Fullerton's office and stood in the bare, expansive room. As Fullerton looked around, he couldn't fail to notice the tell-tale signs of a recent clear-out; the carpet indentations from office furnishings, the scattering of drawing pins and paperclips around the skirting boards, and the bright patchwork of squares on the walls were assorted pictures and maps had once hung. Fullerton collected one of his boxes and handed it to Nicholl, who took it down to the car, leaving Fullerton alone. Around him, Fullerton could almost hear the past echoes of nearly 40 years of military occupation, reverberating between the empty walls. He bent down and collected the other box, remembering his first day in his new office. Fullerton peered through the grubby glass panes at a prominent empty space that was once occupied by an imposing figurehead from HMS Cunningham. The statuesque woman had been dismantled and shipped off to one of the naval museums in Portsmouth many weeks earlier; a relic of the Second World War when the camp was a naval base. He recalled how the porcelain complexion of the lady, dressed in white and blue robes, used to stare straight into his office from her position outside the large Victorian building opposite.

Fullerton heaved the box tightly into his arms and walked out of his office, resisting the temptation to turn around one last time, as he knew that this place also held onto the remnants of some awful memories too.

Fullerton secured the two boxes into the boot of his car. It was as he shook hands with Nicholl that his phone rang. "Excuse me, Rob," he said, removing his mobile phone from a jacket pocket. "Hello?"

Nicholl felt a chill blowing off the Foyle and across what used to be the helicopter landing site. He looked out across the dark, swirling river and thought how much the landscape of the city had changed during his 16 years in Londonderry. The old buildings had been demolished and replaced by newer, smart shops and offices. He could just make out the church spire that once stood opposite a large communications mast, from the small military base that had occupied an old car park, near the city's Masonic lodge.

"Sorry, Rob," apologised Fullerton. "It looks like I start sooner than originally planned. Macleod wants me in tomorrow."

The two men shook hands once more. "Thanks for all your support, Rob, and who knows, maybe in the future, we can work together again. But whatever happens, don't forget, I'm only a phone call away, should you ever need anything."

"I won't, Colin, thanks and good luck."

Fullerton climbed into his car, fired up the engine and accelerated away.

Nicholl watched the vehicle disappear from sight behind one of the old, whitewashed Victorian buildings that had once housed the medical centre and soldiers' accommodation. He collected his thoughts and for the last time, turned around and headed back to secure the building. Time to move on, he thought.

Across the river, a distant siren echoed around the city.

TWENTY-FIVE

Adam Lewis ached all over.

As he inhaled, he felt a sharp pain shoot across the left side of his body. Lewis didn't need to look at or touch his side to know he had a broken rib. The pain he felt was very similar to one he had felt during an army boxing match, and on that occasion, he had suffered two broken ribs from a vicious body assault. The referee had stopped the fight, which he'd lost to a technical knockout.

The blood flow from Lewis' broken nose had long stopped and was now just a dark, congealed mess around his mouth. With every arm movement, he found himself gritting his teeth and fighting the white-hot pain shooting up his right arm from his pulverized knuckles and fingers. He was in a bad way and he had no idea how much longer he could hold out for.

"If I have to ask again, you'll fucking know about it!" White spittle built up at the corners of Boyle's mouth as he spat out the words. "What were you doing at the farm?"

Lewis had spent most of the previous day thinking about the questions he would be asked and the answers he should give. He knew he was living on borrowed time and it was probably going to be down to how long he could sustain their torturing that would determine how long he would live. No one would be looking for him; there would be no search and rescue team coming to his aid. Lewis knew it would only be a matter of time before he was killed, and all he was doing now was making his last moments as painful as possible for himself. There was only so much damage and pain his body could take. But there was something deep inside him that, stubbornly, was not in the least bit willing to surrender.

"I was sent to the farm to meet someone."

"Who?"

"I've no idea; I was shown a photograph and told he would be there."

"Photograph, what photograph?"

"I was shown a photograph and given the location of the farm. I was told the man would be there."

Boyle looked across at Ginty with gritted teeth and a mask of frustration. "Who was the photo of, fucking George Best? Give me a fucking name!" His temper was bubbling over.

Lewis winced with pain. "I don't know his name. I was just given the picture and asked to go find him."

Boyle clenched his teeth once more. His jaw muscles knotted as the veins in his neck throbbed and slowly, his face coloured purple with rage.

"Do you make a habit of taking photos from strangers and not getting any details?" said Boyle, kicking out at Lewis. "Do you think I'm a fucking idiot?" he shouted, putting the boot into Lewis once more.

Lewis opened his mouth to answer but caught the toecap of Boyle's boot on the side of his jaw. He felt one of his upper molars fracture due to the force from the blow. As Lewis fell to one side, he extended his right arm to soften his landing. "AARRGH . . . SHIT! FUCK! BOLLOCKS . . . FUCKING BASTARD!" He landed on his two busted fingers and could no longer mask the pain. Boyle caught Ginty stifling a chuckle as he delighted in their captive's discomfort.

Boyle composed himself. "Who was the photo of and who gave it ye?"

"Look," said Lewis, spitting out a mouthful of blood, "I find people for a living, that's my job." The bitter, coppery taste stayed in his mouth, despite expelling another two globules of sputum and blood. "People pay me good money . . ." Lewis drew in a laboured, painful breath, ". . . to find people."

Using his less damaged left arm, Lewis rolled slowly, pushing himself back into a seated position. Air rasped over his swollen, bloodied lips as he sucked in another breath. "It's none of my business why these people need finding . . ." Lewis paused once more, gritting his teeth as he fought back the pain from his damaged ribs. He tried moving his position, but it only aggravated the fractured bones more. ". . . or even who they are; I take the money and any snippets of detail I need for the job." Again, Lewis spat a globule of blood onto the dirt-covered floor. "I'm paid to find people, not ask questions," he said, feeling nauseous after what felt like an overly long speech.

"Okay then, Pete the finder, why the gun?"

Lewis looked up at Boyle. Wishing he had a notepad and pen, he drew in another painful breath, spat out more blood then answered his captor.

"'Cause some people don't want to be found, and will do almost anything to get away." A fog descended on Lewis' brain as his inability to breathe properly was causing him to become light-headed. He knew it was only a matter of time before he passed out. "And, despite my job, I value my own life and need some protection."

Standing in front of Lewis, Boyle was suddenly aware of his right foot tapping a fast rhythm in the dirt, pushing out small motes of dust. He fought to control his frustration.

"So, tell me about the photo you were given."

The question stumped Lewis momentarily; it shouldn't have, as it was an obvious one. He put it down to not being fully focused due to the intense pain he was in and also fighting off unconsciousness. He masked his lapse by swaying and groaning with discomfort while recalling an image of Sean Boyle.

"Well?" asked Boyle once more, clenching a fist.

The image that forced its way to the front of his mind was the one in which Lewis was standing over Sean after the ambush at the barn, back in 1990-something – the incident that led to his dismissal from the SAS.

"It was an old one," said Lewis, still struggling with the bitter taste of blood in his mouth. "He had brown hair and a ponytail."

Boyle recollected his reunion with his brother Sean on his release from prison. He'd waited with anticipation until the moment Sean was delivered to the house. And recalling their first embrace as free men, Boyle remembered the ponytail.

"Right then, let's say you're telling the truth. What were you told about my brother, Sean?"

Brother? Lewis held his breath. He ran through what he knew so far. He was told Sean was at the farmhouse and no one else, and someone had tipped off his brother to go to the farm. From his present situation, Lewis had worked out days ago that he'd been set up, and now he was waking up to the realisation that he had never been close to getting his hands on Sean Boyle. In fact, far from it, he'd been sent on a wild goose chase across Ireland, finally ending with his capture by the brother of the man he was after. Lewis couldn't help but wonder whether he could have avoided ending up in his current situation if he hadn't been so blinded by revenge.

"Your brother? I've never heard of him. Should I?" said Lewis, annoyed at his own stupidity.

Boyle took a step backwards. Lewis instinctively flinched.

"He was shot dead a few days ago near the Scottish border," said Boyle, swallowing an imaginary lump in his throat. "I got a call to go to the farmhouse; someone knows my business and is responsible for the death of my brother. Then there's ye. Ye turn up, with a gun, looking for Sean. There's a connection here and I means to find it."

Boyle removed the pistol from his waistband and pointed it at Lewis' head. Lewis looked away, for a brief moment forgetting all about his pain and discomfort.

"Were you sent to kill me?"

"No, I wasn't."

"Was the photo a picture of me?"

"No, it wasn't."

"Were you at the farmhouse to kill me?" Boyle's voice rose steadily with each insistent question.

"No, no, I wasn't!"

Boyle squeezed the trigger and fired three rapid shots.

Lewis sat helpless as the rounds whizzed past his ear at over 900 feet per second. The air around his head warmed as he felt them miss him by mere inches. He heard the rounds smash through the wooden wall at his rear.

Boyle put the pistol away again. "Ginty, get the drill."

"Fuck, look, I wasn't after you, I swear!" Lewis failed in his attempt to suppress his panic. He found himself wishing the rounds had blown his brains out. "Look, I wasn't at the farmhouse looking for you, I swear to God. It wasn't you I was after; it was Sean, Sean, your brother."

"Ye'll be doing a whole more swearing in a minute," gloated Boyle.

Lewis pleaded some more. "Think about it, you weren't even at the farmhouse, so how could I have been after you?"

"Maybe ye was early. I was sent there, remember? And ye show up with a gun; maybe ye was early or I was late. It doesn't matter now."

Ginty returned with the drill, which he handed over to Boyle before grabbing hold of Lewis.

Lewis was determined to not make it easy for his captors. He put up as much resistance as he could, with what little strength he had, as Ginty forced him to the floor. The Irishman wrapped one arm around Lewis' neck and wrestled him to the ground. As both men struggled, Ginty reached out and grabbed hold of Lewis' damaged fingers. He squeezed as hard as he could. Lewis yelled out in pain, still trying to resist the effort to get him on the floor. Ginty continued squeezing the damaged digits, only now, he slowly bent them back towards Lewis' forearm. The searing pain and flashes of white light were too much for Lewis as he succumbed and fell onto his side.

"Roll him onto his back," demanded Boyle.

Without a struggle, Lewis was on his back, staring up at the dark rafters and holes in the barn roof. Boyle lowered himself on top of Lewis, pinning him down by kneeling across Lewis' arms. He switched on the cordless drill.

"Please don't," pleaded Lewis.

Boyle ignored him.

Lewis watched as the drill was brought down towards his shoulder. He pleaded once more with Boyle, and again, his pleas were ignored as his rasping, breathless voice was drowned out by the high-pitched whirring from the drill.

Boyle picked a spot on Lewis' shoulder and aimed the drill bit. He pushed the spinning steel into Lewis' soft flesh. The bit tore into Lewis on contact and discharged blood and skin in all directions. Boyle exerted more pressure, forcing the tool deeper into Lewis' shoulder until a high-pitched whining noise could be heard. A noise not dissimilar to a dentist's drill biting into enamel. Boyle had reached bone.

As Boyle ground down further into the bone, Lewis, his face masked in his own blood, passed out.

TWENTY-SIX

Adam Lewis felt a warm liquid splash over his face as he was brought back from the safe, dark oblivion of unconsciousness. He slowly forced his right eye open. The socket of his left eye was filling with warm liquid. As Lewis regained control of his senses, his whole body shuddered with the immediate onrush of pain and coldness. Lewis realised he had been stripped down to his underwear and, as the cloudiness cleared his head, he could now see a figure standing over him. The diminishing light from outside the barn cast a golden aura around the man. How long had Lewis been unconscious? Long enough to be stripped of his clothes. There was still some daylight, was it now late afternoon? All Lewis knew was that it wasn't dark.

Boyle's grinning face came into sharp focus. He was holding something. Lewis realised it wasn't a drill and as he turned his head, spilling the warm fluid from his eye socket, he also realised the liquid was piss.

Boyle finished with a quick shake before fastening his zipper. "Good, ye're awake!"

Ginty handed Boyle the drill once more. "Right, where were we?" He grinned, squeezing the trigger, giving the drill bit a few short bursts. The high-pitched whizzing echoed around the barn as the spinning bit dissipated the aroma of warm blood, until Lewis could detect it around his nostrils.

He was still trying to rid himself of the foul, salty taste in his mouth. It was as he was spitting out the saliva, mixed with urine, that he glimpsed his damaged shoulder. Lewis hoped the blood around the wound was making it appear to be worse than it actually was.

Ginty sat back down on Lewis' waist, pinning his upper torso to the ground. Then Boyle sat on Lewis' ankles, disabling both his legs. Boyle was now looking down at Lewis' kneecaps.

"Any preferences?" Boyle asked. "Not that it matters." He squeezed the trigger and the drill screamed into action once more.

Lewis shouted, but Boyle chose to ignore him, as he lowered the drill. Lewis continued shouting and pleading, but still Boyle remained oblivious and focused on his task. The drill bit hovered over Lewis' twitching kneecap; the soft flesh was tinged a bluey purple, beneath the blood and dirt. Slowly, Boyle pressed the drill bit into Lewis' skin, shredding the top layer as it made contact.

The power died.

"Are ye gonna talk?"

"Yes . . . Yes . . . I'll tell you everything!" Lewis submitted.

Boyle remained seated. "Go on then."

"I do know your brother, Sean."

Ginty turned to look at Boyle, waiting for him to give a signal to stand back up. Boyle tilted his head to one side, motioning an acknowledgement. Once Ginty was on his feet, Boyle followed. Lewis felt a huge relief in pressure sweep over the whole of his body, and as the earlier surge in adrenalin died, the pain, too, returned.

Lewis continued. "Sean killed my daughter and I was after him."

"Okay, I can understand that. But he wasn't at the farmhouse; in fact, he'd never been near it. So why were you there?"

"I was told that's where I could find him."

"Who told you?"

"Does it matter? You won't know him!"

Boyle tightened his grip on the power drill and raised it slightly, mainly as a gesture of intent for Lewis, who now appeared to be growing in confidence. "It matters to me. I've lost a brother and some good men, and ye're the fucking link in all this shit. So, it bloody matters!"

Lewis thought for a very brief moment. He felt he had nothing more to gain by playing dumb. "I was told Sean was at the farmhouse by a British agent. He told me your brother was hiding out there, but all along, the bastard was playing me." Lewis looked straight up at Boyle. "Why were you there?"

Without thinking about the bluntness of the question, Boyle answered, "One of my men was caught, he told me someone was going there looking fer me. They thought it was my safe house."

Ginty looked puzzled at Boyle's candidness.

"Who was it that sent ye?" Boyle asked again.

"What are you going to do with me?" Lewis asked, reluctantly.

"Tell me his fucking name!"

"Does it matter? You can't get to him."

Boyle stepped onto Lewis' kneecap and pushed down hard. "What's his fucking name!" he demanded.

"Fullerton," Lewis spoke, between the bouts of sharp pain, "Colin Fullerton."

Boyle stepped back, handing the power drill and pistol to Ginty. "Put these away."

Boyle then grabbed Lewis and dragged him back to the post he had previously been chained to and re-secured the shackles. Lewis offered little resistance. Once finished, Boyle left the barn, slammed the door shut and refastened the padlock. He was met by Ginty, who was clutching the large canvas bag.

"What do we do now, Billy?"

"I don't know. I need time to think."

"What about him?" Ginty hooked a thumb towards the barn.

"We'll come back tomorrow; be prepared to dig a hole!"

The two men followed the winding track back into the woods and onwards towards their hidden van.

Inside the barn, Lewis sat clutching his knees to his chest. His body heaved from broken bones, split and shredded skin, and numerous bruised punch and kick marks. He started shivering.

TWENTY-SEVEN

Luay Abass' mobile phone played a short jingle. He retrieved the phone from the counter top and thumbed the touchscreen until he could read the message.

Taxi outside 5 mins.

Suddenly, Abass became very nervous. He shielded the phone screen, even though there was only his dad and him in the shop. He shot quick glances left and right. What was he looking for? He had no idea, could they be watching him right now? He felt his head filling with unanswerable questions. Should he ignore the text? Should he take the taxi? What would they do if he didn't? Was the message really for him?

"Are you okay, son?" asked his dad, walking through to the storeroom from the shop.

"No . . . I mean . . . Yeah, I'm fine," he finally managed to say.

"You sure, my boy. You look a little . . . I don't know, you don't look yourself."

"I'm fine Dad, I just need to pop out for a while."

"Why?"

Abass took a brief moment to compose his thoughts as his dad started unpacking a box of digital radios.

"Why do you need to go out?" his dad repeated, looking over towards his son.

"Oh . . . Yeah," said Abass. "Remember I mentioned the placement at Connexion Games? It's just one of the guys going with me." That's it, thought Abass, sticking to his cover story.

"What does he want?"

"He's just texted, asking me when can I pop over."

"Okay," replied his dad, returning back to emptying the box.

"Great," mumbled Abass under his breath, and gaining control of his nervousness.

"Sorry Luay, I never caught that."

"Nothing, Dad," Abass replied, stepping out from behind a shelf and dodging around a pile of stacked boxes to get to his father. He said his goodbye in Arabic, followed by two quick kisses to each of his father's cheeks.

"I won't be late," Abass called back, as he disappeared out of the storeroom.

"Wait, Luay, haven't you forgotten something?"

Abass turned to see his dad holding up his laptop satchel. He retrieved it from his father's grasp, repeated his goodbye and left the store. A rush of cold air wrapped around him like a blanket as he stepped out onto the pavement. Abass looked around the street, furtively searching between the various parked vehicles. A red minicab caught his eye. It drew level with him and the driver leaned out of his window, calling across to him.

"Are you Luay Abass?"

"Yes," Abass answered.

"Great, jump in fella."

The minicab pulled away.

Fifteen minutes later and the silent journey came to an end. Abass took in his surroundings; he was on an estate, dwarfed by tenement blocks. The driver passed on a simple set of instructions before Abass climbed out of the minicab. He headed off towards the entrance of one of the tower blocks. Once inside, he crossed over the large expanse of a reception area, listening to his shoes echoing across the tiled floor, and stopped at one of two lifts.

He didn't have long to wait before he was inside the stale-smelling box and heading up to the tenth floor. Abass stepped out into the concourse and took a moment to orientate himself with his new surroundings, amongst the graffiti-defaced walls.

Flat 1023 was through the door to his left. He pushed the corridor door open, taking care not to catch his hand on the patchwork of smashed, re-enforced glass, only held in place by wire meshing. Once onto the balcony, Abass was exposed to the noises and cold air of an early London evening. This high up, the cold was more penetrating, and the heat he'd gathered from the taxi and lift ride soon disappeared, as the chilly evening air grabbed hold of him.

Abass checked the brass number plate of the first door he arrived at – 1001. He continued walking until he was stood outside the one he was instructed to report to. Abass reached out to knock on the green door, and to his surprise, the door opened before he made contact.

"Hello Luay, don't look so surprised, we have a team in the block opposite watching over us."

Abass instinctively turned around to be confronted by an almost identical tower block, with row upon row of windows, some with lights on and some in complete darkness. He stared for a moment, thinking he might catch a glimpse of the watchers, but all he could see was a hundred or more windows staring blankly back.

"Chai, coffee or water?" Falah offered, grabbing Abass' attention once more.

"No, I'm fine, thanks," said Abass, following Falah to the front room.

"Take a seat then and we can get started."

Abass sat down on the small settee, followed by Falah, who then opened the laptop resting on the cheap, MDF coffee table.

"I need you to watch this before I explain things to you," said Falah, hitting the touchpad and starting up the laptop.

Abass sat through a short clip of a gun battle, something not dissimilar to what he usually saw on the late-night news. Three men being lined up and shot dead quickly followed this. The execution was very graphic, but Abass felt compelled to watch it to the end. The three men fell to the floor like marionettes with their strings cut. A single figure approached the line of bodies and riddled the corpses with more machine gunfire before raising his weapon skywards and letting off one final burst. Once the clip ended, Falah closed the laptop.

"I appreciate it's not to everyone's taste, Luay, but you need to see it, and probably a few more times after we finish."

Falah reached down, over the side of the settee, and produced a black case; he rested it across his lap before opening it. Falah took out a passport, mobile phone and a number of folded sheets of paper, one of which he passed over to Abass.

"Here, Luay, this is your new identity."

Abass accepted the sheet and briefly scanned the pen picture.

"As you can see, we've only changed your surname so as not to overcomplicate things. You're used to answering to your first name, so this will make it easier for you, considering the rest of the information I need you to take on board."

Abass' eyes flickered back to the top of the page. "Luay Mohammed", it read.

"The clip you've just seen is of your brother, Uday's execution in Syria," started Falah. "He was there fighting a Jihad against Syrians, whom the West have armed. A friend emailed you the clip and now you want to avenge your brother." Falah pointed to a paragraph on the second sheet of paper. "This here is a brief history behind your brother's story, backing up his presence in Syria." Falah looked at Abass. "The story will hold up to a reasonable amount of scrutiny, but nothing more in-depth. Which is why we placed in a number of trigger phrases."

Abass looked puzzled.

"The phrases, when checked, will alert us to someone digging deeper into your cover story. If we can't hold them off, we will extract you immediately."

Abass still looked worried.

Falah continued with his briefing. "We know al Dulhaimi has sent some of his followers to Syria, along with a number of other clerics. What we want you to do, Luay, is get inside his special study group over here. Once inside, we need you to find out what he has planned for the UK and, if possible, who will carry out his plan."

Falah broke away from the briefing and stood up.

"I hope you remembered to mention the placement to your family?" asked Falah.

Abass looked up from the paperwork and nodded.

"And did you manage to convince them it was a genuine offer?"

“Yes, it wasn’t easy lying to my family, but I convinced them it was real,” replied Abass.

“Good work, Luay. Because, from tomorrow, this flat will be your new home for the next few weeks. When you’re ready, take a look around and also familiarise yourself with the details on your briefing notes. I need to pop outside for a while,” said Falah, heading for the entrance hall.

Abass stared blankly at the sheets of paper.

TWENTY-EIGHT

Robert Macleod parked his car, locked the door, then darted across the road to the wine bar opposite. Once inside, he scanned the room, seeking a familiar face. On seeing Tracey Scott, he gave her a wave. After he navigated his way around the other patrons to her table, Macleod pulled out a chair and sat down.

"Sorry I'm late, Tracey, the traffic out there is a right . . ."

Tracey Scott cut in. "It's okay, Robert, I've only just sat down myself."

"Good evening, madam, sir. Can I take a drinks order for you both?" asked the immaculately-dressed waiter.

"Tracey?" Macleod looked across at his companion.

"A glass of chardonnay, please."

"I'll have the same, thanks."

"Will sir and madam be dining tonight?"

"Maybe, in a while," said Macleod, dismissively.

The waiter dispensed with his notepad, committing the simple order to memory, and headed for the bar.

"Thanks for your call earlier, I've spoken with Fullerton and asked him to report in tomorrow."

"That's a little presumptuous, isn't it, Robert? You haven't heard what I've found out yet."

"Tracey, you've never let me down in the past, so, if you tell me you've found something, however small it is, I know . . ." Macleod paused, as the waiter arrived back with their drinks. Taking his glass, Macleod raised a silent cheers gesture and swallowed a mouthful of the chilled wine.

"As I was saying, however small your snippet of information may be, I know you won't stop until you have all the facts and that you'd not bother me with trivial matters."

Tracey blushed with pride. "Stop it, Robert, I only do my job." She paused momentarily. "It's not my fault I'm great at it."

The two people acknowledged the comment with an exchange of smiles.

"Well then, Tracey, tell me what you've found out."

"Firstly, I had to confirm that we at least had a body to start with. A quick Internet search confirmed that a man, believed to be working with the British government, was found shot dead on the outskirts of Londonderry. And the date and location match with Strong's statement."

Macleod listened, nodding at the appropriate places.

Tracey continued. "Although I've found the alleged body, I haven't found any particular group claiming responsibility for the shooting, or admitting that he had any affiliation to them."

"That's hardly unusual. We've had similar situations when it comes to establishing the group they've belonged to, and that's usually only to save face. Nobody wants to admit they had an informer in their midst," replied Macleod.

"Yes, anyway, here's one of the first anomalies I came across." Tracey handed Macleod a blue file. "Reading the coroner's report, he links the wounds and bullet fragments found in the body with similar wounds and fragments found on two other murdered corpses. This puts the firearm used into the hands of a Republican group."

Macleod opened the report and speed-read the first page.

Tracey continued once more. "A Loyalist's solicitor and Protestant taxi driver where both killed by ammunition from the same gun."

Macleod beckoned over the waiter and ordered an orange juice for Tracey and a glass of coke for himself.

"I'm guessing you're driving too?" asked Macleod.

"Unfortunately," sighed Tracey.

A thin smile crossed Macleod's lips/ "What else have you found, Tracey?"

"Well, as I was saying earlier, we do have a body, but finding his killer is little harder." Tracey opened the folder on the table in front of her. "Here, on page four, is a list of all the soldiers that served with Captain Roberts, during our timeframe."

"Have you managed to speak with Roberts?"

"Unfortunately not. Captain Roberts was killed shortly after his tour of Northern Ireland. He died during a rescue mission in Bosnia, in 1996."

"Oh," was all Macleod could say.

"I have managed to track down some of the other soldiers though, and to speak with them. Luckily, one of them does remember Roberts going off on a number of occasions and meeting with Fullerton."

The brief moment of deflation was replaced by keen interest. "And?"

"And. He doesn't recall who went along with him."

Macleod finished his wine just as the waiter returned with their order. He thanked the waiter and asked for the dinner menus.

"Well, here's a first. It looks like I have indeed jumped the gun. There's nothing here to link Fullerton with the killing."

Tracey Scott looked across the table at Macleod. "I wouldn't say that exactly . . ." Tracey paused long enough for Macleod to catch on. "Remember, I said the gun had previously been used in two other murders?" Macleod leaned in, listening intently. "Well, after a great deal of digging around, I have managed to find a suspect for one of the previous shootings, with said pistol."

Macleod picked up the folder and with an expert eye, started to speed-read the report once more.

"There's nothing in there, Robert."

Macleod closed the file.

"The reason there's nothing in print is because the suspect was released, as one of a number IRA prisoners released under the Good Friday Agreement and given special leave that he wouldn't be later charged with any unsolved crimes."

Macleod was aware that "special passes" had been agreed between the Prime Minister and Sinn Fein, as one of the terms for a ceasefire, expunging a number of terrorists from future prosecution for outdated crimes. But he still looked puzzled.

"Don't worry, I'll explain. The coroner at the time linked the three deaths from bullet fragments taken from all bodies. A man named Padraig Breen was arrested on information received, and in possession of the gun, but he was never charged." Tracey raised her eyebrows, "Are you still with me?"

Macleod nodded.

Breen was in prison for five years on other charges, but not the murders with our gun, because the murder weapon disappeared. Then, luckily for him, the Agreement happened and he was released with a get-out-of-jail-free card, courtesy of Mr . . . well, you know who!"

Tracey Scott paused to take a sip of her juice.

"Anyway, let's back-track to Breen's first arrest. He was picked up after information was received from one of our informers. For which, said informer was paid £500."

Macleod leaned back in his chair momentarily, before moving in closer for the punchline. Tracey Scott didn't disappoint.

"Colin Fullerton was the informant's handler at the time. I know the link is a little tenuous, but it does put him into the chain involving our gun. I do think, with more time, I'll find something more substantial, as this wasn't the route I was expecting to be going down."

Macleod nodded. "I agree, and for the time being, I still think I have something to question him about. Good job, Tracey."

TWENTY-NINE

Adam Lewis had spent the night attempting exercises to keep himself as warm as possible. His range of movements were limited by his shackles, but each time he'd achieved an exercise, Lewis had executed it to the point of exhaustion. Then, following a short rest, he attempted another exercise. Although he was tired through lack of sleep, he was thankful he hadn't succumbed to hypothermia.

Morning had finally arrived and shafts of warm sunlight, penetrating the gaps in the roof, bathed Lewis' battered and bruised body. It felt like the warmest he'd been since his abduction. Even so, Lewis still sat with his legs pulled tightly to his chest, trying to retain as much core body heat as he could.

After the previous day's interrogation, Lewis had a sense of foreboding about the new day. All through the night, he'd fought back the strong possibility that today would be his last day – his last day, full stop. Lewis had used every last effort to keep himself warm, and had not wasted energy contemplating any final thoughts of what he'd achieved in life or what he would miss out on. Despite his situation, survival had been his main aim. In fact, it still was his main aim. More than ever, he needed to call on all the experience that he had honed over many years of working and surviving in dangerous places.

As the morning sun rose and more light shafts pierced the roof, Lewis heard footsteps outside the barn. He opened his mouth slightly to sharpen his hearing and listened. Both of his captors were talking. Unfortunately, their words were muffled and hard to decipher, so Lewis struggled to understand anything. Slowly, the voices travelled down one side of the barn before gradually fading. Lewis briefly thought back to two days ago when an animal was walking down the very same side. Maybe it had been a very hungry wolf looking for food and it was still lurking outside, and any moment now, it would come to his rescue and pounce on the two Irishmen. Lewis chuckled at his wishful thinking.

The footsteps appeared to be moving away from the barn. Apart from the occasional snapping of twigs under foot, he heard nothing else and eventually he was, once again, alone in the silence.

Lewis tried to imagine ways in which he could attempt an escape and avoid the finality of death. His situation wasn't helped by him being chained to a sturdy support beam. Lewis knew, to have any chance at all, he had to be free from his shackles, but he had already tried everything and it wouldn't budge. That little light at the end of the tunnel was fading fast. He knew it made sense for his captors to kill him whilst he was still chained up, so Lewis tried to figure out a way of fighting back whilst shackled. Unless one of the Irishmen came close enough for Lewis to seize, he had nothing. With the chain still as secure as when he was first restrained, his survival relied solely on him being unshackled.

During his many self-defence classes with the Regiment, Lewis had been placed in many situations where he was expected to escape from an armed captor. His assailants had been armed with a wide variety of weapons and Lewis had practised many blocks and strikes to disarm his opponents. Some techniques were better than others, but they all came with some element of risk. Lewis concentrated on one in particular. It required one of his captors to be standing behind him, holding a pistol to the back of his head, and, as this was a favoured method of execution by the IRA, it may just work. All Lewis had to do was draw the man behind him close enough to pivot sharply and knock away or seize the weapon before it was discharged. The manoeuvre relied on the element of surprise and very quick reflexes. It had worked for him many times during training, but now, cold, tired and battered, the situation was very different. Did Lewis feel up to this? He looked at his gunshot wound then his broken fingers, before finally staring at his damaged ankle. Possibly, he thought, but not with much confidence.

The barn door swung open, throwing up motes of dust and dirt. Boyle walked in quickly, followed by Ginty. Lewis noticed both men were carrying weapons, and with this, he felt his chances of escape take a severe tumble.

Ginty handed Boyle his Glock pistol before walking across to Lewis. In his left hand, he held a pair of bolt cutters. Lewis suddenly felt his chance of escaping rise back up again. He quickly thought through his repertoire of techniques, settling on one in particular. All he had to do now was manipulate the situation to his advantage.

Ginty bent down and snapped the lock free from the chain. He booted Lewis sharply in one side. "Get the fuck up!"

Lewis now knew he had to focus completely on his situation. He forgot about his pain, he forgot about the cold, he pushed from his mind thoughts of hunger and dehydration, concentrating all his energies on escape and survival.

"Don't ye be trying anything stupid, Pete," called Boyle, taking aim with his shotgun at Lewis, keeping him in his sights the whole time.

Lewis remained silent and focused.

Ginty pushed Lewis in the direction of the barn door; slowly, the two men stepped forward. Boyle trained the shotgun on Lewis the whole time, slowly turning before stepping between the two men as they passed by. Ginty collected his pistol and followed on at the rear.

As Lewis emerged from the barn, he lowered his gaze to avoid looking into direct sunlight, as he needed time for his eyes to adjust to the brightness.

"Hold it there," ordered Boyle.

Lewis stopped walking. Looking down, he noticed small pools of water reflecting sunlight from an assortment of muddy footprints and then, he spotted the shovel. The bolt cutters landed on the ground close to the spade, displacing some of the pools of water.

"Okay, follow the barn around to ye left an' keep walking."

Lewis complied, taking deliberate, slow, methodical steps. He gritted his teeth, fighting to block out the pain from his damaged ankle. Still retaining his focus.

"Follow that there track on ye right," barked Ginty.

Both men kept a safe distance from Lewis, not venturing closer than five feet. Lewis felt he could not slow down any further, as it would only antagonise his captors and possibly ruin any chance of escape.

The three men reached a clearing, no bigger than the inside of the barn, at the end of the muddy track. Overhead, grey clouds rolled past a gapping break in the tree canopy. The first thing Lewis noticed was the hole dug in the centre of the clearing; it reminded him of grave, only not quite as deep. In fact, on closer scrutiny, it looked more like a shell-scrape – a type of hole he'd dug many times during his army career. It was meant to offer a soldier, lying in one, protection from enemy shellfire, but this one definitely wasn't for protection. This was to be his final resting place. Lewis pushed the image to the back of his mind, maintaining his focus.

"*I'm not dead yet!*" A quirky, old voice spoke inside Lewis' head as he very briefly recalled a *Monty Python* film. Only he was not lying on a cart being led by a man calling, *"Bring out your dead."*

"Kneel down in front of ye grave," commanded Boyle, as he shoved Lewis with the end of the shotgun barrel.

Lewis ignored the instruction, hoping Boyle would step just a little closer. He didn't.

"I said kneel the fuck down!"

Lewis obliged. As he did, he heard the other man swearing under his breath.

"What is it?" Boyle asked.

"I've left the spade up at the barn," replied Ginty.

"Don't worry about it," placated Boyle. "Go back and get it, and I'll do fer this fucker."

"Are you sure, Billy?"

"Ye, away and fetch it. He'll be dead an' in the hole before ye get back."

Lewis strained to hear what was being said, but heard nothing. He did, however, hear one of the men running back up the track. He felt like he was being given one last chance to escape. Now, more than ever, he needed all his strength and focus to defeat Boyle.

Lewis splayed his fingers and dug them into the ground, trying to give himself a strong platform to spring from.

"Ye may want to say ye prayers now," said Boyle, as he took a step closer and placed the shotgun barrels onto the back of Lewis' head.

Lewis drew in one final deep breath; his whole body tensed as he readied himself. Adrenaline coursed through his veins, blocking out all feelings of pain.

Boyle tightened his finger around the trigger; his face twisted in a grimace as he prepared for the shotgun blast. Slowly, he squeezed the trigger.

THIRTY

Ginty reached the barn. After a short trudge around to the front, he located the tool bag, and lying beside it were the bolt cutters and spade. He packed the bolt cutters away in the tool bag, retrieved the spade, and headed off back down the track.

Click.

Nothing.

Lewis held his breath. It was now or never.

Boyle panicked. Barely a second passed and he desperately pulled at the trigger once more to fire off the second hammer.

Click.

The colour drained from his face.

Lewis heard the second click; the term he was more familiar with was "dead man's click". The first click, Lewis noted, was dull sounding, which indicated that the hammer had struck a damaged percussion cap or simply miss-hit the shell case. The second click, however, was more of a metallic echo, and this indicated that the hammer had fallen onto an empty chamber.

During his time handling firearms, Lewis had heard "dead man's click" numerous times but, the more proficient he became, the less he noticed the distinct sound. The only way to avoid "dead man's click" was to count your rounds as you fired. This gave you an indication as to when you were almost out of ammunition, thus allowing you to execute a magazine change, before you completely ran out. You never wanted to face your enemy with an empty magazine; otherwise, you'd be a dead man.

Lewis used all his strength to push himself up and around to face his captor. Boyle was trying to draw back the shotgun's hammers when Lewis slammed his forehead into Boyle's face. Blood exploded from his captor's nose as the appendage flattened under the force. Boyle was knocked off balance and reeled backwards. He only just managed to remain on his feet.

Lewis continued his assault by slamming his foot directly into Boyle's groin. The violent blow ruptured one of Boyle's testicles. Boyle instantly doubled over and crumpled to the ground. He let out a wail that would normally have been associated with a small child and, as a consequence, released his grip on the shotgun. Lewis knelt down over the prone Boyle, following up the kick with a fist to face. Pain shot up his arm as his fist made a connection, Lewis fought hard to suppress the excruciating agony as he continued pounding Boyle's face until it was a bloody, pulped mess.

Next, Lewis reached for the shotgun. Gripping the barrel, he wielded it like a club, raining blow after bone-crunching blow down onto Boyle's head. With each brutal strike, his skull fractured, tearing vicious rents through his skin until folds of bloody brain spilled from the gaping wound. Lewis ceased his assault, his chest pounding, with his lungs threatening to burst free. He drew in a succession of quick breaths as the adrenaline burst started to wear off, leaving him weakened. Looking down at his own chest, Lewis watched as rivulets of blood streaked down to his naked waist. He let his eyes wander over Boyle's motionless corpse, until he was staring at his pummelled face. Blood flowed into the grass from the folds of damaged brain that filled the battered cavity above his left eye.

Three rapid gunshots refocused Lewis' mind. He looked up to see his other captor approaching from down the track with one arm raised and clenched in his fist was the Glock. Lewis knew the man was not firing from a stable fire position so the rounds could go anywhere. Still, he was not prepared to hang around and be hit by a lucky shot. So Lewis darted behind the nearest tree just as another two rounds struck the large trunk, blasting off splinters of bark and exposing the tree's pale, yellow wood.

Ginty reached the clearing and saw Boyle's motionless figure lying face-up on the blood-soaked grass. He also noticed the shotgun was missing, and ducked behind a sturdy tree for cover.

Lewis pushed the barrel lock to one side with his thumb and broke the shotgun open. One empty barrel and the base of a partly-struck shell-case greeted him. To Lewis' trained eye, it looked like the hammer had failed to make full contact with the shell-case, probably due to either the shell not being seated correctly in the breach or a foreign body blocking the movement of the hammer. Lewis removed the shell-case and inspected it for further damage, and, happy it was okay, popped the shell between his teeth and upturned the shotgun. He shook it and patted it heavily in an attempt to dislodge any obstruction. Lewis was aware that his teeth were incessantly tapping against the hard, plastic shell casing. As the effects of his adrenalin rush wore off, Lewis was once more feeling the elements assaulting his cold, exposed body. He took the shell from his mouth and reloaded the shotgun before slamming both barrels closed.

Ginty peered cautiously from around his cover. Once again, he saw Boyle's lifeless body and then the tree Lewis had taking shelter behind. He shouted, "Ye might as well give up, I'm not going anywhere an' ye sure as hell aren't in any fit state to hide fer long."

Lewis listened. Ginty did have a point, but he was not prepared to give up so easily. He had already dispatched of one of his captors and if he had to, Lewis would die trying to finish the task of disposing of the remaining captor.

Ginty shouted again. "Did ye hear me? Ye ain't going nowhere!"

Lewis clutched the shotgun to his chest; Boyle's blood on the handgrip was now cold. He was also feeling the freezing cold ground under his bare feet and as it crept up his legs, the numbing of his muscles. The sun disappeared behind a smothering of dark rain clouds and with it went the little warmth it offered; Lewis felt the last remnants of warmth leave his bare, exposed skin.

Suddenly, a thought electrified his mind, and for a brief moment, he was back in the farmhouse kitchen. Lewis was falling towards the tiled floor. A sharp pain enveloped his shoulder as he made contact with the floor, but he also caught sight of an object just out of reach. Lewis focused his mind.

Ginty, once again, shouted from behind his tree, only this time, the words were lost on Lewis, as he concentrated on his vision. The tiles became clearer as his head rested on the floor, small black and white squares. No, that was not it. "*LOOK!*" a voice demanded from deep in his subconscious. Lewis looked away from the tiles. A dark object came into view, a black metal object. A black metal object containing something that shone like gold. No, Lewis looked harder; it was brass.

Lewis felt the coldness from the tiles washing over the side of his face; his vision was blurring as he slipped into unconsciousness.

"*CONCENTRATE!*" his subconscious yelled, once more.

Lewis summoned up all his willpower and focused on the black metal object. It was a magazine, his magazine; it was the spare magazine he'd tucked away in his waistband. The magazine had dislodged itself as he'd hit the floor and was now resting beneath the large fridge freezer inside the farmhouse kitchen. Lewis now realised the significance of his vision and immediately tried working out how many shots had been fired from the Glock pistol. Lewis' other captor only had that same magazine fitted to the pistol; and as he had not seen either of the Irishmen with any other pistols, he hoped he had no spares. It was now imperative that Lewis worked out how many bullets were left in the pistol.

Fighting against the freezing cold, Lewis created a mental image and walked himself back through the last few days. Above him, the dark clouds released their load as the first droplets of rain bounced off his bare shoulders.

Lewis counted two rounds fired into the tree he was sheltering behind as he walked through his thought map. Before that came three shots from the lunatic running down the track towards the clearing and now, going further back, Lewis counted the shots fired by Sean's brother.

As the rainfall intensified, Ginty decided to have another look from behind his cover. Slowly, he pressed himself up against the tree, tightly clutching the pistol in his right hand, and then, in one sharp, fluid movement, he bobbed his head out from behind cover. He saw nothing of Lewis. Ginty moved his head once more, only this time more deliberate and slower. Again, he saw nothing of Lewis, just the prone figure of Boyle, whose clothes were now soaked through, as the rain showed no sign of relenting. As Ginty drew his head back into cover, he shot a glance up the track towards the barn. *Was it time to make a run for it?*

"Shit!" he cursed under his breath, as he realised Boyle had the keys to the van.

Lewis recalled Billy firing eight times inside the barn; three when Lewis had been kneeling up, once into the ground before they had started torturing him, and four times into the wall on his first night of captivity. That just left the amount of rounds Lewis himself had fired.

As the downpour intensified, Lewis' hair became matted to his head and his fringe clung tightly to his forehead in a row of small spikes. His torso was awash with rivulets of rainwater, coursing pathways over his bruised and battered body. He felt the rainwater pooling around his bare feet, chilling him right down to the bone.

Despite the cold and the wet, Lewis still managed to recall firing three shots before being shot at in the farmhouse kitchen. He calculated the total and took it away from the 17 rounds he had placed into the magazine before heading for the confrontation. He worked out that there was only one round left in his pistol.

Lewis thought quickly; he needed a simple plan. With each passing second, the rain was getting heavier and, likewise, Lewis was getting colder and weaker. He had to act, and fast.

The rain, he thought. I can use the noise as cover and launch a surprise attack on the other guy.

Lewis slowly peered from behind his tree and scanned the area to his front; he was looking for any signs of where the other captor was hiding. Lewis looked for signs of movement but the rain only made the task harder and he knew he couldn't just sneak out and hope to not be discovered before he'd found his assailant. Lewis knew what he had to do in order to locate his target, and for his plan to succeed. He pointed the shotgun into the clearing and fired in the direction of the track.

Ginty wiped rainwater from his face. He knew, deep down, he had to make a decision, as it was not an option to remain hidden behind the tree. He had to do something. Maybe his prisoner had already passed out. After all, he'd taken one hell of a beating and he was naked; naked in the middle of a freezing cold, soaking wet woods.

The loud retort echoed around the clearing, shattering the silence, and with it, Ginty's train of thought. He grasped the pistol tighter, until it felt like his knuckles would pop.

"Shit, he has the shotgun!" Ginty mumbled to himself, as he risked a quick look from behind his cover. Both men momentarily stared straight into each other's eyes. Ginty moved his head back first, but not before taking another look towards the track.

Lewis had a location and, clutching the shotgun, he moved off as swiftly as his freezing cold legs would allow. He darted between trees and bushes, ignoring the branches that tore into his exposed flesh, slicing his skin and instantly drawing blood. Lewis was almost level with the tree his captor was sheltering behind. Without any shotgun shells, there was only one way Lewis could use the weapon against the other Irishman, so raising the shotgun and holding it like a baseball bat, Lewis stepped forward and swung it with all the strength he could muster.

The shotgun connected with the solid tree trunk and shattered the hand guard, sending the hammer and trigger mechanism flying into the undergrowth.

The Irishman was gone. Fight or flight, Ginty had chosen the latter.

Lewis ignored the pain shooting up his arms, looking towards the track. He just caught sight of his captor fleeing before disappearing from sight.

Lewis breathed deeply, sucking in lungfuls of cold, damp air. He looked down at the damaged shotgun before discarding it into the undergrowth. He moved into the clearing and towards the dead body.

First, he removed Boyle's boots, followed by his outer layer of clothes. Lewis dressed in the soaking wet garments before heading off, back into the woods. He pushed his way through the dense foliage, going in completely the opposite direction to Ginty. Lewis' lungs burned with each step he took, but he gritted his teeth and battled on. I've done it, I've escaped, he thought to himself, and now I've just got to survive until I can get to safety.

Lewis was not ready to give up just yet, as he pushed on deeper into the woods.

Overhead, the dark clouds remained, but at least the rain eased off to a drizzle.

THIRTY-ONE

Luay Abass returned home to the flat after attending evening prayers at the al Dulhaimi's mosque in Whitechapel. Letting himself in, he hung up his wet jacket before heading off to the kitchen.

"Hiya Luay, chai?" offered Falah.

"Yes please," answered Abass, sitting down at the kitchen table.

Falah poured the hot water onto the sweet herbal drink and brought the two small glass teacups to the table. He passed one across to Abass, who immediately stirred the sugar resting at the base of the cup into the dark-red fluid. Abass savoured the sweet taste of his first mouthful before swallowing.

"How did it go tonight?"

Abass rested his glass cup. "I don't know. I went in and readied myself for prayers, when I was approached by one of the elders."

"Did he say anything to you?"

"Not really," said Abass. "He welcomed me to the mosque and showed me to where the prayer mats were kept."

"What else happened?"

As Abass sat back in his chair, he felt the cold dampness of his robe against his shins. The robe caused him more than a chill; the damp material irritated his skin. Abass had not worn a robe since his early teens. He was more used to the feel of ordinary clothes. He missed his trousers, jeans, and the sort of clothes his friends wore. Abass only wore robes on days of important religious events and family birthdays, when he would gather with his whole extended family.

"Again, there wasn't much to tell. I didn't see al Dulhaimi, as one of the other clerics took prayers," explained Abass.

Falah was about to speak when Abass cut in. "It was when I was getting ready to leave that I was approached again." Falah waited for Abass to continue. "Another cleric, younger than the first one, asked me why he had not seen me in the mosque before."

"What did you say to him?"

"I recited the speech written down in the notes you gave me. I think it worked," smiled Abass. "He took me to one side then asked me to show him the video clip."

"And then what happened?"

"That's it. He watched the clip then left me to put my shoes back on and set off home."

"Did he follow you outside? Did you see him talk with anyone else?" quizzed Falah.

Abass finished his drink. "No, I'm sorry. He watched the clip then walked off."

Falah stood up, retrieved the two glass teacups, and took them over to the sink. He stood them on the draining board before turning back to Abass. "Never mind, the good thing is you've made contact with someone from inside the mosque." Falah scooped up his mobile phone from the kitchen table. "Hopefully soon, we'll see al Dulhaimi make an appearance." He excused himself as he left the kitchen and went to his bedroom to check in with control.

THIRTY-TWO

The car snaked along the country lane, its headlights picking out the reflective markers standing in line along the verge. The miniature post stood to attention, warning the driver of the edge of the road with a bright, white flash as the car sped past. Every so often, the car bounced across a pothole, to the annoyance of the driver, Peter Locke.

"Okay, I've sorted it with the hotel . . ."

"Did you explain about the tyre?" interrupted Locke, his focus on the dark road ahead.

"Yes, I mentioned the tyre," replied Brenda, putting her mobile phone back into her handbag. "The receptionist was very helpful. She said they'll keep someone there till we arrive."

The car juddered once more, as the front wheel found another pothole. Locke clenched the steering wheel even tighter, feeling every jolt in the road transferring through the car and up his arms.

"I swear if I hit another pothole . . ."

"Pete!" shouted Brenda. "Look out!"

Locke swerved the car to avoid hitting a large object lying at the side of the road. The car swerved before skidding to a halt.

"What the hell was that?" he asked his wife.

"I've no idea. It may have been an animal."

Locke recomposed himself before depressing the clutch and engaging first gear. Brenda rested a hand across her husband's forearm. "What are you doing?"

"We've got a chalet to get to. We're already four hours late because of the puncture." Locke slid his arm from under his wife's grip. Taking hold of the steering wheel, he prepared to drive off.

"Can't you go back and see what it was laying in the road?"

"Brenda, we don't have time for this," sighed Locke.

Brenda turned in her chair and went to open her door.

"What are you doing?"

"Well, if you won't go back and look then I will."

Locke, once again, depressed the clutch and manoeuvred the gearstick into neutral. After applying the handbrake, he removed his seatbelt and opened his door.

"You win," he conceded. "I'll go and see what it is."

The redness from the backlights lit up most of the road behind the car, including the large shape at the side of the road. Locke walked slowly towards it.

A noise alerted Locke. He turned around to see the car lit up by the interior light and his wife now standing by her open door.

"Can you see what it is, Pete?"

Locke continued walking towards the object. He heard his wife call out once more and again, chose to ignore her. As he approached the object, he realised that the dark shape was a person, probably a man, he guessed, judging by the size of the shape. Subconsciously, Locke's strides shortened as he neared the motionless figure.

He stopped short of the person and looked around for any clues that may explain why there was someone lying at the side of the road. Darkness and shadows stretched out on either side of the road. The trees appeared to bind tightly together as Locke's eyes squinted, behind his gold-rimmed spectacles, as he attempted to pierce the gloom. The cold, dark night offered him nothing. Once again, he focused his attention on the still figure. As his eyes grew accustomed to the night, he was now able to pick out small details on the figure, bathed in the blood-red glow from the car's backlights.

The figure had his back towards Locke and was curled in the foetal position, with his right side exposed to the elements. The man was wearing sodden, ill-fitting clothes, and it looked like there were a number of dark patches around the shoulders, which could be bloodstains. Cautiously, Locke made a final approach.

"Hello?" spoke Locke.

No reply.

"Hello?" repeated Locke, a little louder.

Still nothing.

"Excuse me, can I help you?" asked Locke, kneeling down and reaching out a hand to the man.

Lewis rolled his head, until he faced the man; slowly, one eye opened, focusing on the blurred image leaning over him.

Locke retracted his hand in a swift motion and stood up straight. He gazed down at Lewis as his eye closed and his head fell back away. A plume of vapour rose from his mouth as he exhaled a tired breath.

"Brenda," Locke shouted, "fetch my jacket and the picnic blanket from the car!"

Brenda climbed back into the car and, kneeling on her seat, grabbed the blanket from the back seat before taking Locke's jacket from off the rear passenger handrail.

"And Brenda, phone for an ambulance," he added.

THIRTY-THREE

The Garda officer parked his patrol car behind a row of three ambulances, locked it up and darted across the hospital through-road, narrowly avoiding a departing taxi. As he approached the Accident and Emergency entrance, the automated doors parted, allowing him to move unhindered into the inside of the St Patrick's Hospital. An old man dressed in pyjamas and a thick dressing gown extinguished a cigarette and followed the officer inside to the reception area.

The two men exchanged pleasantries as the officer looked for the reception desk. Then the two men parted company; the old man shuffled off towards a line of three lifts and the Garda officer approached the receptionist.

The officer had only recently started his shift. He had been sat enjoying his first cup of morning coffee when he was tasked with checking out a late-night admission.

The receptionist chatted animatedly on the telephone as the officer approached and he waited patiently for her to finish the call. From a corridor off to the left, a trio of nurses passed through reception, en-route to the car park. One of the nurses smiled at the officer as they passed by him. He returned a smile, watching as the automated doors opened and the nurses exited the building. He turned back towards the receptionist, who was still talking on the telephone. A clock on the wall behind her showed it was half-past eight in the morning.

The Garda officer removed his notebook from a pouch on his utility belt and flipped through it to the notes he had taken that morning. The receptionist finished her call then looked up at the officer.

"Good morning, officer, can I help you with anything?"

"Hello," said the Garda officer, checking the woman's name badge, "Barbara, we received a call late last night, concerning a male admitted with gunshot wounds."

The receptionist typed a few details into her computer, waiting for the screen to refresh. "Here we are," she said, reading from the screen. "He arrived at 2:46a.m. and is under the care of Doctor McEvoy. If you take the lift to the fourth floor then follow the signs to the Intensive Care Unit."

"Thanks for your help, Barbara," replied the Garda officer politely.

He turned and headed for the row of lifts.

After introducing himself to Doctor McEvoy, the Garda officer was taken off to a private room, occupied by Lewis. He stood silently at the end of the bed as the doctor checked on her patient.

"How is he, doctor?"

"There's no real change from when he was admitted last night," she replied.

"Do you have an update on his injuries, doctor?" asked the officer, before taking out his notebook.

"Please, call me Andrea," requested the doctor, opening a bedside drawer and removing a blue folder. "The patient has been treated for a possible shotgun wound to the right shoulder, from where a number of pellets were removed. He has also received treatment to the left shoulder and the underlying muscle for an injury that was possibly caused by a drill."

The police officer scribbled away as the doctor dictated from the folder. "Two fingers have been dressed and splinted. This is the result of damage from an unknown, blunt-force trauma. The knuckles were damaged beyond repair. He has also suffered a fractured ankle and two broken ribs, and I might add, despite his injuries, he's extremely lucky the damaged ribs didn't puncture a lung."

The Garda officer paused from writing to look down at Lewis. His face, especially around the eyes, was bruised and swollen, his skin a patchwork of blue, red and purple. He also noticed two white patches, one on a cheek and the other on his neck. The officer knew these patches were used to cover stitches. He pointed towards Lewis with his pen. "Someone's certainly gone to town on him."

The doctor followed the line of the pen until she too was staring at Lewis' face. "Yes, he has suffered – the patches cover two slashes. One has six stitches and the other, five. Someone has taken a serious disliking to this man."

The doctor opened the cupboard below the bedside table drawer and removed a large, plastic bag. "These are the clothes he was wearing when he was brought in. Unfortunately, there's no identification in any of the pockets."

The Garda officer took the bag from the doctor. "With your permission, Andrea, I'd like to photograph your patient and take his fingerprints. There's a chance he may already be in our system, which will, at least, give him a name."

"No, it won't be a problem. He's heavily sedated so won't be waking up anytime soon."

The officer tucked his notebook away into a pouch before removing a digital camera from a jacket pocket. He switched it on, leaning closer to Lewis. The image on the display came into focus. "Smile for the camera," whispered the Garda officer.

THIRTY-FOUR

Luay Abass arrived at the mosque ready for Isha, night-time prayers. After entering the place of worship, he proceeded with his preparation for Salah; prayers. He followed a group of men into a large, tiled room, not unlike an oversized bathroom, where he waited for a vacant washing space. Like the other men in the room, he was waiting to carry the ritual of wudu, the act of cleansing one's body before prayer. Finally, a space became available at one of the taps.

Abass started his cleansing ritual by washing his hands up to his wrists, three times, taking care to massage the water into the gaps between his stubby fingers. He then rinsed his mouth, followed by cupping handfuls of water to his nose, sniffing up the water and blowing it out again and, as with his hands, he carried out this action three times. After washing his arms, as far up as his elbows, Abass washed his face, followed by drawing a wet hand over his hair. He started at his fringe and finished at the nape of his neck, quickly followed by his ears. Once Abass had washed his feet three times, he finished off wudu by running a wet finger between each of his fingers and toes. All of the cleansing was done in a very precise, but hurried, manner, as the whole process had to be completed before any one part of his body had time to dry.

Once Abass had finished, he padded, barefoot, into the main prayer room and took his place on the last row of adult males, almost opposite where the imam would be seated. Behind him, children were forming another two rows, and to the rear of the children were a scattering of women. Abass knelt down and waited for the imam to arrive and begin prayers.

The tap on his shoulder took him by surprise. Abass sat back on his heels and turned to see the imam from the previous night, the one he'd shown the video clip too.

"Come with me, you have been requested to join in with the private prayer in the next room."

Abass fought to contain his nervousness as he rose shakily to his feet. Without speaking a word to each other, the two robed men walked around the rear of the prayer group then headed for a black door at the far side of the prayer hall.

As the door was closed behind him, Abass noticed there were six men of similar age also present; each one sat cross-legged on a large, woven mat, in a semi-circle. Sat in front of the young men, upon a decorative, gold leaf, throne-like, high-back chair was the head imam. He was dressed in crisp black robes, adorned with a tightly-wound black turban.

Abass recognised the man instantly, as he'd only being studying his photograph an hour before. In fact, Abass had studied this man's facial features the most from the folder of assorted images given to him by the MI5 agent.

Abass was now sat in the presence of Mustafa al Dulhaimi.

THIRTY-FIVE

Luay Abass returned to the flat almost an hour later than the previous night. He fed his key into the door lock and turned it. As he stepped over the threshold, Falah popped his head around the kitchen door to greet him.

"Is everything okay, Luay? I was expecting you home earlier," said Falah, sounding like a concerned parent.

Abass removed his jacket and placed it on an empty coat hook before answering. "Yeah, everything's fine, I just need to get out of these robes." He ducked into his bedroom and pushed the door shut behind him. Abass fell back against the door in a subconscious effort to keep the outside world out and on the other side. He sighed deeply, closing his eyes and allowing the back of his head to fall against the chipped paintwork of the bedroom door. Abass wasn't ready for his daily interrogation yet.

"Would you like a drink?"

He heard Falah's voice so loudly that he thought he must have been standing just the other side of the bedroom door.

Abass summoned up the strength to push himself away from the door and took the few steps towards the edge of his bed. He dropped down like a sack of potatoes and proceeded to remove his shoes.

"Luay, did you hear me?" Falah now sounded like he had his face pressed to the door.

Feeling like he was getting slowly suffocated, Abass took several deep breaths before speaking. "Yeah, sorry. Can I have a strong coffee please?"

"Okay."

The next sound Abass heard was that of running water from the kitchen tap as the kettle was being filled, so unless Falah had sprinted to the kitchen, he hadn't been standing at the bedroom door at all, thought Abass. Maybe his troubled mind had churned out the scenario, as he was beginning to feel the pressure.

Abass removed his robe and put on a tracksuit before joining Falah in the sitting room. As he entered the front room, Falah pointed a remote control towards the television; the screen went blank.

"There you go," said Falah, indicating a mug of coffee placed on a magazine, lying atop of a small table beside the settee. Abass retrieved the mug before sitting down. He took his first mouthful and felt the hot coffee warm him.

"How are you feeling?" asked Falah.

Abass' shoulders drooped as he slumped back in his seat. He raised the mug to his lips and, after blowing across the surface, downed another mouthful, keeping the mug up to his face, using it to hide behind. Falah watched on, aware that Abass was beginning to withdraw into himself. He needed to keep the communication open between them.

"Has something happened, Luay?"

Abass peered across the top of the mug and in a hushed voice, replied, "I don't think I can do this anymore."

Falah edged himself forward in the chair to Abass' left-hand side. "Why don't you tell me what's happened and let's see if we can work something out." Falah had seen these self-doubting traits before in a few of his previous recruits. Falah hoped he could help Abass overcome his fears quicker than usual, as this operation, unlike previous ones, was very time-sensitive.

"I don't feel comfortable with this situation. I don't think it's for me anymore."

"Look, Luay, I'll level with you, we don't have much time to stop al Dulhaimi. We are under enormous pressure to achieve a positive outcome from this operation." Falah watched as Abass slunk his shoulders, allowing his neck to drop down and his head to tip forward.

"I need you to talk to me, Luay, so that we can work our way through this."

Falah waited a moment for his words to sink in. All the time, Abass' posture remained passive and he continued to stare at the floor.

"In less than three weeks, al Dulhaimi is going to carry out a major attack somewhere in London and we need your help to stop him. We need you to find out when and where it's going to happen. We came to you, Luay, because we believe in you and we think that you are the one person that can see this through and help prevent a catastrophe."

Abass looked up. "I thought I was one of a small number of people that could help. Why can't you go to one of the others for help?"

"You were one of a small number, but I'm afraid we just don't have time to set this all up with someone else, Luay. With your background and your father's fighting spirit, we were sure you could pull this off."

Abass opened his mouth to reply, but the words stuck in his throat. Falah's words had pricked a nerve.

"What has my father got to do with this?"

"We know of his fight against a corrupt regime, of his detention and of the effort to free him from incarceration. And we see those traits in you. How many protests have you been involved with, Luay?"

Abass reflected on Falah's words. "I could never do what my father did; he's stronger than I could ever be."

"I'm not asking you to be your father, or even try to better what he achieved. All I'm asking is for you to take what you know about him and use it to give you strength."

Abass' mouth felt parched as he struggled to come to terms with Falah's words of encouragement. The agent sat silently, waiting for Abass to reach a decision. Falah watched on as Abass' brow furrowed and felt he should remain silent until Abass was ready to speak.

"I'm sorry but I don't feel like I can do this anymore," replied Abass, after much thought.

"Why don't you tell me what happened tonight at prayers and then we can see what we can do," said Falah, in a sympathetic tone, placing a hand on Abass' shoulder.

Abass raised his head once more, but only to take a sip from his coffee mug.

Falah sat back before pushing on. "Luay, I understand that you have doubts, but unless you talk to me, I don't know how I can help you."

"You can help by taking me away from this. I'm not cut out for this situation or this type of work. I'm not a spy; I work in a shop selling iPads and MP3 players."

"Not many people are cut out for this type of work, I'm afraid. You have to look at the bigger picture and what we are trying to achieve. Talk to me, let's see if we can work something out."

Abass placed his coffee mug down before using his hands to cup his forehead. His lips twitched as he mouthed a silent prayer. Falah watched on in silence.

"I was taken into a private prayer room. Al Dulhaimi was there, as were a number of the others that you'd shown me in the folder. I was scared," said Abass, eventually.

Good, thought Falah, he's talking again.

"Why?"

"I felt isolated in that room. I was alone with some very bad men and I had no idea what was going to happen to me."

"It couldn't have been easy for you, Luay, but you do have the panic button, remember? It was stitched into your robe; it's there for your safety. You only have to press it and it'll send out an alert with details of your location. Help will never be far away. You have to trust me on that."

"I didn't feel helpless in that way. The whole situation made me feel claustrophobic. Once the door was shut, I felt like the whole room was closing in on me. It was as if I was trapped and couldn't escape. My breath was being squeezed from me and I couldn't contain my panic."

"I know the feeling." Falah felt like he was making progress. "When I worked on my first assignment, I felt completely uneasy. Being alone with someone you're meant to be spying on and in their environment takes a great deal of self-belief, inner strength and courage to help you cope. I think deep down, you have these qualities, Luay." Falah watched as Abass' concentration spiked. "You deal with people on a daily basis in your store, having to adapt your approach with each customer, in order to be as helpful as possible. These skills are what can help you cope with this operation. What you have is a natural talent with people. All I'm asking is for you to explore and adapt that talent even more." Falah paused to take a drink, letting his words sink in. "So, tell me what happened and let's see how we can work out a solution for your issues, Luay."

Abass sat back in his seat, looking straight at Falah with a renewed sense of vigour. "We prayed for a short while, and then one of the other imams gave us a lesson from the Qur'an."

"About what?"

"The imam talked about not letting the West suppress our beliefs."

"I don't recall that being written in the Qur'an."

"It's not, unless you twist your interpretation. It's all down to how you word your understanding by then making it appear that the word of the Prophet fits in with your explanation," explained Abass. "I may not be a worldly-wise person, but I do have a grasp on when someone is trying to push an agenda, and in that brief time, the imam put forward a very twisted but convincing argument."

"Did anything else happen?"

"Not until the end. I just sat and listened. I don't think we were meant to participate; I think we were all there to listen."

"Was al Dulhaimi involved in the lesson?"

"No, he just sat in silence, watching over us. He let the other imam do the talking. But at the end of the lesson, I was asked if I still had the video clip."

"Did al Dulhaimi ask you this?"

"Yes. He took me to one side to explain that one of his followers had mentioned what happened to my brother, the clip, and that he wanted it."

Falah looked puzzled. "He wanted it? As in wanted to see it?"

"No," explained Abass. "He wanted the clip. He asked me to transfer it to his phone."

Falah's face lit up. "You mean he gave you his number?"

"No, not exactly. He had me send it to one of the other imam's phone."

"Do you still have the number?"

"No, I'm sorry, he asked me to delete it straight away, watching me as I did it."

"What about memorising the number?"

"It all happened so quickly. It started with 0-7-9 and I think there were two 66s in the number," said Abass, apologetically.

"No problem, I will need to have your phone though, as I can still retrieve the number from the internal memory. It shouldn't take longer than half an hour, as I have my laptop in my room."

Without question, Abass handed over his mobile phone.

"What did he want to know about your brother?" asked Falah.

"He explained that he'd heard about his death in Syria. He was curious as to how he got there, who helped him, where he was staying, and what group he was helping. In fact, he asked just about every question you'd prepared me for."

"Did it look like he believed you?"

"I think so. He was very repetitive with his questions; it was obvious he was trying to trip me up. I think I managed to sound convincing." Abass paused, first looking into the empty space above Falah's head, and then into his eyes. "The man seems to look deep inside you. He has dark rings around his eyes so, when you look at him, it looks like there's an unnerving emptiness to his face. Plus, he shows no emotion; he can be very intimidating without saying a word. I told him the reason I was there and what I wanted to do, but he wasn't that bothered. It made me think I'd overdone the vengeful brother, but I'm sure I didn't."

"And I'm sure you didn't either, Luay. His next move should be to check out your story and then, maybe, we'll see some progress," explained Falah. "Did anything else happen?"

"That's it, I'm afraid. He let me leave after that, saying he looked forward to seeing me again."

Falah stood up beside Abass, resting a reassuring hand on his shoulder. "You did very well tonight, especially for someone new to this game. I think you more than held your own in that room, especially given the circumstances. And," continued Falah, as he pocketed Abass' mobile phone, "I really think you've made some noteworthy progress. You should be very proud of yourself, Luay."

Abass was flushed with pride, just like Falah had intended. Although Abass didn't feel completely at ease, he did feel that, tonight, after talking with Falah, he had conquered a big, personal hurdle.

"Why don't you unwind whilst I make a phone call." Falah patted Abass' shoulder. "You did very well tonight, my friend."

THIRTY-SIX

After clipping his personal radio to the small strap above his breast pocket, Sergeant John Clegg closed his locker, secured the door, then left the small changing room for the refreshments room. The room was once the kitchen of a house that, over half a century ago, had been converted into the village's police station. It still retained some of the features of the one-time family home, like the chimney breast in the old kitchen. The fireplace had been bricked up many years ago, but the prominent feature now held a notice board. The morning sun spilled in through a large, wooden-framed window, partly obscured by a row of iron bars. Inside the sparsely-furnished room was a sink, fridge, microwave and table. On entering, Clegg was greeted by the station's only female officer, sitting at the table and eating a bowl of cereal. "Morning Sarge," she said, between mouthfuls of bran.

"Morning Colleen, do ye want a coffee?"

"No thanks, Sarge, I'm running late this morning. Once I've finished this, I've got last night's incident reports to file away, and that's before I go to St Joseph's to help with the bicycle awareness scheme."

Clegg dropped a teabag into his mug before raising it up to the spout on the wall-mounted water boiler; a step up from the small station's old kettle. He filled the mug with hot water. "I don't envy ye with all those screaming kids. Give me an armed robber any day," chuckled Clegg.

"Like we get them around here. Still, someone has to do the boring stuff," Colleen replied, as she took the bowl to the sink and rinsed it out.

"I tell ye what, to save time, I'll do the reports for ye."

"Cheers Sarge, if it's no bother."

Clegg stirred a spoonful of sugar into his tea before removing the teabag and dropping it into the waste bin beside the fridge. He opened the door, took out a milk carton, sniffed it and, happy it was still fresh, poured some into his mug.

"It's no bother," said Clegg, leaving the room.

After a short walk past two holding cells that were once the old drawing room, Clegg was behind the front desk. Either side of the front desk were two doors. Behind one was the interview room and opposite this, behind the other door, was the only office in the station, which was shared by both the station sergeant and inspector.

Clegg opened the office door and stepped inside. Before crossing to his desk, he flipped the light switch on, illuminating a fluorescent tube that flickered rapidly before settling into a constant glow. He placed his mug down beside his computer and switched it on. Sitting himself down at the desk, Clegg waited for the machine to come to life before tapping in his password to log into the system. After the machine went through its own slow start-up procedure, he scanned through the reports displayed on the screen. Two stolen cars, one assault outside a Chinese takeaway, one driving under the influence and . . .

Clegg opened the file, reading through the report. Moving the cursor and clicking an icon, he opened the attached photo file, wincing, then muttering under his breath, "Nasty . . ."

After reading the report a second time, his eyes picked out a selection of words from the document – drill, gunshot, stitches, broken, broken, broken. Clegg left his desk and shuffled around the office to the filing cabinet tucked away behind the door. He opened the top drawer, labelled missing persons/OTR, on the run, and lifted out the most recent file, cursing under his breath that he hadn't added it into the station's system yet.

Once Clegg had sat back down at the desk, he printed out the previous night's reports, only retrieving the one that had sparked his interest. Clegg reached for the telephone and, holding the handset tightly, stabbed out the number jotted down in the file. Was this nameless man the Adam Lewis reported missing less than a week ago, he thought.

The call connected.

THIRTY-SEVEN

Colin Fullerton had given up on the television. He finished his third cup of coffee, aware that it was still only half-past eleven. The four walls of his MI5 rented apartment, close to King George's Park, were slowly becoming more and more claustrophobic as the days dragged on. Fullerton made his mind up; he needed to get outside into a wide, open space to clear his head.

He grabbed his thick winter jacket and keys before leaving the apartment. After negotiating three flights of stairs, he was outside, taking in the noises and smells of a busy metropolis. The dark clouds gathering overhead made the likelihood of Fullerton returning from his walk dry very remote. Still, turning up his collar and turning sharply left, he set off. He headed in the direction of the small local park.

The previous night had been yet another restless one. Fullerton had set his mind to recalling everything he could about the incident he'd been suspended over. It had played on his mind since walking out of MI5 Headquarters that there was more to this than a tenuous involvement with a missing pistol. His intuition was telling him that James Strong was somehow involved in this fishing expedition. Fullerton thought about the events of the shooting of one of his informers, but unless Adam Lewis was involved in some way, he was baffled as to why Strong would want to put his own career on the line. Especially given that shortly after the event, James Strong's reward from Fullerton had been a move into a much better position. If Strong was the connection, Fullerton was thinking that he'd been kissed on the cheek by Judas.

Still, what was done was done, thought Fullerton. Now his priority was damage limitation, and apart from Lewis, there was not anyone he could think of that had any tangible evidence against him. But still, something did not sit easy with Fullerton. He could not help wondering what exactly Macleod had uncovered. The department head must have something, otherwise why had the suspension happened, thought Fullerton. He knew he'd taken risks every time he had "turned a blind eye" for payment, or carried out a "behind closed doors" secret deal, but Fullerton was sure he'd more than covered his own back at the time. The uncertainty knotted his stomach and twisted his mind.

Perhaps it was scare tactics, Fullerton thought. It could be payback. 'After all, I did sleep with . . . ' Fullerton chuckled to himself.

Unsurprisingly, due to the imminent bad weather, the park was almost empty. The trees lining the border of the park held onto scatterings of yellow, brown and orange-coloured leaves. Fullerton decided to walk along the leaf-covered path that followed the treeline around the park.

He took the quiet time he had to himself to recall the circumstances leading to his indiscretion. Having cast his mind back, he remembered he'd received permission to return to England from Northern Ireland to attend the funeral of an old spy who he'd been involved with his formative years within the service.

After the funeral, the small gathering had returned to a hotel on the outskirts of Kensington. The old spy and his wife had taken to running the quaint hotel after his retirement from the service. His widow had spoken with Fullerton, expressing her surprise at his heart attack, and the circumstances in which she had found him in one of the guestrooms.

Macleod, another one of the old spy's former protégés, had been involved in an on-going operation and so, had requested his wife attend the service on his behalf.

Fullerton recalled how the pair had got chatting and later, under the influence of much alcohol, had slipped away together.

The secret tryst had only remained a secret for a few months, as Macleod's wife had raised details of the liaison during a heated argument. There had been two outcomes of this revelation: one, Macleod divorced his wife, and two, Fullerton had been informed. He would most likely see his time out in the service in Northern Ireland, with Macleod being reassigned elsewhere.

Sidestepping a dog turd, with his hands dug deep into his jacket pockets, Fullerton decided on a second lap of the park. His fingers were beginning to feel the effects of the cold, so he balled them into tight fists.

His mobile phone started ringing.

"Hello?" he answered, breathing a plume of vapour out across the mouthpiece as the cold took hold of the rest of his body.

The voice on the other end of the line spoke briefly to Fullerton; the message was good news for him. He smiled and felt a brief respite from the chill.

"Thank you, Sergeant Clegg. I need to sort out a few things first, so I should be with you sometime early tomorrow morning."

Fullerton halted on the spot and, with military precision, executed an about-turn before heading out of the park. He still held the phone to his ear as his pace quickened.

"No, thank you, Sergeant. I'm very grateful. I'll definitely be there before you finish your shift."

Fullerton disconnected the call just as he stepped through the park gates. He was about to put the mobile phone back into his pocket when it rang again. He held it up in his hand, staring down at the display screen. The name flashing up on the screen was "Macleod".

Fullerton held his thumb over the green telephone symbol, wavering. He moved his thumb to the red symbol then back to the green one, as the ringing steadily rose in volume.

Overhead, the clouds finally relented and the first drops of rain descended from the heavens. Small splashes peppered the display screen.

Fullerton pushed his thumb down.

THIRTY-EIGHT

Robert Macleod had worked through his lunch break in order to arrange the final details for a new recruit to attend the Metropolitan Police's Advanced Driving course. With the details finalised, Macleod turned his attention to his now cold cup of coffee. The milky film resting on top of the brown fluid looked far from inviting. The soft tapping at his office door was a welcome distraction.

At Macleod's request, Tracey Scott opened the door and entered the office. She was immaculately dressed in a dark-blue trouser suit. In the crook of one arm, she carried three slim folders, which she placed on the corner of Macleod's desk. Macleod motioned for her to sit down on the cushioned chair nearest his desk.

"I'm sorry, Tracey, I'd offer you a drink, but it's been one of those days."

"Don't worry, Robert, I've come straight from the canteen so I'm fine."

"Anything nice?" asked Macleod.

"Not really, just the usual bland offering," answered Tracey. "The reason I've popped in is to update you on Fullerton."

Macleod opened a desk drawer and removed the notebook he had used for Strong's statement. He flipped it open at the next free page. "Okay, Tracey, what do you have for me?"

"I have something. Unfortunately, it's not exactly what you're after."

Macleod hid his disappointment as he watched Tracey open one of the folders.

"Firstly, I think I've identified the other soldier involved in the shooting. I've managed to track down more of the SAS soldiers who served in Northern Ireland at the time of the incident." Tracey removed a photograph from the folder and handed it over to Macleod. "Three of the soldiers I spoke with named the same man, Adam Lewis."

Macleod studied the photograph, identifying the embossed markings across one corner. He recognised the image as one taken from a passport.

Tracey continued. "Unfortunately, all I've managed to find of Lewis is the photo. I do know that over the last eight years or so, he has travelled in and out of this country at irregular intervals, mainly to Dubai and Oman, and then on to Iraq, where he has been working for a private security company called TSGS, Trojan Safeguard Security."

Macleod placed the photograph down and scribbled some notes.

"From my research, he's been working in Iraq since late 2003, and that's where it ends. He left Iraq about two months ago and seems to have disappeared."

Tracey handed Macleod two more photographs. "These were taken at passport control at Heathrow. The dates are on the reverse."

"And you have no idea where he is now?"

"Not a clue. He doesn't show up on any local authority listings and the only address he has for his bank account and a motorcycle registration are an old one in the northeast. I've asked for the motorcycle details to be checked against the transport camera system but at the moment, it's a 'needle and haystack' situation."

Macleod was about to open his mouth when Tracey cut in. "The northeast address was knocked down over a year ago, so it's safe to say he's moved out!"

Macleod smiled, despite it not being the news he was after.

"Have you thought about checking police and medical databases?"

"I have, and he's not in the UK. I've put in a request for help locating him through the European channels, and there's also a worldwide request being processed. But as you know, it could take weeks for information to come in from so many different areas. And I've had no indication Lewis has had contact with either, yet."

"Okay. What else do you have?" asked Macleod, indicating to the other two folders.

Tracey drew in a deep breath, curling up the sides of her mouth. Macleod strained to mask his concerns. She let out her breath as she reached for another folder.

"I'm still no closer to finding anything concrete linking Fullerton with the shooting. It could be that Lewis is our missing link, but until he resurfaces, we'll not know. What I have discovered though is that Fullerton had been taking money due as payment for information gleaned from informers for himself."

"Are you sure about this, Tracey?" Macleod didn't doubt she'd be mistaken, but as a matter of course, he felt obliged to ask.

"Yes, I am, and the good news is it is a definite, as well as being supported with documented evidence. I stumbled across it quite by accident." Tracey handed over four photocopied sheets of paper. "These are records of payments made to informants by Fullerton. They list the amounts, when, and who to, etc. If you look at the one highlighted on page two . . ."

Macleod located the page and read the name highlighted. "Peter Coyle."

"Yes, that's him."

"£3,000?"

"£3,000," repeated Tracey. "Quite a large sum for information that didn't lead to anything. Not one find, arrest or attack prevented."

"I appreciate that, but even I know not everything you're told by an informer leads to anything substantial," answered Macleod.

"I know that, you know that, hell, even Fullerton knows that. But, on this occasion, what he may or may not have known was Peter Coyle had been dead almost a week before the payment was made."

Macleod looked up from the sheet. "What do you mean, dead?"

"Coyle had been shot dead by the Ulster Volunteer Force earlier in the month, but due to an oversight, he'd remained on a list of paid informants."

Macleod scanned through the sheets of paper once more, noticing more highlighted names. "And these?"

"Those, Robert, are other payments made by Fullerton to other informants that, for one reason or another, were not in a position to supply any information. Out of the forty-seven payments I've traced, so far, only two were for genuine intelligence."

"How much are we talking about?"

"I've estimated the cost at around £78,000, and that's only the few I've managed to check through fully. Who's to say there aren't more false payments, or even destroyed documentation, going back many years. Londonderry recently closed down and all original documentation went to Lisburn, making it harder to piece together a paper trail. I only came across these when I was cross-checking the evidence relating to the pistol."

Macleod made a note of the amount before sitting back in his chair. He held the sheets of paper in one hand and the photograph of Lewis in the other. "This is really something I can run with, Tracey, but what about this Lewis fella, and what about the shooting?" Macleod remained upbeat about the revelations uncovered, but to him, the shooting carried more gravitas. "Do you think you can find him?"

"Honestly? It's hard to say. I'd like to think I can, but unfortunately, I don't think he wants to be found."

Macleod handed back the sheets of paper, only retaining the photograph, which he placed into his notebook, before returning both items to the desk drawer.

"You've done very well, Tracey. I'll call Fullerton and give him the *good* news about the fraud investigation. In the meantime, I want you to find Adam Lewis."

Tracey stood up, gathered together the folders, shook hands with Macleod and left his office. Once the door closed, Macleod allowed his shoulders to drop, followed by a deep sigh of disappointment. He took solace in the fact that Tracey had uncovered something with which he could end Fullerton's career with the service for good, and probably any future employment, especially within the security environment. Unfortunately, it wasn't the evidence he was after. More than anything, Macleod wanted Fullerton behind bars – *no more than what the lying, cheating and murdering bastard deserves.*

He plodded slowly around his desk until he was stood in front of a portrait of the Queen. Below the portrait was a brass plaque with the inscription: *"HM QUEEN ELIZABETH II, sovereign of Great Britain and Northern Ireland"*.

"Where the bloody hell are you, Adam Lewis?"

THIRTY-NINE

The nurse wrote down the results of the two o'clock observations of her patient. Before removing the black armband and the grey clip attached to the patient's index finger, she noted the steady improvement in his blood pressure against the results of her previous visit. The nurse unplugged the machine, replaced the patient's record chart, and wheeled the machine out of the room.

Very slowly, Adam Lewis opened his eyes.

The room was bathed in the soft hue of low lighting, so it didn't take long for Lewis to accustom his eyes to his new environment. He felt dizzy and light-headed as he took stock of his surroundings. His last memory was that of losing his footing at the side of a road. He'd seen the road through a gap in the trees, and had fought his way through the undergrowth towards it. He remembered falling and his head coming into contact with the cold, wet tarmac, and then nothing.

As Lewis explored the room with slow, deliberate eye movement, he knew he was in hospital. As the foggy haze lifted from inside his head, Lewis took stock of his condition. He followed the assorted wires and tubes attached, by a series of pads and surgical tape, to a large machine on the left side of his bed. The machine displayed a number of flashing lights and four numbered readings. Despite the itchy sensation in his left arm, Lewis resisted the urge to remove any of the tubes or wires.

As more sensation returned, Lewis felt his right hand and foot were both tightly constrained and weighed down. It didn't take him long to work out that both his hand and foot were protected by plaster castings. His pain was subdued, probably thanks to the fluid dripping from a suspended plasma bag next to the monitoring machine. Lewis immediately realised the drugs he was being drip-fed were not nearly enough, as an electrifying pain radiated from his shoulder as soon as he moved his arm. A sudden image of a tall, shadowy figure flashed through his mind; the figure was holding a drill. Lewis blinked hard, shaking the tortuous image from his mind. He gave up on the notion of moving and surrendered himself to just staring up at the ceiling. Very slowly, his eyes closed.

Two hours had passed since Lewis had first opened his eyes. The nurse returned once more to monitor his progress.

"Can you get me a drink of water please?" Lewis asked in a parched whisper.

The nurse continued wheeling the machine into position. "Let me set this up first," she answered. "Then I'll get you a drink and let the doctor know that you're awake."

For a brief moment, Lewis thought of the difficult questions he'd soon be answering. *What's your name? Where are you from? Where have you been? Who shot you? Who's been using you for DIY practice?* Lewis closed his eyes and waited for his water.

The nurse returned with a jug of water and a plastic beaker, resembling a young child's drinking cup, complete with a spouted lid. She placed the jug down on his bedside tray table and gave the cup to Lewis. He raised an eyebrow with a quizzical look etched on his face.

"You don't want to spill water on yourself," explained the nurse.

Lewis manoeuvred his left hand into a position to accept the beaker, taking extra care to not to entangle any of the paraphernalia taped to his arm. He took steady, shallow sips from the beaker, savouring each plastic-tasting mouthful.

The nurse waited until Lewis had finished drinking before taking the cup from him and attaching the black armband and grey clip. She depressed a button on the machine and the armband immediately inflated. Lewis watched as two red digital numbers on the machine steadily climbed as the armband tightened. He recalled using a similar machine during an advanced first aid lesson, whilst serving with the SAS.

"Is it the top one or bottom one that measures the pressure in the arteries when the heart beats? Systolic or something . . ."

Before he received his answer, a doctor entered the room. "Good afternoon, sir," spoke Doctor McEvoy. "I'm very pleased to see you awake."

"Believe me, you're not half as pleased as I am, despite all the pain," replied Lewis. "Doctor . . ."

"McEvoy."

The doctor, dressed in smart trousers and a blouse, collected Lewis' charts and, removing a pen from a breast pocket, turned to the latest entries.

"How long has he been awake, nurse?"

"When I came in at four o'clock, he was awake, but he was still sleeping during my two o'clock checks."

Dr McEvoy turned to Lewis. "Well then, Mr . . ."

Lewis remained silent.

"Okay then, do you have a first name?"

Lewis stuck with his assumed alias. "Pete. My name's Pete, doctor."

"Well, Pete, as you can imagine, you've caused quite a stir. I don't think I can ever recall having someone admitted with your level of injuries. How are you coping with the pain? I have you on the highest dose of pain relief. Is it—"

"Where exactly am I, doctor?" interrupted Lewis.

"You're in St Patrick's Hospital in the beautiful town of Carrick-on-Shannon. Do you remember how you ended up here, Pete?"

Lewis sipped more water as the nurse removed the observations machine, and excused herself before leaving the room.

"I'm not going to pry into your private life, Pete, that's not my job. But it only makes it harder for my staff and I if you don't let us know how your injuries and pain levels are affecting you," explained the doctor.

Lewis looked up at the doctor. "I'm coping fine."

"Okay then. But if you don't mind me saying, you're a little out of the way to be a tourist. We're not a place of particular interest either. We're just a sleepy Southern Irish town that nobody usually bothers with."

Again, Lewis just stared blankly at the doctor.

Dr McEvoy replaced Lewis' notes before returning her pen to the breast pocket. "No matter, Pete, I know you need your rest. Besides, asking questions will be the job of the Garda."

This time, Lewis spoke. "Have they been in?"

"We have an obligation to report admissions that have your nature of injuries. They sent an officer out to check on you."

The doctor removed a small, slim, white box from the wall behind the bed. "This is to call the nurse should you need anything."

"Thanks."

"I'll leave you to get some rest, Pete. I'm off shift in a couple of hours, but I'm back in again tomorrow. When I return, I'll have to report your change in condition to the Garda," Dr McEvoy explained, as she walked towards the door. "It's in both our interests that you continue resting for now, as you've been through a great deal already."

"Thanks, doctor," was all Lewis could think of saying.

Once again, he was left alone with his own thoughts.

FORTY

Adam Lewis had managed to sleep for almost four hours before he woke up once more. The room was still bathed in a cool glow from the low lighting, only this time, the heavy curtains at the window had been drawn. He reached for the buzzer by his hand and pressed the large red button. Above his bed, a red light came on, and a similar light outside his room illuminated.

One of the duty nurses was alerted to Lewis' call by a buzzer sounding at the nurses' station. She checked the panel of lights to see which room was requesting attention. As she set off down the corridor towards Lewis' room, a shout escaped one of the open wards.

"I'll be in to see you in a moment, Mr Connor," replied the nurse.

"Hello Pete, what can I do for you?"

Lewis turned in the direction of the nurse. "Do you have a phone I can use? There'll be people back home worried about me."

"Yes, we do," she answered. "It's on a trolley back at the nurses' station; I'll go fetch it for you."

"I don't suppose I could borrow some money, it's just . . ."

"Don't worry, I'm sure I can stretch to a couple of euros for you." And with that, the nurse left the room.

Lewis dredged the depths of his memory in an attempt to find the number he was after. Luckily, the number was for a landline and hadn't changed in over 20 years, so Lewis had been calling it long before he had owned a mobile phone, which meant it didn't take him long to remember the number. It also helped that the six digits formed a distinct U-shaped pattern on the dialling pad, following on from the last number 1 in the area code. The rest of the code he would get from the operator.

After raising his bed into a sitting position, the nurse gave the telephone handset to Lewis. She deposited three one-euro coins and waited for him to give her the number.

"It's okay. I need the area code so I'll ask the operator to connect the call for me, thanks." Lewis managed a crooked smile from his swollen features.

"Just buzz when you're done," she said, after dialling the number for the operator, leaving Lewis on his own.

"Hello, can you connect me to a number please. It's a Londonderry one, I don't know the area code. Thanks"

The call connected.

"Hello Danny, is that you?"

The voice on the other end sounded surprised as he recognised the caller. Lewis held back on the pleasantries and cut straight to the reason for his call. "Look, mate, I'm in deep shit! I need your help!"

Lewis also decided not to go into the details of his situation, as there would be plenty of time for that later. Right now, he needed urgent help.

"I'm in a hospital in Carrick-on-Shannon, St Patrick's, the doc said. I need you to come and get me ASAP, in fact, fucking quicker than that!"

Lewis screwed his face up at the pain from his shoulder. At least the shotgun wound pain was subsiding. The drill wound, however, was a different matter. Lewis wondered how many painkillers he'd need to help make his escape.

"The local police will be here sometime tomorrow morning to talk to me, so I need to be outta here."

Lewis listened as Danny Kelly explained his situation. "Surely you've not had that much to drink. Remember, I've seen you drive after a skinful, never mind just a couple of whiskies!"

Again, Lewis listened before cutting in. "Looka Danny, the boyos caught me, I've been shot and tortured." Lewis decided to give his friend snippets of information. "When the cops get here tomorrow, I won't be able to play dumb for too long before they start smelling bullshit. I desperately need you to come and get me, mate."

Lewis lay his situation on the line for Kelly, before breathing a huge sigh of relief. "Cheers, Danny, you're gonna save my fucking neck. Can you also bring me some clothes. I can't do a runner in this gown, not with me arse hanging out!"

The two friends shared the joke; only it was Lewis that winced in pain.

After Kelly hung up, Lewis buzzed for the nurse.

FORTY-ONE

Colin Fullerton had been summoned to the unfamiliar surroundings of MI5 Headquarters. After getting directions and exchanging pleasantries with a number of colleagues, he made his way to Macleod's office. As he passed by James Strong's office, a small, Middle Eastern man was coming out. Unfortunately, he closed the door before Fullerton had chance to glimpse inside at his accuser; at least that's who he thought was sticking the knife deeper into his back.

Fullerton knocked on Macleod's door and was immediately beckoned to come in. After stepping into the office, he noticed Macleod was sat behind his desk, with a blonde lady sitting on a comfy chair to his immediate right. Fullerton also noticed the same portrait of the Queen hanging on one wall, the very same portrait Macleod had taken to Northern Ireland all those many years ago. He suppressed a chuckle.

"Good morning, Colin," said Macleod. "This is Tracey," he said, indicating to the blonde-haired woman. "Tracey, this is Colin Fullerton."

Introductions over, Macleod offered Fullerton a seat across the desk from him.

"I hope you don't mind me not offering you tea, Colin, but this won't take too long."

"Not *even* for old times' sake," replied Fullerton, with a hint of sarcasm in his voice.

Macleod didn't allow himself to rise to the bait. He merely removed a sheet of paper from a file on the desk in front of him. He turned the sheet to face Fullerton and rested a pen across it.

"This is a copy of the department's disciplinary procedures and a brief explanation of the charges brought against you." Macleod pushed the pen and paper closer to Fullerton. "I want you to read through it and sign to say you are aware of the allegations made against you. There are two copies; one for you and one for admin. I'd appreciate it if you sign both please."

Fullerton collected the sheets of paper and pen then proceeded reading. He hid his surprise well, as he digested the details printed on the sheet. He was expecting to read something relating to the shooting of Gerard Logan, not the theft of money. With a modicum of relief, Fullerton reached into his jacket pocket and retrieved a pen. Macleod ignored the blatant attempt at a snub.

"As you have just read and are now aware, the allegations made against you are 'the misappropriation of Government funds in relation to the paying of agents, in Northern Ireland, for intelligence-based information', and in particular, Peter Coyle on 4th April 1991."

Fullerton returned his pen to his pocket and regarded Macleod passively. The department head continued with his narrative from a separate witness statement.

"It is alleged you paid Peter Coyle the sum of £3,000 for information relating to a suspected weapons dump. It has since been brought to our attention that at the time and date you signed to acknowledge payment, that Coyle was in fact deceased."

Macleod paused, staring across the table at Fullerton; neither men blinked. Without dropping his gaze, Macleod continued. "You will be escorted from here to an interview room where you will have chance to provide a statement and make known any information that may refute the allegations made against you. After that, Colin, you will be escorted from the building and will continue your suspension whilst the investigation is underway. As per the conditions of the disciplinary code, your suspension will be on full pay. Do you have any questions?"

Fullerton shook his head.

Macleod broke his stare first. "Tracey, can you leave us alone for a moment please?"

Macleod waited for the door to close.

"Before you go, I require your official ID card. You will be informed at a later date when the hearing will be scheduled for."

Macleod held out a hand.

Fullerton stood up, removed his photographic identity card, and placed it into Macleod's outstretched hand. Before taking it, Macleod spoke. "I can't say I'm not enjoying this, Colin. Nothing gives me greater pleasure than seeing you on the verge of losing your job and all the perks and benefits that go with it."

Macleod took the card from Fullerton and dropped it into a desk drawer. "Colin, you once fucked my wife, now I'm fucking your career," he said coarsely.

A loud knock interrupted Macleod. "That'll be your escort, Mr Fullerton, do have a nice day!" he said sarcastically.

Fullerton turned and headed for the door. With his hand on the handle, he turned and looked down at the seated Macleod. "You know, Robert, she wasn't even that good. Pity!"

Tracey Scott passed Fullerton on the way back into the office. She was immediately drawn to the look of anger etched across Macleod's weary face. She chose not to say anything.

"Tracey, I want you to forget about the missing money for a while. Pass it on to someone you know will get to the bottom of it. I want you to concentrate all your efforts on locating Adam Lewis. I want Fullerton to pay dearly for his crimes."

FORTY-TWO

Luay Abass approached the block of flats with a heavy heart. His shoulders were drooped and his head lurched forward, as he dragged his heels. He reached a hand towards the graffiti-covered door and paused. He stood frozen for a few brief seconds before taking a number of steps backwards. Abass slowly raised his head until his eyes were scanning the mass of windows and balconies. They came to rest on his flat and, as usual, the lights to the place were on, glowing like a sodium beacon in the cold, bleak night.

Abass turned up his jacket collar and walked away from the flats. Following a path to his left, he wandered to a children's play area. A gang of half a dozen teenagers occupied the far side, sitting and standing around the base of a slide. Some of the teenagers were smoking and, as far as Abass could see, two of them were drinking from cans that looked too big to be pop cans.

Abass took a moment to take in his surroundings. A tower block on one side of the play area, another block on the other side, a further block behind him, and finally, a row of three shops in front of him, just beyond the play area. The lights were still on in the off-licence and the mini-mart, but the shutters were down and padlocked on the florists. Abass thought to himself, who in their right mind would open a florists on this estate?

As one of the teenagers produced a bottle of vodka and passed it around the group, Abass took a seat on the nearest bench and cast his mind back to that evening's prayer meeting.

Once again, he'd been requested to attend the private meeting in the side room. And, once again, al Dulhaimi was present at the meeting. He had taken his place on the throne-like chair at the head of the semi-circular group of young, male Muslims. The imam that Abass now knew as Ali Hashim, al Dulhaimi's right-hand man, according to his intelligence pack, was sat on the floor, immediately in front of his leader. Abass had taken his place at one end of the semi-circle. He'd counted nine people in total in the private room.

Tonight, as a deviation from prayers, Hashim had produced a laptop, which he proceeded to set it up in front of the group, so that all the young men where in a position to see the screen. Hashim played a short video clip. It was only morbid curiosity that compelled Abass to stare transfixed at the screen. On any other occasion, Abass would have felt repulsed by what he had seen, but under his new persona, he felt it was his duty to watch the clip out to the end. After all, how could he report back if he'd failed to carry out his task properly?

The one scene he still found impossible to shake from his mind was the decapitation. The scene had lasted less than 30 seconds, but would stay in his mind for many more days to come. As sick and revolting as the images were, it was the noise that played most heavily on his mind. The sounds made by the victim, as the masked captor furiously hacked away in a saw-like motion across his throat, were noises he would normally have associated with a very distressed animal. The high-pitched whining was only partly drowned out by the sound of gurgling as blood had filled the victim's mouth. There was a brief moment of silence, followed by shouts, cheers and chants, praising Allah. Abass was sure he'd heard one of the other young men wretch at the moment the executioner held up the head as some kind of sick trophy.

Once the screen went blank, Hashim proceeded to justify the preceding acts of violence with a quote from the Qur'an.

"Qur'an 8:12, I will cast terror into the hearts of those who disbelieve. Therefore strike off their heads and strike off every fingertip of them."

Hashim twisted the quote into a statement from their God, justifying the execution they had just witnessed. He also explained how he expected Muslims in all countries to rise up against their Christian oppressors and mete out the same sort of justice. Abass felt his stomach turning as he listened to the bile pouring from Hashim's mouth. *How much longer must I put up with this?*

"Qur'an 2:191, And kill them wherever you find them, and turn them out where they have turned you out."

Once again, Hashim twisted the quote from the holy book into another attack on those infidels that had set foot on Muslim soil. He made references to Iraq and Afghanistan in particular.

Abass listened intently as Hashim pulled passage after passage from the Qur'an, cleverly manipulating the words and meanings to suit his own twisted beliefs.

The small group of young men were then shown another video clip, only this time, it was segment after segment of military strikes, in what could only be guessed were Muslim towns and cities. As the video clip went on, the strikes were replaced with images of wounded and dead men, women and children. Most of the scenes had small symbols in one of the corners. Abass took these to be the logos of the various television news stations reporting the military strikes. Judging from the graphic content, Abass also surmised that the majority of images were not from British news sources, as this would have been deemed unsuitable for British broadcast. As the footage finished, the video clips were followed by a selection of stills, mainly images of troops abusing or mocking prisoners in their care. Abass recognised a number of images from their appearance on national news channels, including one of an American female soldier pointing at a naked man's genitals, and another that was proved to be nothing more than a hoax, but was passed off as proof of British military abuse by a tabloid newspaper.

Hashim concluded the film show with one final quote.

"Qur'an 3:151, Soon shall We cast terror into the hearts of the Unbelievers."

Abass was not in the least bit surprised he only spoke the quote without offering any spin or translation because, even to him, the quote was pretty much self-explanatory and needed neither.

The teenagers were now running up the slide and jumping down from the other side. Abass watched as one of the girls raised an arm, launching an object across the play area. The shattering of glass let him know that she had disposed of the vodka bottle. The group cheered at the sound of breaking glass.

"Get off me fucking tits!" The words travelled across the play area as Abass watched one of the girls lashing out at one of the boys. She caught his hand that held his cigarette. The object arced across the slide like a firefly diving for cover.

"You fucking bitch!" shouted the boy, as he left the group to retrieve his cigarette.

Abass watched on as the boy wandered across the playground, kicking at the ground, until he bent down to collect the cigarette. He held it up for inspection before throwing it back to the ground. Abass averted his eyes as the boy caught sight of him and hurried across towards the bench.

"Excuse me, mister, do you have a fag I can have?"

Momentarily, Abass was oblivious to the voice, so the young boy spoke again. "Excuse me, geezer, can I bum a fag offav ya?"

Abass looked up at the boy. The first thing he noticed, in the ambient street lighting, was his acne, as it spread over both cheeks and down onto his chin. He was dressed in baggy, ill-fitting clothes and sported a baseball cap, pulled down low over a bandana.

"Well then, do you have a fag or not?"

"I'm sorry, I don't smoke," replied Abass.

"Has he got any, Mickey?" one of the group shouted from across the play area.

"Nah, he don't smoke," Mickey shouted, setting off back towards his gang of friends. He turned back. "Have you got a few quid then?"

Abass stood up, turned in the opposite direction and headed out of the play area at a fast pace.

It was another hour before Abass finally returned to the flat.

FORTY-THREE

The Garda officer checked in with the nurse on duty at the reception desk of the Intensive Care Unit. The nurse briefly scrutinised the officer's ID before pointing him towards Adam Lewis' room. As the officer walked away, the nurse dialled an extension number and passed on a brief message to Dr McEvoy.

Lewis was just finishing his breakfast when he heard a light tapping on his open door. He looked up from his tray but before he had chance to speak, the Garda officer entered his room. Lewis physically slumped with disappointment. This wasn't the visitor he was expecting – where the hell was Danny Kelly?

"Good morning, sir," said the Garda officer, politely. "It's good to see ye awake and hopefully recovering well."

"Yeah, thanks," was all Lewis could offer, masking a nervous sense of worry. Lewis pushed the mobile tray away from his bed. "Would you?" he asked, indicating to the tray.

The Garda officer moved the tray to the end of the bed.

"Thanks," said Lewis. "I'm afraid I can only offer you water."

The officer smiled. "It's okay, I've already had my fill of coffee back at the station. He checked his watch, removing a large black folder from inside of the case he was carrying. It was 9:28a.m.

At that moment, Dr McEvoy entered the room. "Good morning, officer. I had the receptionist call me when you arrived as I'm in surgery most of the day." The doctor collected Lewis' notes and scanned the night-time observations. "If there's anything you want to ask me?"

Happy with Lewis' progress, Dr McEvoy replaced the file. She stayed beside the bed, looking across at the Garda officer, watching him arranging his paperwork.

"If you wouldn't mind confirming the causes of the injuries please, doctor."

"Not at all. From the pellets removed from the left shoulder, I can conclude that the injury was the result of a shotgun blast. The right shoulder received muscle and bone damage from the result of an attack with a drill."

The officer scribbled down an abridged version of the doctor's comments.

She continued, leaving Lewis feeling like he wasn't in the room. "There are a number of lacerations to the face, caused by a sharp, bladed implement. And finally, we have a number of areas that have been on the receiving end of blunt-force trauma. These are consistent with a beating of some kind. Those areas are the ribs, ankle and fingers."

The Garda officer continued his note-taking, thanking the doctor for her help. She excused herself and left the room.

The officer remained seated. Lewis was used to questioning in difficult situations, but in this case, the evidence was pretty overwhelming, and so his responses had to be believable enough to buy him some time until Kelly arrived, and without giving too much away. He felt like he was in a very difficult position, which wasn't helped by his urge to fidget, and which he fought hard to combat. Lewis hoped Kelly wasn't too far away.

"Quite a list of injuries you've got there, fella," the Garda officer piped up. "Someone don't like ye, that much is obvious."

For the moment, Lewis chose to remain silent.

"The doctor says ye name's Pete. Well then, Pete, how did all this happen to ye?" The Garda officer waved his pen like he was drawing an imaginary outline around Lewis' body. He then read the list of injuries from his notebook, pointing towards each one with his pen.

"That's some beating you've taken, Pete. Care to tell me how all this here happened?"

Lewis gave the question time to sink in as he mentally prepared his answer, wanting to keep as close to the truth as possible, so as not to overcomplicate things. He recalled that he was once given a piece of advice about making a lie sound more believable. It went along the lines of; *relate the story to something you have actually done, as it will be easier to remember the details and you will appear more convincing when you're telling the story.*

"I can only remember bits and pieces at the moment; my head is still swimming and isn't thinking clearly yet," answered Lewis.

"Well then, fella, let's start with what ye do remember, then we can go from there and hopefully, we'll help fix that memory of yours."

"Okay. Well I was in Derry with a couple of mates having a drink. I'd had a few too many when I'd got chatting with this lady."

The Garda officer interrupted. "Right then, Pete, let's take it back again. What are the names of your friends?"

"Tony McMahon and Jon Gittens." Lewis gave the names of two obscure footballers he'd remembered once playing for the team he supported.

"Okay. And what was the name of the bar you were drinking in?

"I'm sorry, I don't remember which one, you see, we'd been in quite a few that night and I was . . ."

"Yeah, worse for wear. Never mind, what about the lady then, what was her name?"

"I'm afraid I don't remember that either," said Lewis, trying to sound sincere.

"Okay then, carry on."

"Anyway, this lady asked if I had anywhere we could go. I said I had a room at the Waterfront Hotel. As we left to get a taxi, I was jumped from behind by a couple of men in the car park. They bundled me into a van and the next thing I remember is waking up tied to a post in a shed somewhere."

"Do ye have a description fer the men that attacked ye? Can ye remember anything about them at all, however small the detail?"

Lewis knew he was on safe ground describing Boyle and his accomplice, as one was dead, and unlikely to be found in a recognisable state, and the other had probably disappeared for good. So he gave the best description he could.

As the Garda officer wrote down the description, he recognised a familiar pattern emerging. He'd been taught a similar method of how to give a full description of a person.

He interrupted Lewis. "Pete, can I stop ye fer a moment? Have ye ever served with the police or the military before?"

"Why?" Lewis asked.

"It's the way ye describing these men. The pattern is familiar; age, build, colour of hair and eyes, distinguishing features . . ." The Garda officer let the sentence trail as he looked at Lewis for an answer.

Lewis had used the method he'd been taught during his army service. It was only as it was read back to him that he realised he'd switched to autopilot and reeled off the descriptions.

"Oh, you mean A to H?"

"Is that what ye call it?"

"Yes, it is." Lewis then filled in a few more of the missing headings. "Elevation, face, gait . . ."

"So, Pete, were you in any of the services?"

Lewis realised he couldn't give anything other than a truthful answer. "Yeah, I was, I was in the army. I served about 11 or 12 years ago." Lewis thought for a moment. "Maybe that's why I was grabbed, because I used to be a British squaddie. I mean, I still walk with a military bearing, even after all these years, and with my accent, I probably stick out like a sore thumb."

The Garda officer carried on with his questioning. "When you woke up in this shed, did ye have any idea where they had taken ye?"

"Not a clue, it was in some woods somewhere."

"Well then, what do you think these men wanted with you?"

"As I said, they must have gotten it into their heads that I was a squaddie and wanted to reach me a lesson."

"But why the torture, and to the extreme lengths they've gone to?"

"From what I remember, it started off as a sick game. I think they were getting some kind of twisted thrill from it all."

"Okay, I might be able to understand that. But why did they bring ye all the way out here? I mean, Derry is a big city, there's plenty of places they could have taken ye to that were a lot closer."

Lewis paused to take a sip from his baby beaker. The Garda officer sat watching patiently.

"I honestly have no idea. That's something you're gonna have to ask them."

"It looks like I will," said the Garda officer. "What else can you tell me about the shed and its location?" he asked, turning over to a fresh page in his notebook.

FORTY-FOUR

Colin Fullerton arrived at the Garda station.

After finishing his interview the previous day, Fullerton had wasted no time in returning back to his apartment and packing an overnight bag. Once done, he headed for the ferry port at Liverpool and made the late crossing to Dublin, where he checked into a hotel.

After an early breakfast, Fullerton had set off for the Garda station. Sitting in his car across the road from the station, he checked his watch – it was approaching 11:05a.m.

Fullerton stepped out of his car and crossed the road. As well as the station being nothing more than a converted house, from his earlier visit, Fullerton was aware that an old, obscure CCTV camera was its only protection. Shielding his face as best he could, Fullerton proceeded inside, nonchalantly resting his right arm against an object hidden beneath his jacket. On entering the station, Sergeant Clegg, who was standing behind the reception desk, greeted him. The two men exchanged pleasantries before Fullerton was invited into the side office.

"Did you have an easy journey?"

"I did, thanks, and mainly due to the rain holding off," Fullerton answered.

Clegg, sitting at his desk behind the computer, tapped a number of keyboard keys before hitting the print icon. The printer groaned into action; the clattering from the ink dispenser whirring across a sheet of paper filled the small office. Next, the mechanical wheels presented the paper into the collection tray at the bottom of the printer. Clegg turned in his chair to retrieve the single sheet. He turned it the right way up and handed it to Fullerton.

"Here, take a look. It's not a pretty sight," warned Clegg. "Is it your missing friend?"

Fullerton accepted the sheet of paper, noticing his hand quivering slightly. He composed himself before looking at the image. His eyes darted furtively across the image, looking for some distinguishing feature that would tell him he was indeed looking at an image of Lewis. He was sure the man in the picture was Lewis, only the purple and red swellings, and closed, puffed-up eyes were hiding his identity really well. Fullerton now concentrated on particular areas of the image, taking in the full extent of Lewis' facial injuries. He now noticed butterfly stitches holding together two slashes, and that one side of his bottom lip was more swollen than the other. It was also split in three places, with each split being no bigger than a metal staple. Both sets of eyelashes were closed tightly together and still crusted with dried blood from the damage around the sockets. Fullerton was under no illusion that if Lewis' eyes had been open, they would both be badly bloodshot.

"Not nice, is it?"

Fullerton wasn't surprised by the brutality of the violence used against Lewis. He did, however, wonder how Lewis had survived.

"It does look awful," was Fullerton's first response. "Yes, it is him. How is he? How did this happen? Whereabouts is he?" Fullerton asked the sort of questions he'd expect a close friend to ask.

"All in good time. Now then," said Clegg, taking the sheet of paper back, "do ye know of anyone who would want to inflict this level of violence on ye friend?"

Fullerton lightly shook his head. "No, I'm sorry, I wouldn't know of anyone who'd want to do this to Adam. I shouldn't say this, but he does have an issue with his temper when he's had a drink. Where was he found? Was it near a pub or bar?" Fullerton asked.

Once again, Clegg chose to ignore Fullerton's questions.

"Ye see, my colleagues are very concerned for ye friend. He sustained more serious injuries than the ones ye saw in the photograph," explained Clegg.

"What sort of injuries?"

Clegg held back with the details. "The report says, 'serious, life-threatening', and not the sort you would associate with a bar fight."

"I'm sorry I appear unhelpful, Sergeant, but this has come as quite a shock to me. All I know is we'd arranged to meet up and Adam failed to show. I then decided to come and speak with you."

Clegg took one final look at the image of Lewis before filing it away inside his missing person's file.

"I hope ye can understand the gravity of this incident . . ."

"Oh, I do, Sergeant," interrupted Fullerton, with mock concern. Clegg waited a moment before continuing.

"We all want to get to the bottom of this, and not just for Adam's sake. If ye know anything, no matter how small or trivial ye may think it might be, it will only help if ye mention it."

Fullerton nodded in acknowledgement. "I fully understand, Sergeant, but you have to know that this whole episode comes as a terrible shock to me," said Fullerton, feigning worry.

Clegg stood up, negotiated his way around his desk towards the office door. Resting one hand on the handle, he gestured for Fullerton to leave.

"The good news is he's still here in the south and not too far away," started Clegg. "If ye take ye sel' off to Carrick-on-Shannon, it's about a two-hour drive from here. Do ye have a satnav or one of them there apps on ye phone?" Clegg asked, as Fullerton walked out of the office.

"Yes I do, it's in the car."

"Good, I'll give you an address and postcode. But just so ye know where to look," Clegg led Fullerton to a large map, hanging up beside the main door to the station, "this is where ye need to go."

Fullerton followed Clegg's finger until he could see his destination on the map.

"See, it's not too hard to get to. Once you get there, just go to the local station and someone will take ye to the hospital. I'll call ahead so that they are expecting ye."

Fullerton and Clegg shook hands. "Thank you, once again, for all your help in finding my friend, Sergeant. I'm indebted to you and your fine force," said Fullerton from behind a veil of insincerity, before leaving the station.

He climbed back into the car. Once seated, he reached across to the glove box. After opening it, Fullerton lifted out a black car manual to reveal a dark-blue case stashed away beneath it. He took it out and rested it on his lap; on the lid were four small dials. He dialled in a code and opened the lid. Next, Fullerton removed a pistol from his waistband and, satisfied things had gone well and he hadn't had to resort to a desperate, messy plan B, he returned it back to the case. After re-securing the lock, Fullerton placed it back in the glove box.

He fired up the engine, engaged first gear, and released the handbrake. Fullerton accelerated away, heading for Carrick-on-Shannon.

FORTY-FIVE

A lady dressed in a green overall pushed a food trolley into Lewis' room. "Oh!" she said, as she halted the trolley. "I have the gentleman's lunch."

The Garda officer stood up. "It's okay, we were just finishing here," he said, closing his notepad.

The catering assistant wheeled the bed-tray stand from the end of Lewis' bed and guided it into position just over his waist. She collected his meal from the trolley and placed it down on the tray in front of him.

"What would you like to drink?"

"Coffee will be fine, thanks."

The lady turned back to her trolley and poured Lewis a coffee.

"Ye be taking it easy there now, Pete. I'll check out these details and will come back to speak with ye some more," the officer said.

"Okay, thanks, and I'll be here waiting for you," replied Lewis, as the officer left his room.

The catering assistant placed a plastic beaker of coffee down beside Lewis' lunch, before following the Garda officer out of the room.

Lewis picked up a spoon and cut into his meal. He lifted the first spoonful to his mouth, just as the room door opened once more. His bruised and swollen face lit up.

"Am I glad to see you or what?" he beamed.

Before closing the door, Danny Kelly placed the holdall he was carrying down on the nearest chair.

"I thought he was never going to leave," said Kelly.

"How long have you been here? I thought you would've been here earlier, what kept you?" asked Lewis.

"Long enough, me auld mucker. I was held up, a big crash, I couldn't turn around, just had to sit it out. Anyway, I'm here now. Jeez, what the hell happened to ye?" asked Kelly, taking a seat near the bed.

"It's a very long story," answered Lewis, as he guided another spoonful of food into his mouth. "Are those the clothes?" he asked, between chews, pointing towards the holdall with his spoon. With each jaw movement, Lewis felt a dull pain throbbing around the side of his face and up behind his left ear.

"Yeah, there's a pair of jeans, some socks and a sweater. I've also thrown in a pair of old trainers as well. I hope you ain't too bothered about fashion," said Kelly, with the flicker of a smile on his lips.

Lewis attempted another three mouthfuls of food before succumbing to the pain. "I'm due my next dose of medication in an hour."

Kelly checked his watch. "At half-past one?

Lewis nodded his head. "Once I've had them, we can get out of here."

"I'm guessing you already have a plan then?" asked Kelly, as he helped himself to some of the chips from Lewis' lunch plate. "Care to share it with me?"

"It's pretty simple really; you fetch a wheelchair and I get in it. Then you push me out of here. I'll tell the nurses I need some fresh air."

Lewis refilled his baby beaker with water from the jug on his tray. "I don't suppose you saw any wheelchairs on your way up here?"

Kelly looked up at his friend, who was now holding a beaker of water. "No thanks, mate," he smiled. "I'll stick with the chips."

Lewis looked puzzled. "Wheelchairs?"

"Sorry, mate, what do you need it for?"

Looking at his plastered foot, Lewis replied. "I can't shuffle out on that, it'll take too long."

"Got ye," said Kelly. "Yeah, there's a few down the corridor next to the lifts." Kelly reclined back in his seat. "Anyway, tell me what happened to ye."

FORTY-SIX

Colin Fullerton guided the car into the hospital car park and drove slowly down the narrow channels, until he spied an empty space and parked. The dashboard clock displayed 1:20p.m. before going blank as the car was switched off.

Fullerton had decided to visit the hospital before going to the police station, as he wanted to confront Lewis on his own and without a police officer present. As this was the only hospital in Carrick-on-Shannon, the chances were very high that this was the place where Lewis was recovering. Fullerton chose to leave his pistol in the glove box, as he could not risk being caught with it in such a public place, plus, he figured Lewis would be in no position to offer up any form of resistance. Fullerton weaved a path through the parked cars towards the hospital entrance.

***

Danny Kelly reversed into the double doors, bumping them open with his backside, turned around, and pushed the wheelchair towards Lewis' room. As he passed the nurses' station, he smiled at the only nurse sitting behind the large counter. Kelly nodded his head down towards the wheelchair to indicate to the nurse that he had found one.

On entering the room, Lewis was passing back an empty medication pot after taking his painkillers and antibiotics. The nurse looked across at Kelly with both eyebrows raised.

"I'm just taking him outside for some fresh air," explained Kelly, as he parked the wheelchair beside the bed. "That is, if it's okay with ye, nurse?"

The nurse looked at Lewis. "As long as you aren't outside for too long."

"I promise to have him back in half an hour, scout's honour," said Kelly, as he touched two fingers to the side of his head in a mock salute.

The nurse smiled. "I suppose half an hour won't hurt." Checking her watch, she noted the time before filling in Lewis' medication chart. "Just make sure he's back before two o'clock, when the doctor does her afternoon rounds."

"I will."

"Can you help me up, mate?" asked Lewis, reaching an arm out for support.

Kelly grasped Lewis under his armpit and helped him transfer from the bed into the wheelchair. The nurse watched from the door, which she held open for the two men to leave.

"Don't go too far," she said.

"We won't," replied Lewis.

***

After flashing his fake ID card at the reception staff, Fullerton headed off towards the lifts. He stepped inside one and hit the button for the floor where Intensive Care was situated. Fullerton shared the lift with a porter and an old man in a wheelchair, who were in animated conversation, and paying little attention to Fullerton. The lift came to a halt. Fullerton stepped out, leaving the two men to their musings. He turned sharply and headed off towards ICU.

***

Outside the hospital, the Garda officer parked his patrol car as close to the entrance as he could. He switched off the blue flashing lights, climbed out and made a dash for the entrance. The officer excused himself as he bumped into a pregnant women, almost knocking her off her feet. Once he was happy she was steady on her feet again, he headed off at speed towards the lifts.

The Garda officer trapped his hand between the lift doors before it had chance to fully close. The doors reopened and the officer leapt inside.

The call to the station had been received 10 minutes earlier. The officer had been busy transferring Lewis' statement from his notebook to computer when he was called into his chief inspector's office.

The chief inspector had explained that after Lewis' fingerprints had been entered into the analysis system, a match had been found. Lewis' prints matched those taken at a farmhouse in Altnakereen, the location of a double murder. After an extensive forensic search, fingerprints, blood samples and DNA swabs had been taken and catalogued. Lewis' blood group was a match for one of the samples taken from the farmhouse kitchen, as were his fingerprints.

The lift doors opened and the Garda officer swiftly exited, racing off towards ICU.

***

Lewis clutched tightly onto the holdall resting across his lap, as he and Kelly waited for the lift to arrive. The slow rumblings of the car echoed up the lift shaft as it approached their floor. A muted bell sounded and the doors opened.

"Shit!" mumbled Lewis.

"What did you say?" asked Kelly, as he stooped down to his friend's level.

"Quick, get me inside," said Lewis, trying to hide his face behind the sports holdall.

Kelly pushed the wheelchair into the empty lift, turned, and pressed the button for the ground floor. The doors closed before the lift began its slow descent.

"That copper rushing out of the other lift was the one who interviewed me. I wonder what his hurry was."

***

Fullerton opened the door to Lewis' room. It was empty.

"Fuck!" said Fullerton, scrunching his face into a scowl. He looked back down the corridor to the nurses' station. The one nurse behind the counter was chatting on the telephone.

"Can I help you, sir?"

The voice came from Fullerton's other side. He turned and came face to face with the ward sister. He flashed the fake ID.

"Yes, hopefully you can. I'm looking for the man in this room. Do you have any idea where he is?"

"Yes, he left with a friend to go outside for a short while. You've just missed him."

Fullerton looked down both sides of the corridor. "Which way did he go?"

"I'm not sure, I think they went that way." The sister pointed in the direction of a corridor running parallel to the one Fullerton had just walked down.

"Thanks," said Fullerton, walking away from the sister at a brisk pace. The sister reached for the door handle to Lewis' room and pulled it shut. As she turned to walk away, she almost collided with a Garda officer racing towards the room.

"I'm sorry, sister," apologised the officer, reaching for the door handle.

"My, he's popular today."

The officer spun around as he caught the words spoken by the sister. "I'm sorry, what did ye say?"

"I was just saying how this patient is popular today. One of your colleagues was here moments ago asking for him, and that was just after a friend of his turned up to take him outside for some fresh air."

The officer's brow furrowed and his eyes narrowed. "What do you mean 'one of my colleagues'?"

It was the sister's turn to look perplexed. "I've just spoken to him. He asked about the patient's whereabouts."

Reaching for his radio, the officer asked, "Which way did he go?"

"Down there. The same way as the patient went with his friend."

The Garda officer was sprinting off down the corridor before the sister could finish her sentence. He spoke into his radio, just as he caught a glimpse of a man leaving through the exit door.

"Tango Control, this is PC 1400. I need immediate backup at the hospital. I have reason to believe a suspect is trying to escape."

The officer buzzed the exit door open and raced across the landing in four stretched bounds, ducking into the lift before the doors had chance to close.

"I'm sorry, I didn't know . . ." said Fullerton, frantically hitting the door close button.

"That's okay," the officer panted, between drawing a lungful of air. "You didn't know what?"

Fullerton slipped his right hand into his pocket, wrapping his fingers around a small solid, thin, steel tube. In one silent, swift move, he withdrew the self-defence weapon from his pocket and drove the steel tube into the officer's temple. He made contact with the trigeminal nerve and, as a result of instantly disrupting the flow of the body's natural fluids, rendered the officer unconscious, causing him to collapse to the floor instantaneously, as his legs buckled beneath the weight of his body and equipment. Fullerton pressed the button for the next floor up, as he did not want to risk opening the lift door onto the reception area and someone seeing the unconscious police officer.

The instrument Fullerton had used against the officer was a Kubaton. His was disguised as a pen and was a very effective weapon when used against the body's pressure and nerve points. Fullerton always carried the pen with him, but this was the first time he had cause to use it against anyone. He was very impressed with the results.

Before stepping out of the lift, Fullerton pressed the button for the top floor. He watched as the doors closed and the lift began its slow ascent. He adjusted his dark glasses, a last-minute quick disguise, and headed for the stairs.

***

Kelly helped Lewis into his car. Once both legs were safely inside, he closed the rear passenger door. Next, he pushed the wheelchair to one side, climbed into the driver's seat, turned the engine on and carefully pulled away from the hospital. Kelly switched the car stereo on and without turning around, spoke across the seats to his reclined backseat passenger.

"A bit of *Summer of '69* for the journey?"

Lewis just smiled and closed his eyes. It was going to be a long, bumpy ride back to Londonderry.

***

Fullerton stepped out of the hospital doors opposite the main car park; he knew he had little chance of finding Lewis now, so he trudged back to his car. He did keep looking around, just in case – just in case what, he thought to himself, he's long gone.

Fullerton approached and unlocked his car. As he sat himself inside, the first of two patrol cars arrived at the main entrance, their sirens blaring out across the car park, causing several people to turn to see what was happening. Fullerton reversed his car out of the parking bay, selected first gear and accelerated away, totally oblivious to the wheelchair stood idly next to the empty bay on his passenger side.

All Fullerton could do now was catch the ferry back to England and return home to London.

***

Four hours after escaping from the hospital, Lewis was back in Northern Ireland and heading for Kelly's home. Outside the car, heavy rain pounded down on its roof and lashed against the windscreen; the wipers fought relentlessly to keep visibility to an acceptable level. The noise from the downpour drowned out the car stereo. Lewis slept silently on the back seat.

Kelly lit another cigarette as the blurred white spots of another approaching car drew level and then passed by, throwing up more water for the wipers to deal with.

FORTY-SEVEN

Luay Abass arrived back at the flat.

After the last incident, Falah decided not to fuss over Abass as much, leaving him to settle into his own rhythm once he was home, and then only talk to him when he appeared good and ready.

Falah was nonchalantly flicking through the television channels when Abass came into the front room.

"Hello Luay," said Falah, finally settling on a channel.

Abass made a "humph" sound as he dropped down into the corner chair. Falah glanced across the room and in that moment, decided Abass' demeanour was an obvious indication to stay clear for a while. He fought the urge to say anything and continued watching the television.

Abass sat in silence for fifteen minutes before he spoke.

"When a suicide bomber blows himself up, why does his head nearly always remain intact?"

Falah muted the television. "I'm sorry, Luay, what did you say?"

"When a suicide bomber detonates his vest, why does it destroy everything but his head?"

It wasn't the sort of question Falah was expecting to answer during a repeat of *Top Gear*, but he gave it a go.

"Honestly, I couldn't give you an exact answer, but I do think it has something to do with the way in which the explosives are packed, which in turn, impacts on the direction of the blast."

"What do you mean?"

"Well," said Falah, resting the TV remote on the coffee table, "the explosives are placed in a vest in such a way that once detonated, the blast explodes out, away from the body, and the pressure generated pushes the head upwards and away from the blast."

Abass furrowed his brow with a quizzical look on his face. Falah thought for a moment.

"Okay, think of a bottle of champagne. If you shake the bottle up, causing the gases inside to expand, the liquid has no place to go, so the build-up of pressure forces the cork up out of the way." Falah decided to switch the TV off. "Why do you ask?"

Abass still looked distracted. "Um," he said, as if looking for inspiration from the ceiling. "We were shown more suicide bombings tonight."

"I see. Was al Dulhaimi present again?"

"No, not tonight," said Abass, shaking his head. "I also noticed four of the other students were also missing."

"Do you know which ones?"

"I'm afraid not," said Abass, momentarily looking at the floor, as if he had disappointed his friend. "We still haven't been properly introduced or allowed to talk to each other."

"Wait here a moment," said Falah, getting up from his chair and leaving the room.

A minute later, he returned, clutching a black folder. "Here, Luay," he said, handing the folder across to Abass. "Take a look through these photos and see which ones from your class were missing."

Abass accepted the folder and slowly began looking through it. Each page contained two photographs of males and females entering and leaving the mosque. Most were single shots, but occasionally, there was a group photograph of upwards of two people.

Falah excused himself and left for the kitchen to put the kettle on.

Next door, Abass flicked through the black folder. After his first invite to the private prayer room, Abass and Falah had spent almost three hours going through photo after photo, until they had identified Abass' other prayer group members. And later, Falah had arranged a folder that contained all the photographs the group appeared in. This was the folder Abass was now scrutinising.

Falah returned with the drinks. "Any luck?" he asked, before sitting down.

"Not yet," replied Abass. "Oh, one other thing," he said, matter-of-factly. "We have to take our passports in tomorrow so they can arrange visas for Turkey."

FORTY-EIGHT

The early morning sun struggled to penetrate through a wall of grey rainclouds. Even the birds were noticeably absent as the new day dragged itself from the clutches of a rain-soaked night.

Danny Kelly finished sealing the hospital gown into carrier bag after carrier bag, until he was convinced the garment could not be seen through the flimsy plastic material. He took the package, along with the rest of the household rubbish, and stuffed everything into a large black bin-bag. After securely knotting the bag shut, he took it all outside, ready for the weekly collection. In one hour, it will be collected and away from here for good, he thought.

After washing his hands, Kelly sat down with a mug of tea and two slices of toast. Lewis was still sleeping upstairs, so Kelly used this time to catch up with his newspaper.

Both men had arrived back at Kelly's house late last night, under the cover of darkness. Kelly had helped Lewis upstairs to the spare room, where he'd struggled to get him out of his clothes and into bed. Lewis had been so frustrated with his casts that he'd been tempted to smash both of them off. Lewis felt a little better once Kelly had returned to the bedroom with a large glass of brandy, which he quaffed down in one mouthful. Kelly left his friend to get some sleep and returned downstairs to his own glass of brandy and the comfy chair opposite the television. Within an hour, he too was fast asleep.

***

Tracey Scott arrived at her office with a folder tucked under one arm and a coffee beaker and keys grasped precariously in her other hand. She nudged her office door open with her elbow then flicked it shut with the heel of one foot, as she walked to her desk.

The coffee and keys were the first items to be released, followed by the folder. Tracey pressed the power button to start her computer before crossing over to the filing cabinet and retrieving Fullerton's case file.

After typing in her password, Tracey browsed her emails. She responded to the few that only required a "yes or no" reply; the rest could wait, she thought.

It was as Tracey was scanning through an assortment of police bulletin reports that something caught her eye. She moved the cursor and clicked on the relevant report, which opened, filling her computer screen with information. Tracey jotted down a few salient points, got up from behind her desk, and left the office.

***

Lewis slowly opened his eyes. Blinking as the outside light flooded in, he could just make out the shape of a blurred silhouette of someone standing over him. Gradually, Kelly's features came into focus, although most of his face remained in shadow. Lewis recognised his friend.

"What time is it?" asked Lewis, stifling a yawn.

"It's just after 10. Here," said Kelly, extending an arm, "I've brought you a drink."

"Thanks, mate. I don't suppose . . ."

"Yes, I've found some more. Here ye go." Kelly handed over a strip of painkillers."

After Kelly's mother had died, he'd left her room more or less as it was whilst she was alive. He'd tidied up the room, packing away her clothes for a charity shop, but all her personal effects had remained in the room, tucked away in an assortment of boxes. To ease the severe pain she'd been in, prior to her death, Kelly's mother had been prescribed various doses of painkillers and antibiotics, and it was these he was giving to his friend.

Lewis popped two tablets from the foil wrapping with his good hand, reached for the glass of water on the bedside table, and washed down the tablets with lukewarm water.

"Do you think you can manage some food?" asked Kelly.

Between sips of coffee, Lewis answered, "Yeah, I think so, but nothing too heavy, mind."

"Don't worry, I was only making toast," smiled Kelly.

"Thanks again for coming and getting me, Danny, I really appreciate it, mate."

Kelly sat down on the corner of the bed. "About that, Adam, I wasn't going to ask anything until you were stronger . . ." Kelly's eyes wandered before settling on Lewis' face. "I was watching the morning news . . . and, Adam, I need to know what's going on."

Lewis looked puzzled. "What's the news got to do with anything?"

"You're the main story, Adam."

The colour from Lewis' face drained as he rested the coffee mug on the bedside table. "What do you mean 'main story'?"

"The Garda are saying you're wanted fer questioning. They have reported ye missing from hospital, but say they want to talk to ye in connection with a double murder at a farmhouse in Altnakereen."

Lewis wanted to speak but his mouth was suddenly parched. He grabbed the glass of water and swallowed large gulps.

"Who have ye shot, Adam?" asked Kelly, still perched on the corner of the bed, trying to remain calm. "Does this have anything to do with Sean Boyle?"

Lewis swallowed more water. Shaking his head, all he could say was, "I've been set up. Someone's setting me up!"

"What do you mean, Adam?"

"I've been set up!" said Lewis, through gritted teeth. "I haven't shot anyone."

"Well, who's setting ye up and why?"

"I don't know . . ." Lewis' eyes widened. "Wait . . . Fullerton. The fucking . . ."

Kelly waited patiently as Lewis pieced together his fractured memories. He watched on as his friend's eyes darted rapidly from side to side, sorting through a broken timeline of events from the past weeks.

"Where were the shootings?"

With the news item fresh in his mind, Kelly answered, "Altnakereen."

"Altnakereen," repeated Lewis. "That's where Fullerton told me Boyle was hiding out."

"Sean Boyle?"

"Yes, I was told that's where I could find him."

"Adam, Sean Boyle was shot dead in Northumberland."

Lewis sank down into his pillows as the painkillers began taking effect.

"Fullerton sent me there on a wild goose chase. I was shot by one of the farmers and then taken to a desolate barn out in the sticks somewhere."

"Who took you?"

"From what I can remember," Lewis winced, as pain from the drill wound to his shoulder reminded him of his time in captivity, "I think it was Sean's brother. He wanted to know what I knew of Sean's death." Lewis massaged his shoulder momentarily. "He had it in his head that I had something to do with it."

"So, this Fullerton fella sent you to the wrong place?" Kelly stood up. "It still doesn't explain the deaths though."

Lewis turned his head towards Kelly. "I know it doesn't, but I'm going to get to the bottom of this . . ." His speech slurred as his eyes slowly closed.

"Get some rest and when you're stronger, we'll talk again and try to figure something out."

Kelly left the room, gently closing the door behind him.

***

Tracey Scott knocked on Macleod's door waiting for an invitation to enter. It came and so she opened the door and walked in.

"Good morning Robert."

"Morning Tracey, take a seat," replied Macleod, pointing at the vacant chair across the desk from him.

Tracey declined. "It's okay, this won't take too long."

"Right then, fire away. What do you have for me?"

"It's Adam Lewis, he's resurfaced." She chose her words carefully. "Well, in a way, he's turned up."

"What do you mean 'in a way'?" asked Macleod, with a furrowed brow.

"I was checking through some of the daily bulletins when I came across one concerning Lewis." Tracey passed a sheet of paper across to Macleod. "Apparently, he's wanted for questioning in connection with two deaths at a farmhouse in the Republic of Ireland. His current whereabouts are unknown since he disappeared from a hospital in Carrick-on-Shannon yesterday."

Macleod scanned through the contents of the bulletin.

"Right, I see. Let's get Fullerton in today and get this investigation moving. Can you set things up, Tracey, while I speak with Fullerton and invite him back in for questioning?"

Macleod reached for his telephone as Tracey turned and left the office.

***

The monotonous ringing eventually roused Fullerton from his sleep. After his long journey back from Ireland, he had just collapsed onto the sofa in an exhausted heap, not even taking the time to remove his clothes.

Fullerton reached out until his fingers rested on the mobile phone. Before bringing it up to his ear, he checked the caller ID and then accepted the call.

"Hello Robert." Fullerton listened for a short while before speaking. "I hope you don't mind if I wait until this afternoon. I had a rough night last night and I wouldn't want to face a hearing smelling of booze."

Fullerton waited for Macleod to speak again before answering. "How about I come in at five? I should be okay by then." He checked his watch; it displayed 11:06a.m.

"Drink some coffee and be here at two o'clock!" was Macleod's final word on the matter before he disconnected the call.

FORTY-NINE

September 1994

Colin Fullerton stepped into his office. He shut the door on an empty corridor. The clock in his office showed it was very late, 12:10a.m. The only other person in the building was the duty officer, and he was tucked away downstairs. He removed his jacket, hanging it up on the tall, slender rack beside the filing cabinets. Then he dragged his feet over to his desk and slouched down into his chair. Next, he leaned down to his right and opened the bottom drawer, took out a pack of cards from his trouser pocket, and he dropped them into the open drawer.

Then he collected a small bottle of whisky and a glass tumbler, before pouring himself a healthy measure. The first mouthful barely touched the insides of his mouth. His evening chill was soon forgotten, as the amber liquid warmed its way down his throat. Fullerton topped up his glass before returning the bottle to its hiding place in the bottom drawer.

He leaned back in his chair, toying with the tumbler, whilst contemplating the card game he'd just returned from. Fullerton played cards fortnightly, tasks depending, with a number of special branch officers, across at the local police station. They all gathered in a back room, taking it in turns to provide refreshments. On this occasion, Fullerton had lost nearly £800.

A gentle knock on the office door refocused Fullerton's attention.

"Come in."

One of Fullerton's agents entered the office. "Sorry to bother you, sir. I saw your light on and wanted to drop this off."

The agent reached into a jacket pocket, producing a brown envelope, which he handed across the table to Fullerton.

"It's payment for one of my informants. We had arranged a meeting, as details of a weapons dump he gave resulted in a significant find and two arrests. Unfortunately, he failed to appear, so I'm returning it back to the safe."

Fullerton accepted the envelope. "Leave it with me and I'll sign it back in for you. Who was it for?"

"Peter Coyle."

The agent left the office. Fullerton crossed over to the solid steel safe in the corner of his office. Dropping down to one knee, he dialled in the combination then twisted the handle and heaved the door open. Inside was an assortment of brown and blue banknote bundles, and a small ledger precariously slotted into one side. Fullerton removed the ledger and opened it on the required page. He placed the envelope inside the safe before seeking the corresponding entry. Once he'd found it, Fullerton returned to his desk for a pen.

Pen poised over the entry, Fullerton read the amount, £3,000. His hand wavered. He looked back at the safe and then at the brown envelope.

£3,000.

Fullerton's hand slowly wrote in the ledger.

Paid!

FIFTY

Ali Hashim tapped gently on the door and waited.

"Come," boomed the voice from the other side.

Hashim entered the room with his head bowed low. As he approached the desk, he was aware that all eyes from five men seated down one side of the room were upon him. Stopping a few feet short of the desk, he raised his head and addressed the seated figure on the other side.

"Imam Dulhaimi, we have a problem with one of our students," said Hashim.

"Tell me, Ali, what exactly is wrong?"

"I have just received a call from a distressed mother; she is concerned about her son. After prayers last night, he failed to return home."

Al Dulhaimi sat back in his chair, waiting for Hashim to explain himself.

"She waited up most of the night for him and then checked his room this morning. She informs me that when she checked his room, a bag and some clothes were gone. He has now been missing for over . . ." Hashim checked his watch; it was 2:30p.m., " . . . 18 hours. After calling around his friends, out of desperation, she called me to ask if I would know of any reason for him taking off."

"Do you, Ali?"

"No, Imam. But Mohamed is one of the students chosen for our Prophet's next mission."

Rolling his eyes, al Dulhaimi gave some thought to the situation. Hashim stood in silence, waiting patiently in front of the imam. The other men too sat in silence watching al Dulhaimi.

"What steps have you taken, Ali?"

"I've called the others from Mohamed's group and asked if they know what has happened. If Mohamed has spoken to them about his actions, and if they know anything of his whereabouts. Each one of them was unable to offer any information."

"Do you think he's changed his mind?" probed al Dulhaimi.

"That could be the case, Imam Dulhaimi," said Hashim. "Until we find him though, we will not know for sure."

The five seated men followed the conversation between al Dulhaimi and Hashim like tennis spectators, their eyes flicked from one to the other as each man spoke.

"So, this leaves us one short?"

"It did, Imam,"

"Did?" asked a puzzled al Dulhaimi.

"Yes, Imam, I have looked at the other students and found some possible substitutes."

"A substitute," said al Dulhaimi, clasping his hands together and resting them on top of the desk.

"Yes. I know how much this mission means to you. With all the preparation we have done, it would be such a shame to call it off."

"I wouldn't dream of calling it off," protested al Dulhaimi, as he unclenched his hands and stood up. The imposing figure, dressed in immaculately-pressed robes, stepped out from behind his desk and approached Hashim. The seated men took this as an indication to avert their eyes. Standing face-to-face, al Dulhaimi was a good foot taller than Hashim.

"We have had too many failed missions recently; this one has to go ahead."

"That is why I've drawn up a list of suitable replacements."

"And where is this list?"

Hashim produced a sheet of paper, which he handed to the imam. Al Dulhaimi took the list and scrutinised the names.

"Why is this student on the list?" asked al Dulhaimi.

Hashim looked at where the imam was pointing and read the name.

"He's only been coming to this mosque for about three weeks."

Hashim turned around as al Dulhaimi started pacing away from his desk.

"I know, Imam, but he has shown unwavering willingness and great promise since his arrival, and unlike our other students, he has expressed a need for striking back at the Infidels.

"Hmm," pondered al Dulhaimi. "I may have misjudged your choice, Ali," he added, padding back to his desk.

"No, no, Imam, you are right to question. I have only proposed suitable choices; the final decision rests with you."

"I trust your reasoning for adding this student to the list, and if it truly is his time to step forward and serve the great Prophet then he should have his chance."

Hashim let out a soft breath of relief.

"Inform him immediately. We do not have much time before the great day is upon us and we strike with fire deep into the heart of this corrupt city.

Hashim excused himself.

In his office, Hashim wasted no time in seeking Luay Abass' phone number. The moment he had it, Hashim was calling the student to pass on Imam al Dulhaimi's wishes.

FIFTY-ONE

Colin Fullerton arrived at MI5's Headquarters at 3:45p.m.

He was greeted at the door by a security guard, who took his details before issuing him with a visitor's pass.

"If you would be so kind as to take a seat, Mr Fullerton, someone will be down shortly."

Another man, about 20 years his junior, was buzzed through the internal security door and made his way towards Fullerton.

"Hello Colin, I'm Martin Bailey your representative through the disciplinary hearing. Please, follow me."

After shaking hands, the two men disappeared inside the inner sanctum of Thames House.

"In here, Colin," Bailey indicated, by way of opening a door. "I've been given half an hour to go through any questions you may have about today."

Fullerton squeezed past Bailey and into the room. It was sterile and brightly lit from one long, tubular light, directly above a table in the centre of the room. Four chairs were placed around the table, two on either side, and in one corner of the room stood a water dispenser.

"You know, Martin, I quite fancy a coffee, would you mind doing the honours?"

Bailey placed his briefcase down on the table.

"How do you take it, Colin?"

"Just with milk, thanks."

Fullerton took the time he was alone to scrutinise his surroundings, which weren't too far removed from a police interview room. There was a voice recorder stored inside a built-in wall cabinet, and two mounted security cameras, the leads of which disappeared into the wall above the cabinet. Finishing his look around, Fullerton was disappointed there was no two-way mirror. He already had images in his mind of his conspirators hiding away in a room, pointing and whispering amongst themselves whilst watching over his downfall. Still, they could always watch on the recording, he thought.

Bailey returned with two plastic cups of a liquid resembling dirty dishwater. He set one down in front of Fullerton and retained one for himself. Bailey then took the seat beside Fullerton.

He spun his briefcase around until he could see the combination dials then rotated them to the correct three digits. After clicking open the briefcase, he proceeded to remove a handful of pens, a notepad and a thick, hard-backed document.

"What's that?" asked Fullerton. "I hope it's not the list of charges against me!"

A thin smile flickered across Bailey's lips. "Good grief, no, it's a copy of the Code of Conduct."

Fullerton rolled his eyes. He puffed out his cheeks and exhaled deeply, rasping his lips and hoping his advisor wasn't a "wet behind the ears" novice to disciplinary matters.

Someone knocked at the interview room door.

"Come in," Bailey responded to the tapping.

The door opened, just wide enough for Macleod to pop his head around. "How long do you need, gents?"

Bailey turned to face Fullerton, who in turn, was glaring at Macleod. He broke his stare, whispering something to his representative.

"We're fine to start right away."

"Good," said Macleod, opening the door wider, allowing Tracey Scott to step into the room first. Macleod closed the door behind him and joined the three people at the table.

Macleod spoke. "Good afternoon, Colin. I trust you're feeling much better since we last spoke?"

Fullerton chose to remain silent.

"Okay, Tracey, if you can start the recording equipment please. Then we can begin."

Tracey opened the top desk drawer and removed two remote controls. She aimed them at the machines. A small, red light flashed briefly on the side of the cameras, indicating they were both on, while the voice recorder gave out a loud audible buzzing to indicate it too was on.

Macleod opened the first of three folders he'd brought to the interview. Looking across the top of the folder at Fullerton, he very briefly summed up the reason for them all being present.

"Colin, you were requested to attend today, as it has been brought to my attention that during your period of supervision of the Londonderry section, a number of financial irregularities have surfaced. As head of the department and main signatory to these payments, I, today, need to establish your level of knowledge and or involvement in these irregularities."

Fullerton rested his arms on the table and linked his hands together in a prayer-like gesture, as he looked on impassively at Macleod.

"Anyway, this is your opportunity to put your side across, and for me to ask you questions regarding these matters."

Macleod continued with his calm, disciplined tone, even when Fullerton changed his facial expression to one of boredom. Fullerton's attempts to goad a reaction from Macleod were having very little effect.

"The interview will be recorded, both verbally," Macleod indicated to the cabinet containing the voice recorder, "and visually." Again, Macleod made an indication to the cameras positioned in the room. Fullerton turned briefly to look at both pieces of equipment; his only reaction was to raise his eyebrows slightly.

"If it is found that there is a case against you, Colin, then you will be afforded copies of both recordings in order to prepare a defence. If not, they will be retained in archives or destroyed in accordance with our Codes of Practice."

Fullerton looked on blankly.

"Do you understand, Colin?"

Fullerton shook his head slightly.

"Colin?"

"I'm sorry... yes," replied Fullerton, stiltedly. "Yes... I understand. Yes, Robert, I fully understand. My apologies, I was miles away."

Macleod remained unfazed by his obvious tactics.

"Right, Colin, let's get started..."

***

Strong was just finishing off typing a memo when his secure telephone rang. He tapped a final full stop before reaching for the handset and lifting it to his ear.

"Hello."

Strong's eyes narrowed, as he found himself nodding along, listening to the caller. He chose to take mental notes rather than reach for a pen and paper, as he didn't want to interrupt the caller.

"Mm. Right. Okay, Hassan, I'll collect the rest of the equipment and we'll meet for coffee in . . ." Strong looked across at the wall clock. "It's half-past four now, let's say in one hour. Where are you now?"

Strong turned the handset away from his ear briefly as he mapped out, in his mind, possible meeting places.

"Right, Hassan, I'll meet you at the bookshop."

He ended the call, closed down his computer and hurried from his office to the room Falah's operation was being controlled from. Once there, Strong collected a sports bag from a locked cabinet. Before securing the door, he checked the contents of the bag; happy, he resealed the combination lock. Next, Strong crossed over to a small desk containing three telephones. Lifting the handset from the middle telephone, he punched in an extension number.

"Hi Tim, we have a green light. Can you send up a communications team, please?"

Strong left the room, hurrying away to find Macleod.

***

Fullerton raised the sheet of paper once more, scrutinising the contents highlighted in yellow. His eyes followed the entry from the number in the margin on the left, across the line, to the signature on the right. Fullerton rechecked the amount, £3,000, once more, before switching focus to the signature.

"Yes, it does look like my signature," said Fullerton, looking directly across the table at Macleod. "Do I remember signing it? Well, that's the thing, you know yourself, Robert, we sign a great number of documents whilst running an operations room, and given how long ago this was signed, I couldn't possibly say, in all honesty, that I did indeed sign it."

Fullerton handed the sheet of paper back to Tracey.

Macleod carried on.

"The logbook, dated the same day as your signature that appears on the cash release form, shows that at the time the payment was authorised, you were the officer on shift."

Tracey handed Fullerton another photocopied sheet of paper, which he reluctantly accepted. He knew exactly what point Macleod was going to make, so didn't attempt reading the document. Instead, Fullerton waited for Macleod to say that it was evidence that he was on shift that day.

"As you can see, Colin, you signed to say you came on shift at 0730 hours and again, to say your shift finished at 2300 hours. So, according to this log report, you should have been the person responsible for signing over that money," Macleod confirmed.

"Again, all I can say is that as it is such a long time ago, I can't recall authorising that payment," responded Fullerton.

Three loud raps at the door echoed around the brightly-lit room. Macleod turned in his seat. "Come in."

Strong opened the door just wide enough to poke his head in through the gap. He motioned with his head for Macleod to come over to him. Before getting up, Macleod announced a halt to the meeting.

"Paul, take Colin to the canteen and we'll use this time for a 15-minute break."

Fullerton and James stood up before leaving the room. As he passed by Strong, Fullerton looked him straight in the eyes; neither man spoke a word to each other.

Macleod turned to Tracey. "Can you leave us, please."

Tracey nodded, switched off the recording equipment, gathered up her paperwork, and silently slipped out of the room, closing the door behind her.

"Right, Strong, what do you want?"

"I received a call from Hassan, less than 10 minutes ago. Abass has been asked to buy an evening suit and take it with him to the mosque tonight."

Macleod's brow furrowed. He regarded Strong with a puzzled look etched on his face. Strong remained where he was with his back pressed up against the closed door, awaiting questions.

"What do you mean 'buy an evening suit'?"

"Abass was called around lunchtime and asked to buy an evening suit and take it with him to evening prayers," said Strong.

Macleod waited for the punchline and Strong didn't fail to deliver.

"He was told one of his group had dropped out of a planned visit and he was been given the honour of replacing him." Strong paused momentarily. "He's to take the suit with him for the visit planned this Friday."

"That's two days away," said Macleod.

"I know."

Macleod leaned back in his chair.

"Jesus, two days. Your guy has certainly delivered." Macleod stood up, adjusted his jacket, and crossed over to Strong. "Do we have a target location yet?"

Strong slowly shook his head. "Not yet, we're still going with plan A, arresting all suspects before they set off for their target."

Macleod opened the interview room door for Strong to lead the way out.

"What do you have in place so far?"

"The operations room will be up and running within the hour, and I'm about to take these to Hassan." Strong lifted the sports bag. "I also need authorisation to put the Met's designated firearms units on immediate standby."

Macleod looked over to Tracey Scott, who was standing at a drinks dispenser machine. He nodded gently to acknowledge her presence.

"You get off to your meeting, Strong, and I'll work on getting the other resources in place."

The two men shook hands before parting company. Tracey took this as her cue to approach Macleod.

"I'm sorry, Tracey, something's come up. Can you take over for me and finish quizzing Fullerton?"

"Yes I can, do you want me to keep him here for you once we're through?"

"No, it's okay to let him go," said Macleod, as he turned to leave. "One thing though, ask him about Adam Lewis and see if it provokes any sort of reaction in him. I'm guessing it probably won't, as he's trying to play this situation as cool as you like." Macleod took a step, then added as an afterthought, "Just try and trip him up, Tracey, ruffle his feathers so he doesn't have it all his own way." He winked. "You know what I mean."

Tracey Scott smiled as Macleod hurried away.

FIFTY-TWO

Luay Abass arrived back at the flat, carrying his newly-purchased evening attire. He locked the front door and headed straight to his bedroom.

"Excuse me," Falah called from the front room. "Can you pop in here for a moment, Luay, please?"

Abass stopped in his tracks. Feeling like a naughty child caught sneaking in from school, he swapped the suit from one hand to the other, as he turned around and padded into the front room.

Falah was sat on the floor behind the coffee table. Spread out across the table were a number of everyday items that Abass recognised easily; the other space-aged gadgets, he hadn't a clue what they were.

"Please, Luay." Falah indicated for him to sit down at the coffee table.

Abass carefully lay the suit out across the sofa, before making himself comfortable on the floor at the coffee table.

"Do you have your mobile?"

Abass zipped open a tracksuit pocket. "Yes, it's here," he said, reaching in for the object and holding it up for Falah to see.

Falah took the phone, stashing it away in the sports bag. "Don't worry, you'll get it back."

Falah then picked up a mobile phone from the table and handed it to Abass, who took the item, looking curiously at it, turning it around so that he could inspect all sides. Nothing stood out; it looked exactly like his own phone – a simple touchscreen phone, no lasers, no secret knives or guns. Abass didn't know if he should feel disappointed or not.

"I made a note of your phone and had this one made for you. It's exactly like your old phone; the only difference is this phone has a GPS tracker fitted inside."

Abass looked puzzled.

"I'm giving you some equipment so that you can summon support, similar to what you had sewn into your robes. All of the items are reactive, so will only work once activated," explained Falah.

"Why's that?" asked Abass.

"It eliminates the chance of the items being discovered, should someone decide to use any sort of detecting equipment. I know you've already told me they haven't used anything previously, but this late in the game, we can't take any chances."

Falah reached for one of the boxes on the coffee table, flipped open the lid and switched it on. The screen lit up. Falah entered a security code, before bringing up a map of the local area. He then turned the machine so that Abass could see the screen.

"Luay, I want you to turn the phone on, just as you would your normal phone."

Abass obliged by depressing the power button. The screen flashed brightly, followed by the appearance of the network logo and then coloured ribbons danced across the screen, before it settled on his home screen, complete with a picture of his family.

Abass' face lit up in astonishment.

"I cloned your phone when I uploaded the video clip," answered Falah. "Now, I want you to call my phone."

Abass scrolled through his contacts until he came to the required number.

Falah picked up his phone, accepting the call before swiftly disconnecting it. "There you go, just like a normal phone. Now, I want you turn the phone off again."

Abass carried out the request.

Once the screen was blank, Falah spoke. "Press the camera button for me."

Abass pressed the button, keeping his eyes fixed on the blank screen, not really sure of what he was waiting for. Nothing happened.

"There you go," said Falah, pointing at the screen in front of him. Abass turned to look; he was now staring at a flashing red dot, superimposed over the map. He looked at Falah.

"Okay, to reset it, press and hold the camera button for 10 seconds."

Abass obliged.

"Don't worry about having to reset the phone; we'll only be interested in knowing your location, and as you saw, it gives off an almost immediate signal."

Next, Falah picked up a set of misbaha beads, used for counting the recitals of Allah's name during prayers. The beads come in either a hoop of thirty-three or ninety-nine, this being the total number of times the Prophet's name is recited in three different guises. Abass possessed a hoop of thirty-three.

"Here you go," said Falah, handing the hoop over to Abass.

"Do I swap these also?"

"Please," answered Falah. "Just leave your originals in your bedroom for safe-keeping."

The hoop was made up of thirty-three beads – twenty-nine dark-coloured beads and four red beads. The red beads were on opposite sides of the fastener, with each red bead separated by a dark bead. All the beads were wooden.

"I need you to be very careful with those beads, Luay. They will only work once and cannot be reset. Do you understand?"

Abass nodded his head slowly as he loosened his grip on the beads.

One of the red beads is joined to the nearest dark-coloured bead; all you have to do to activate the GPS is break the beads apart."

Again, Abass nodded.

"We will be keeping a close watch on you the whole time; we just need to know from you when to act. I'll explain more once we've finished going over the kit."

Falah picked up another black box, about the size of a spectacle case, which he opened and removed a black button from.

"I'll stitch this one onto your suit," said Falah, balancing the button on a finger for Abass to see.

"How does it work?" he asked.

"To send a signal, you only have to squeeze the two flat sides together. Once the contacts make a connection, the GPS is operated. What I'll do is stitch it onto the inside pocket of your suit jacket, as the inside button is larger than normal buttons, so it will be secure and out of sight."

Abass looked on like an attentive schoolboy.

"Our main aim is to avert a catastrophic event, and hopefully catch al Dulhaimi as close to any form of weapon as possible, so I'm asking you to be extremely patient tonight and only activate these devices once this situation arises."

Abass nodded.

Falah continued. "Should you leave the mosque for another location, which we are expecting you to do, as al Dulhaimi won't compromise his own mosque, then the same applies there. Try and hold out until al Dulhaimi is in attendance." Falah then reiterated the mission. "Our first aim is to prevent an attack by this group of extremists and secondly, to arrest al Dulhaimi."

"What if I panic?" asked Abass.

"I'm asking you to hold your nerve, Luay, and trust that support will only be moments away from you. If it happens, it happens; we may disrupt their plans on this occasion and have to plan for another day, but your safety is paramount. All I'm asking is for you to be stronger than you've ever been and see this through to the very end." Looking at Abass and seeing a worried young man, he added, "Do this for your father. I'm sure one day, when you're able to talk about what you've achieved, it will make him even prouder of his son."

Abass regarded the other items on the table. "What about the other things?" he asked, changing the subject.

"Don't worry about the rest, you have enough on your plate without me bogging you down with even more technical jargon," answered Falah, pushing himself up onto his feet.

Falah gathered up the suit from the sofa before turning back to Abass. "The three GPS devices are for you to summon help. Use whichever one you can, or all three if you get the chance." Falah then, for a final time, repeated the mission outline. "But only activate them if you feel compromised, or when everyone is gathered together and you are aware of the presence of any form of weapon, and preferably, when al Dulhaimi is there too."

Abass watched Falah hang the suit on the back of the living room door and then unzip the covering to get at the jacket. He took the jacket out and sat back down on the sofa. Falah reached for the needle and thread from off the coffee table. At that moment, Abass realised that was the one item he'd failed to see. He consoled himself with the thought that it was black thread, and not the easiest thing to spot.

"We'll have teams watching your every move once you leave for the mosque, but as you know, once you're inside, we can only help if you signal for it. You'll be the only person who knows what is going on."

While Falah spoke, Abass fidgeted with the mobile phone.

"I tell you what, Luay, I'll make us a drink while you go and have a relaxing shower. I'll finish this off in a moment."

Abass got to his feet and padded into his bedroom. After pushing the door shut, he sat down heavily on the edge of his bed. He felt his shoulders slump. Bowing his upper body forward and barely able to raise his head, Abass stared into the mirror on the dresser. He felt like the person looking back at him had aged 20 years in the space of a few days. Abass fell back, spread-eagled on the bed. From the kitchen, he heard Falah filling the kettle.

FIFTY-THREE

The man in the long, dark coat had ditched his car in a darkened side street, deciding to continue the rest of his journey on foot.

Turning out of another terraced street, the man kept his head down and his pace brisk. He paid no attention to the small group of youths standing beneath a lamppost, smoking cigarettes and kicking a can between them. Likewise, the youths paid no attention to the man in the shabby coat.

As he stepped off the pavement to cross the road, the man didn't fail to notice that the kerbstones were painted orange, white and green, as were all the streetlights. From a number of the lampposts, there also flew the Irish tricolour flag, and from a couple of others, a solemn, black flag fluttered in the night air; a symbolic reminder from a past funeral of a newly-ordained martyr to the Cause. The man was fully aware he was walking through an Irish Republican housing estate, and was conscious of not drawing attention to himself.

The man crossed an open area at the end of a row of houses. Standing in the centre of the tarmacked space, twisted and burnt, were the remnants of a car shell with the seat springs visible. The whole frame was a mixture of fire-damaged black, and multitudes of orange rust from the constant downpours. Decorating the end of one house was a full-length mural, painted by one of the estate artists, depicting the images of a crouched man in a long overcoat, waving a white hanky, with a small group of people behind him, carrying a younger man. The whole scene was from an incident that had taken place nearby on 30th January 1972, Bloody Sunday.

The man followed a pathway that disappeared between two houses. It emerged on the other side at the bottom of a series of steps, leading up a steep hill towards what looked like castle battlements; these were the old Derry walls. Halfway up the pathway stood a lonely figure, watching out across the housing estates stretched out below. The man in the shabby coat continued up the steps until he was level with the other man.

"Do you have a light?" asked the man in the shabby coat, taking a packet of cigarettes from his coat pocket.

"Only if ye have a spare, mister."

"Are you happy with B&H?"

"Yeah, I is. Now, who are ye? I was expecting Tom."

"No Logan, Tom's busy so he sent me."

Logan accepted a cigarette from the man before lighting both of them. "Here, ye may as well keep 'em," he said, tossing the book of matches towards the man.

The man pocketed the cigarettes and matches.

"Tom tells me you have a problem?"

"Did he not say what it is?"

"I want to hear it from you, Logan. Just so I'm clear on things."

Logan studied the man stood in front of him and couldn't help but notice the strange question mark-shaped scar beside one eye.

"Well then, Logan, what's the problem?" the man in the shabby coat prompted.

"It seems I'm owed some money."

"And why's that?"

"I've been passing on tip-offs to Tom and I've not seen any compensation for it."

The man sucked on his cigarette. The tip burned brightly in the night air then he blew out a long plume of smoke before dropping the cigarette to the floor. The man twisted his shoe down onto the cigarette, crushing all the burning tobacco.

"Maybe someone else got in there before you and the cash was passed to them instead."

"I don't know what's going on. All I knows is I should have got me a big pay-out last week and when I contacted Tom, he said I'd already had it. I'm risking everything for ye an' I don't like being stiffed."

"I can look into it; find out what's going on."

Logan cut in. "I don't care fer ye looking into it. I just want what I'm owed."

"How do I know you aren't just making this up in order to get more money?"

"Check with the peelers. When I was supposed to be picking my money up, they had me in the back of one of their vans on some shit-stupid charge. I never made the meeting."

The man dug his hands deep into his pockets. "Look, I'll check all this out and if you're correct in what you're saying then I'll personally see that you get what's owed."

"Thanks, mister," said Logan, holding out a hand.

The two men shook hands before setting off in different directions.

As he walked away, Colin Fullerton was already formulating a plan to stop Logan from causing any more waves in his lucrative little scheme. The last one to cause ructions had proved easy to silence, so Fullerton wasn't worried about Logan.

FIFTY-FOUR

Colin Fullerton waited for a gap in the traffic then, clutching his newspaper, he made a dash across the road. One irate driver gave him a blast of his horn, but Fullerton just waved his newspaper in acknowledgment.

After a brisk 10-minute walk, he was opening the door to his apartment. Fullerton dropped the newspaper onto the dining room table and walked through into the kitchenette. He flipped the lid on the kettle, filled it with water, seated it on its platform, and switched it on. He rinsed out a mug from the draining board before spooning in coffee, sugar and powdered cream.

Coffee in hand, Fullerton returned to the dining table, sat down, and opened his newspaper.

The muffled sound of his mobile phone ringing inside his jacket pocket filtered across the room. Fullerton cursed himself for leaving the bloody thing in his jacket. He sat staring at his jacket, waiting for the ringing to stop, which it did. Fullerton now waited for the four beeps, signalling that the caller had left a message. They didn't come. Instead, the phone rang once more.

Fullerton turned back to his newspaper, muttering under his breath, "Leave a bloody message."

Once more, the ringing stopped, only to restart seconds later.

Fullerton pushed himself up from his chair.

"For God's sake," he moaned, stomping across to his jacket.

He delved into a pocket and claimed the mobile phone. Accepting the call, he raised the phone to his ear.

The colour drained from his face.

"Adam," he said, softly. "This is a . . . er . . . surprise."

Although Fullerton was, at some time, expecting a call from Lewis, being caught off guard like this was a shock to his system. Fullerton composed himself as he crossed back to the dining table, sitting down once more.

"I can't say I'm in the least bit surprised to hear your voice again, Adam, you're a hard man to shake off. Well then, go ahead and have your say. I'm all out of fighting."

Lewis then let rip and bombarded Fullerton with his threats.

"All I can say, Adam, is you'd better be quick then. My past is fast catching up with me," replied Fullerton. "It's also probably safe to say that it won't be too long before someone's knocking at your door either."

As the colour returned to Fullerton's cheeks, his eyes seem to sparkle as ideas flowed through his mind.

"Wait a moment, Adam," said Fullerton, standing up and walking across to the living room window. He looked out of the window at a restricted view of London, easily picking out the Houses of Parliament and, beyond that, the London Eye. Above the cityscape grey, rolling clouds threatened rain. Fullerton gripped the curtain cord with his free hand, drawing the curtains. Once closed, he flicked on the room lights from the nearby switch.

"Right, I need you to listen to me while I explain my situation and how it affects you. I'm being investigated on some jumped-up fraud charges, but I think there's more to it. I think it's just an excuse and what they're really doing is digging around for something much bigger." Fullerton sat back down at the dining table. "I think they know about Logan."

Lewis drew a blank so Fullerton threw out some reminders. "You must remember Logan, the informer you killed, the tape recording, and the shell casing. Is any of this coming back to you?" Fullerton paused, allowing Lewis time to think. "Just how hard did they beat you?" he asked, sarcastically. If they are digging around my past, looking into Logan's death, it will only be a matter of *when* not *if* your name comes to light."

Lewis tried interrupting, but Fullerton continued talking over him.

"Yes, I'm fully aware of the evidence you possess and that it goes a long way into giving you an alibi." Fullerton paused, to allow Lewis to vent his spleen. Once he'd finished his rant, Fullerton finished his short speech.

"Do you have an alibi for Altnakereen?"

Fullerton held his ear close to the phone. The only sound he could hear were deep, rasping breaths and then muffled movement. It sounded like Lewis was struggling to move around in, what he could only guess to be, a bed.

"I can give you that alibi, Adam," said Fullerton. He continued, as Lewis failed to respond. "I can tie up all the loose ends and make this all go away." Fullerton tried to make his offer of false hope sound as convincing as possible. "I know I'm going to receive some form of punishment for the fraud, that's inevitable. What I don't want is a long prison sentence for what happened to that lowlife, Logan." Fullerton listened, as Lewis' breathing slowed to a more rhythmic, calmer pattern, but still, the silence continued. "I have a fool-proof alibi for the both of us, which only requires a small part to play from your good self, and in exchange, I can point the Irish police away from you and towards a very convincing patsy. All I ask is your trust and confirmation that you will meet me face to face so that we can go over our stories."

Fullerton moved the phone slightly away from his ear as Lewis launched into a foul-mouthed list of reasons why he shouldn't trust the deceiving bastard. Fullerton listened, waiting for his moment to re-engage with Lewis.

"I know exactly how I've behaved towards you in the past, Adam, and for that, I'm truly sorry," lied Fullerton. "We desperately need to put it behind us and you need to hear what I have to say, for both our sakes." After a long silence, Fullerton guessed Lewis had calmed down, giving him a chance to reiterate his terms. "I need you to get back to London, so that I can go over my plan, with you, face to face." Fullerton paused, expecting Lewis to interrupt. He didn't. "You tell me where and when, and once you've listened to what I have to say, you can do whatever it is that you deem is in your best interests. I'll fight the Logan case and you can deal with the backlash of Altnakereen." Fullerton sipped his lukewarm coffee. "I know you're a wanted man, Adam, and not just because your blood and fingerprints were found in the farmhouse." Fullerton allowed the snippet of information to sink in. "I also know how resourceful you can be, so I have every faith in you returning to London safe and sound.

"Once you've had time to think and agree that it's in both our interests for you to return, you need to know that time is against us. It's imperative that you return within the next few days, four at most.

Fullerton had finished his coffee before Lewis offered his answer.

"Good. Good call, Adam. You know it's for the best. Call me on this number when you have a time and place in mind."

Lewis cut the call, leaving Fullerton staring at his silent phone. He pondered his choices before scanning through his contacts list. Pausing on a name, Fullerton made the call. It connected on the second ring.

"Well hello, my old friend," said Fullerton, in an overly-cheerful tone. "Tell me, what's the going rate these days to have a problem removed?"

Fullerton reopened his newspaper as he waited for an answer.

***

Lewis lay in bed, staring up at the ceiling. The pain from his damaged eye socket and the aftereffect of shouting and swearing at Fullerton had left him with a searing, stabbing pain at the sides of his head. He shut his eyes tight, forcing his eyelids closed, desperately trying to blank out the agony. White stars danced against the blackness.

Despite his painful condition, Lewis contemplated dealing with Fullerton once more. He didn't trust the man one bit, but in order to finish with him once and for all, Lewis knew what he had to do; despite all of his reservations, he must go back to London and face this treacherous nemesis.

For now, Lewis needed to rest. But later, he would speak with Kelly and work out a way of getting back to London.

FIFTY-FIVE

James Strong finished briefing the inspectors from the Counter-Terrorist Specialist Firearms Unit assigned to him. Before sending them away to brief their individual teams, he reiterated one important item.

"I can't emphasise this enough, guys; our man will identify himself by immediately dropping to his knees and placing his hands on his head. Once it is safe to do so, he is to be removed from the situation and brought back to this location."

Strong watched for the nodding of heads before excusing himself and leaving the room. In the corridor outside the briefing room, Strong met with Macleod.

"It looks like everything is on track and ready to go, Robert. I'm just going to pay a quick visit, before showing my face in the control room," said Strong. After his brief exchange, he continued on his way to the toilets, leaving Macleod in the corridor.

Strong spoke with the control room commander for reassurance that things were on course and that no changes had been reported. Satisfied he was abreast of everything, Strong collected his radio and firearm and said his goodbyes, before heading out to the vehicle park to meet with his team.

Outside, in the sodium-lit courtyard, police officers and covert agents in various guises were checking equipment and loading vehicles, ready to disperse. The chatter was muted, as the mixture of departments worked together on the preparations.

The police inspector in charge of the three-man, armed surveillance team he was attached to met Strong. The three officers were of Asian descent; two officers were dressed in traditional Muslim robes and headdresses, and the third, the one currently introducing himself to Strong, was dressed in a dark-blue tracksuit. The group exchanged pleasantries before climbing into the rear of a transit van.

Inside the van was an array of monitors, computer screens and radio equipment. Sitting behind one bank of monitors was an MI5 communications officer, going through her various checks.

"Hello Jennie, is everything okay?"

"So far, so good," she replied.

Strong allowed the firearms officers room to squeeze past him and take up positions on the bench seat at the far end of the van. Once they had passed, he pulled down a folding seat, sitting, squeezed in behind the comms officer.

"Inspector, would you mind doing the honours and letting the driver know we're ready to go," said Strong.

The firearms officer turned and put his hand on a small, sliding hatch. Drawing it across a fraction, he passed on the message to the driver. The driver, in turn, radioed the large group and informed them all to prepare to move off. Moments later, the transit van led the convoy of four vans from the courtyard, out into the busy afternoon traffic. Once in the flow, the vehicles separated, heading away to their respective holding positions.

Ten minutes later, the marked firearms units set off in their highly-visible BMW estate cars. And then, 20 minutes after the initial departure of the surveillance teams, the unmarked CT-SFU vehicles departed. The three off-roaders soon disappeared into the flow of traffic outside the now deserted courtyard.

***

Falah answered his phone.

"Everything's fine this end, James," said Falah, checking his watch – 4:22p.m.

"There's no change. Abass will leave at five and head straight to the mosque, taking his suit with him."

Falah held his phone close to his chest as he peered around the kitchen door, looking down the passageway. Abass' bedroom door was still closed. Falah pushed the kitchen door until it was almost closed, but still allowing him a sliver of a gap to peek through.

"Yes, as it's approaching, he's getting jittery. We've spoken about his role and I've deliberately kept things simple, so as not to add any more pressure on him.

Falah heard Abass leave his room.

"Okay, James, I have to go. Bye."

Abass pushed the kitchen door open.

"Everything is in place, Luay. You have our full support, in position, and ready to back you up," said Falah, putting his phone away.

Abass was dressed in his robes and holding the suit carrier.

"Do you have everything, Luay, beads, mobile?"

Abass nodded, taking the beads from a pocket with his free hand.

Falah collected the kettle and crossed to the sink. He filled it up before asking, "Do you want a drink before you leave?"

"No thanks," said Abass, pushing the beads back into his pocket.

***

The man in the blue tracksuit was the first to see Abass leave the flats.

"Standby. Standby," he spoke into his covert microphone, before setting off behind his target. The operator was now shadowing Abass and ready to relay their asset's movement through a series of colour codes. Each road was given a spot code, a colour and number, at prominent junctions, allowing Abass' progress to be followed by those involved in the covert operation.

"This is Victor One, that's the package mobile on foot, intending brown 12."

As Abass followed the pathway towards the shopping arcade and then the junction beyond it, the officer following him behind again radioed. "That's the package confirmed towards brown 12."

Another officer was shadowing Abass' movements, following at a safe distance, and at the junction designated brown 12, another surveillance officer was waiting for Abass. Once at the junction, Abass' planned route was left into the next street, before heading down towards the junction further down the street, and turning right onto a main road leading towards the mosque.

Abass turned as expected and Victor One reported the change in direction. "That's the package left, left towards brown 13."

The officer behind the shops watched as Abass passed by him, oblivious to the fact he was being followed. Across the road, the officer who had been standing on the junction was now shadowing Abass.

"That's the package brown 13, intending brown 14."

Abass checked the street was clear of traffic before crossing over and onto the main road. After another glance around, he darted across to the other side of the main road and continued on his route to the mosque.

"That's the package complete, brown 13 towards 14."

Abass arrived at the mosque 20 minutes after leaving the flat. Once inside, he was soon aware the regular prayer gathering wasn't going to be taking place. The whole place was silent – none of the normal hustle and bustle of people readying themselves for prayers. The entrance area was empty of the usual gathering of chatting men. Beyond the entrance hall, more signs of emptiness became apparent to Abass. The shoe mats were now visible, due to the almost complete lack of shoes and sandals. Also, he noticed the washrooms were devoid of any activity.

Abass was met by one of the imam, who took the suit carrier from him.

"Follow me," he said, leading Abass away to the private side room.

FIFTY-SIX

Inside the room, Luay Abass met with four other young males and a further imam he'd recognised from evening prayers.

"Now that we are all here, I have a few jobs that need doing before we can start this evening. Follow me, please." The imam led the young men from the private room to a store cupboard. He opened the cupboard and proceeded to remove rolled-up camp beds, which he handed out.

"Take your bed into the main hall and lay them out along the far side. I will be through shortly."

The young men and Abass walked through to the main hall and found themselves a space at the far side. Moments later, the imam entered, carrying a pile of blankets.

"Help yourselves to one of these," he said.

They each took a blanket back to their own camp bed and stood around, unsure of what to do next. They waited and watched the imam.

"The beds are very simple to assemble. Unroll them so they are flat on the floor then push the four metal legs into the holes along the two sides. Once you've made your beds, please, come back through to the prayer room."

Abass proceeded to assemble his bed, still unsure of what was going to happen tonight. Looking around at the others setting up their camp beds, Abass saw the same emotionless look on each of their faces. The silence was palpable. He wondered whether it was because they knew what was destined for them. As the last-minute replacement, he knew very little of what was planned for each of them. And, taking the lead from the other three young men, Abass carried on in silence, shying away from striking up a conversation. As he crouched down to push the legs into their holes, he felt the mobile phone, in his robe pocket, fall against his thigh. He resisted the urge to take a peek at it to check the signal. As the first three of the group completed their task, they headed back to the prayer room. Abass finished assembling his bed and soon followed.

When he re-entered the room, he took his place on the mat. This time, standing at the front of the room was Ali Hashim. He was standing beside the laptop that had previously been used to show the killings and bombings three nights ago.

"Before we begin, I want you to watch this short film." Hashim clicked play then stood to one side.

The film started with someone sitting in the front of a van. The image bounced around as the vehicle drove down a busy road. From the lights and signs that Abass could see from the distorted images, he guessed the video footage was taken from a holiday resort somewhere. The cameraman switched angles, from filming the road to a brief glimpse of people walking in groups down one side of the road, all the way around to two men sat in the rear of the van. The two men smiled and gave the camera a thumbs up.

After about five minutes, the van stopped. The cameraman carried out a panoramic sweep, taking in as much of the outside as he could. Abass could see neon signs, advertising pubs and clubs, revellers in various states of dress; some walking, some stood talking and some dancing. The amount of bikinis and scanty T-shirts convinced him it was a holiday resort somewhere, but as the signs were mostly in English, he was still unsure of the exact location.

The cameraman turned to film two men in the rear of the van. Unlike the revellers, both men wore long-sleeved shirts, buttoned fully. They gave a final thumbs up before climbing out of a side door. The cameraman followed them as they weaved a path through the crowds towards one of the clubs, a good way down the road. The cameraman used the zoom to follow the two men. As a result, the image became less stable and the focus switched between blurry and sharp. One of the men stood outside a club, beside a large, colourful board advertising "241" cocktails, while the other one went inside.

Abass watched as people, shouting and cheering, made their way to and from the club. As a small group of girls, dressed as fairies, briefly obscured the man standing by the sign, suddenly, there was a large cloud of dust coming from the inside of the club, followed, a micro-second later, by the sound of a loud explosion. In the dust and confusion, Abass lost sight of the man by the sign. The cameraman trained the camera on where he thought the man was, and then there was a bright orange flame. The screen went blank.

Hashim was standing beside the laptop holding something. Abass had been so transfixed by the video, he'd not seen Hashim leave and re-enter the room. All the young men turned to Hashim, who was carrying what appeared to be a canvas waistcoat. Holding it up with outstretched arms, he allowed his students to take in every detail of the item.

Abass followed the criss-cross of wires across the front of the vest until they disappeared into four bulging pockets on the front. It didn't take him long to realise he was looking at a bomb vest.

"We have all night to familiarise ourselves with this, my brothers," said Hashim, holding up the bomb vest. "And plot the path Allah has chosen for each of you, for tomorrow night at eight o'clock, you will all achieve martyrdom."

Abass rested his hand on his mobile phone.

FIFTY-SEVEN

The red Vectra pulled level with the mosque. The driver made eye contact with Luay Abass before gesturing with his hand for him to get into the taxi.

The mosque had been under surveillance from the moment Abass had entered until he had reappeared again, outside. Abass was the fourth person to be collected by the red taxi and each time, the taxi had taken the same route to its destination. James Strong was fully aware of the anti-surveillance technique that was being carried out. Each time the taxi made its journey along the chosen route, it would pass through any number of checkpoints, where someone would be monitoring the vehicles following. If a vehicle was flagged up by more than one checkpoint on each of the journeys, there was a good chance that vehicle was following their taxi. Fortunately, these tactics didn't easily catch out Strong. So far, his operation was running smoothly and undetected.

"Standby. Standby," alerted the trigger officer across the road from Abass. "The package is now complete in the red taxi; the plate number is confirmed as Tango-Lima-Zero-Two-Romeo-Delta-Charlie. Mobile, intending brown 13."

The taxi accelerated away and, as on each previous journey, without indicating, turned right at the first junction.

"That's the package confirmed towards brown 13."

A blue Focus slotted in, two cars behind the red taxi.

"Victor 3, I now have the package. Mobile, brown 13, towards brown 15 at 25."

The officer in the Focus took over the following of the red taxi and let the control room know the direction of travel and the vehicle's speed. Two streets parallel from the small packet of vehicles, a silver Mondeo shadowed their movement.

The red taxi stopped for traffic lights. While the cars waited, a motorcycle weaved its way to the front of the column of traffic. Stopping alongside the red taxi, the rider rested a foot on the ground as he waited for the lights to change. Once the lights changed and the taxi accelerated across the junction onto its familiar route, the motorcyclist sped in front of the package of vehicles and took up a position at the front.

With the silver Mondeo following on a parallel street, the red taxi was now contained in a standard box formation by the surveillance unit. The officer in the Focus continued to relay location reports as the journey progressed.

After yet another manoeuvre, once again, without any indication, the taxi stopped outside a large tower block. The tower block was at least 50 feet away from the main road. The large, grey edifice stretched up into an evening sky, awash with dark, rain-filled clouds. Over three quarters of the building was illuminated by varying shades of lights, as the residents settled into their evening routines.

The driver turned to Abass, just as a transit van drove past. He spoke to his passenger.

"You need to use the left-hand side lift and go up to the fifth floor, then follow the signs to flat 510." The driver turned back, releasing the central locking, allowing Abass to vacate the taxi. "Have you got that, 510?"

"Yes. 510. Thanks."

Abass climbed out of the taxi. Walking tentatively towards the tower block, he followed another man who was also heading for the main lobby.

"Thanks," said Abass to the man wearing a blue tracksuit, holding the door open for him.

Inside the graffiti-daubed lobby, Abass looked around for the lifts, which he found tucked away in the far corners, opposite each other. Once he had approached the lifts, Abass noted that the one on the left serviced the odd-numbered floors, while the one on the right serviced the even-numbered ones. He took his place in front of the left one and pressed the call button. Abass waited for the lift to arrive, aware that the man in the blue tracksuit was now standing only a few feet behind him. The heat from wearing his robes over the top of his evening suit was starting to have an effect on Abass. As the numbers counted down on the small display panel above the doors, he felt the first beads of perspiration rolling down the back of his neck.

The lift arrived and the doors opened, enveloping Abass in a waft of stale air; this only made his perspiration worse. The two men stepped into the lift.

"Which floor?" asked Abass.

The man in the blue tracksuit scanned the number panel. "Fifteen please." He chose the top floor, allowing him to see which floor Abass would select.

Abass pressed the fifteen button, followed by the five button. The doors jolted shut as the lift slowly ascended.

The lift slowed to a stop before the doors opened. Abass squeezed himself out of the lift and into the open space of the fifth-floor foyer. The air around the open space was cold, and a welcome change from the stale, claustrophobic box he'd just left.

Abass quickly stepped outside onto the balcony, drawing in lungfuls of more cold, night air, in an attempt to cool and calm himself down. Gradually, slowing his intake of cold air, Abass set about looking for flat 510.

The officer in the blue tracksuit exited the lift on the seventh floor, removed a mobile phone from a zipped pocket, and dialled a number.

"Our friend is on the fifth, I'm going down to six."

He ended the call as he pushed open the glassless doorframe, leading to the stairwell. A pungent odour of stale urine invaded his nostrils as he descended the steps to the next floor.

Outside the tower block, another taxi pulled up. Two men dressed in neatly-pressed robes climbed out of the taxi, paid the driver through his side window, before turning and walking towards the tower block. Both men carried rucksacks slung across one shoulder.

One of the men opened the lobby door, and they both disappeared inside. They looked around for the lifts before heading across to the one on the right-hand side. Once the lift was summoned and the two men were inside, one of them pushed the button for the fourth floor.

Outside the foyer, on the fifth-floor balcony, a man smoking a cigarette leaned out over the railing, staring out across the London nightscape. He turned to his right as a man approaching caught his eye.

Abass checked the numbers of the doors drawing closer to the cigarette smoker. 510. He had arrived.

The man flicked the cigarette out into the night, which arced upwards before falling in a spiralling motion towards the ground.

"Luay," said the smoker, extending a hand.

Abass shook the smoker's hand, nodding his head in acknowledgment.

"Go straight in, first room on the left."

Abass turned and entered the flat, closing the door behind him. The man who had just greeted him produced a cigarette packet and proceeded to light another one. He leaned out over the railing once more.

"I have details of the tower block," said the operator inside the surveillance van.

"Great," answered Strong. "Pass on brief details to each team leader and give them a heads up."

Checking out the floor plan of level five once more, the operator prepared to transmit.

FIFTY-EIGHT

Luay Abass was greeted, once more, with a handshake, only this time, it was accompanied with kisses to both cheeks. On entering the room on the left, which he now knew to be the living room, he counted five people in total, but no al Dulhaimi.

After greeting him, the imam offered Abass a seat.

"We're waiting for one more of our brothers then we'll begin our preparations."

A small glass cup of chai was offered to Abass once he was seated. He sipped the sweet, golden, aromatic tea whilst looking around the room at the other seated young men. Abass immediately noticed how calm everyone looked, despite the silence. To him, things had moved along so fast. Two days ago, he'd been informed that he had been selected for a special mission, and then, only last night, he was given the details. The four young men were to be taken into the heart of London's theatre district, where each of them would be told which theatre to target. And at 8:00p.m. exactly, they were to strike their thunderous blows. It suddenly struck him that, apart from first names, he knew nothing about these other men. He had not fraternised with any of them outside of the mosque, and during attendance, they had all barely spoken two words to each other. He wondered if they were so calm because they had already made their peace with the Prophet and accepted their fate.

The front door opened, and the last man entered the living room. Once more, the imam offered the new arrival a seat in the overcrowded room, quickly followed by a drink.

"*As-salamu alaykum*," the imam greeted the whole room. The room responded as a chorus, "*Alaikum as-salam*."

"We have two hours to prepare ourselves, brothers," began the imam. "The rooms have already been prepared for your arrival and convenience. Each of you may cleanse in the bathroom. The two bedrooms are to be used to fit your equipment and the kitchen," the imam indicated to a blue door behind him, "is where you can record a message for our Western Infidels."

Thinking the imam had finished, Abass was about to stand.

"Have any of you brought mobile phones with you?" added the imam.

All four men raised a hand.

The imam was handed a bag, which he took to each of the four men. Stopping in front of each of them, he extended his arms, allowing them to drop their phones into the bag. Abass fumbled for his phone. He held it out in his hand, looking at the buttons along one side, as the imam shuffled along to him.

"It's okay, Luay, drop it in, I'll switch it off for you."

Abass placed his phone into the bag with the others.

***

James Strong was waiting patiently in a van parked behind a convenience store, four streets away from the tower block.

"That's everyone in position, James," said the MI5 communications officer, relaying a message he'd just received.

Strong looked at one of the monitors; a fresh feed from the tower block opposite the target location. In his mind, he plotted the locations of the surrounding teams. The three CT-FSOs he had transported where in situ inside the target location, on the floors above and below Abass. The unmarked CT-FSU vehicles were interspersed with other vehicles within a hundred-metre radius of the target. The marked BMWs were further away, stacked up, with engines ticking over, in a supermarket car park almost half a mile away.

The only location Strong could not plot was that of Abass. Apart from the fifth floor, his exact location would not be known until he could activate the GPS equipment. It had been decided that he would not be using any form of tracking device that emitted a passive signal, so as not to alert anyone at Abass' location.

Across the network of estates, Hassan Falah sat silently waiting and watching a map on his laptop screen. The map displayed was of the area containing the tower block and Abass.

Falah's phone sat on the coffee table beside the laptop. Whilst he waited, he recalled the instructions he had given Abass before setting him off on his way. Falah methodically recalled every detail, right up to the moment he had shut the door behind him.

The laptop screen glowed a soft blue hue, casting shadows over Falah's face. He remained transfixed, waiting for the GPS to be activated.

FIFTY-NINE

Colin Fullerton stared at his watch, strumming the table with his fingers, wondering how much longer after half-past five he should wait.

"Sorry I'm late," apologised a voice behind him.

Fullerton spun around in his seat.

"You're a fucking half-hour late," he spat out.

"I'm sorry, the bloody council is digging . . ."

"I don't give a fuck," interrupted Fullerton. "Just shut up and listen!"

A waitress approached the table. "Can I get either of you two gentlemen a drink?" she asked curtly.

Fullerton looked up at the waitress as his anger subsided.

"Can I have a brandy, please?"

"And a pint of lager."

"We have Kronenburg, San Miguel . . ."

"San Miguel's fine, thanks."

Both men sat in silence, waiting for the waitress to return with their order. She placed fresh coasters down before standing the glasses down on the table, and left the receipt on a small, black tray in the centre of the table.

Fullerton swallowed half his drink in his first mouthful. "I need a job doing," he said, placing his glass down.

"I gathered that from your call."

Fullerton responded to the sarcasm. "Well, I didn't ring for your scintillating conversation."

The other man tilted his pint glass. "Touché."

"I'm having a meeting with someone, in the next few days, and I need him dealing with."

"Whereabouts are you having this meeting?"

"I don't know yet," said Fullerton, as he finished his drink. "I'm waiting for a call."

"Okay then, who's the guy?" The man paused. "I gather it is a guy we're talking about?"

Fullerton nodded. He removed a photograph from his jacket pocket and slid it across the table.

"Adam Lewis. It's not a great photo, but it's the best I can get."

The man reached for the photograph and examined the face.

"I'll be in touch once a time and place has been arranged. I will want you waiting for him."

"It's gonna cost ya," was all the man said.

Once again, Fullerton reached inside his jacket, only this time, he brought out an envelope the thickness of a deck of cards. The man swiftly scooped it up, removing it from sight. He opened it below the table.

"There's five-thousand now and another five once he's gone." The man looked across at Fullerton. "Don't bother asking. It's non-negotiable."

As Fullerton stood up to leave, he took out his wallet and removed a £20 note, which he placed on the black tray. "Here, have another drink on me," he said. "I'll be in touch, Stan."

Stan Norman looked on impassively.

As Fullerton left the wine bar, he briefly wondered how many times he'd used Stan Norman to do his dirty work. He gave up counting, as a mini cab drew up.

SIXTY

The black fishing vest was lifted slowly and deliberately above Luay's head. He positioned his arms up towards the sleeveless openings, as the garment was carefully lowered down over his head.

Once it was in place, the helper secured the fastening straps one at a time, down the middle of Abass' back. Abass couldn't help wondering if this was what it felt like when a magician was strapped into a straitjacket. *But then, had Dynamo tried escaping from a bomb fastened to his body?*

The helper then held up a crisp, white shirt. Abass fed his left arm into the first sleeve until it poked through the buttoned cuff. Before slipping his right arm into the sleeve, the helper fed a long wire that was attached to the vest, down into the sleeve. At the end of the wire was a black tube, no bigger than a grown man's thumb, with a grey button at the tip and a small crocodile clip fastened to the side of the tube. Abass slid his arm into the sleeve, before meticulously pushing each button through its tiny slit to fasten the shirt.

The helper opened the crocodile clip, fastening the tube onto the shirt cuff. Once Abass had his jacket on, the tube would be obscured from view. The idea had been taken from the covert "press to talk" buttons bodyguards frequently used. Only with this set up, Abass was aware that once the safety pin had been removed from the bomb's battery pack, the button was then a live switch. All he had to do was push the button to connect the live circuit. At the mosque the previous night, Abass was told that the safety pin was to be removed once he was given the name of his theatre.

The helper handed Abass his jacket before gesturing for him to leave the room. The whole dressing ceremony had taken place in complete silence, and now Abass left the room, still without uttering a single word.

The imam met Abass in the passageway. "Have you filmed your message yet, Luay?"

Abass shook his head. "Not yet."

The imam reached down for Luay's jacket. "Here, you go to the kitchen and I'll put this in there," he said, taking the jacket from a reluctant Abass and indicating towards the front room.

Abass watched on as the imam and his jacket disappeared from view. He turned, pressing one hand against the prayer beads in a trouser pocket, before sloping off to the kitchen.

Inside the room, it resembled a small photography studio, with a tripod-mounted camera at one side, which was flanked by two shaded spotlights. Everything pointed towards a chair in front of the opposite wall, behind which hung two flags – a black flag and a green one. Both flags displayed white Arabic script, which Abass roughly translated as short verses from the Qur'an.

The helper operating the camera greeted Abass then ushered him towards the empty chair. It was as Abass seated himself that he noticed a second man, whom had previously been obscured by the lighting, stood beside one of the spotlights. He was holding a large card with a prepared statement for Abass to read to the camera.

"When you're ready, just read this, inserting your name where the blanks are. And if you pick up the holy book at your feet, holding it in your left hand as you speak. Thanks."

Abass quickly scanned through the writing, absorbing the message as he digested the words. It made no reference to the potential target; it was just a direct message to whomever the recipient was to be, explaining that his action had been carried out as Allah's wish against an infidel that had had a Jihad placed upon them.

"Okay, when you are ready, my brother," said the man behind the camera.

Abass paused for a moment.

"Is everything okay?"

Abass' brow furrowed, then he spoke.

"When will I know where I'm to strike?" Abass asked.

"That will come in good time, brother," replied the cameraman.

"Will Mustafa al Dulhaimi come to see us ahead of us leaving on our mission? Will he bring with him Allah's blessings before we proceed?"

"You ask questions I cannot answer, brother. You have been given the honour of carrying out the Prophet's wish. Whatever else happens is not for us to know, we are merely humble followers."

"But wouldn't it be right for our leader to be here before we go?"

"Again, my brother, I am not the one who can give you answers. Read your message then speak with the imam. Please brother, we have others waiting."

Abass stood up.

"What is wrong, brother?"

"Nothing. Nothing. I just want my beads," said Abass, reaching into his trouser pocket. He gently eased out the garland of black and red beads, fighting to control a nervous shake. The hairs on the back of his hand stood up. Abass sat back down slowly, feeding the beads through his clammy fingers and thumb.

"Okay. When you're ready, brother, just read from the card."

Abass looked up at the card and then at the helper holding the message. As he did, his finger and thumb found the two joined beads that Falah had shown him. He took hold of the beads with both hands either side of the join.

"My name is Luay . . ." he started, just as he pulled the beads apart.

SIXTY-ONE

James Strong sat patiently beside the communications officer, gently bouncing his back against the rear support of the uncomfortable seat he occupied. He stared at a monitor, displaying a hybrid map of the surrounding area, plotting likely escape routes around the estate.

A small, red dot flashed up on another monitor, along with the border, to alert the watcher. The comms officer turned to Strong; the look on her face was enough – she did not have to say anything.

"Right, pinpoint his exact location," confirmed Strong.

"Standby. Standby. This is Zulu control, we have an activation. Location to follow."

The comms officer's fingers danced across her keyboard. The images on her screen changed perspective with each stroke, until they finally settled on a translucent image of a section of one floor in the tower block. The comms officer cross-referenced the image on that screen with one of an electronic blueprint on another screen.

"The fifth floor, flat 510," she announced.

With officers already above and below the fifth floor, Strong confirmed the missing piece of intel.

"Alpha team from Zulu control, secure five-one-zero. Alpha One acknowledge, over."

The reply from inside the tower block was immediate. "Alpha One, roger, secure five-one-zero. Roger, out."

"Bravo team from Zulu control, prepare to move on Alpha One's command. Bravo One acknowledge, over." Strong ordered the plain clothes CT-FSU to ready themselves for deployment.

"Bravo One, ready to move. Roger, out."

"Charlie team from Zulu control, go mobile towards Alpha One's location. Charlie One acknowledge, over."

"Charlie One, roger. Go mobile towards Alpha One's location. Roger, out."

The sergeant sitting in the passenger seat of the first BMW estate car gave the okay for his driver to pull away.

"Charlie team, prepare to move. Moving now," he ordered through his personnel radio.

The other two marked police vehicles followed behind. The small convoy of vehicles set off at a fast pace, but without their sirens and lights on, in order to maintain the element of surprise. Their task was to block off the three main road junctions surrounding the target location. They had to make sure no one else got into the area, but more importantly, no one got out.

Inside the tower block, the three plain-clothes CT-FSOs raced towards the fifth floor, congregating in the foyer, close to the lifts.

Alpha team's leader, the CT-FSU officer wearing the tracksuit, spoke into his covert radio. "Bravo team, go, go, go!"

"Bravo One, roger, out," came back the crackled reply through his earpiece.

The tracksuited team leader moved off, closely followed by the two CT-FSU officers wearing the robes. They pushed through the door onto the balcony; a rush of cold air enveloped their bodies, causing one officer to shiver slightly.

As each floor was set out in an identical numerical order, the officers were aware they needed to turn left towards flat 510. They set off towards their target.

Standing outside of 510 was the chain-smoker, gazing out across at the cityscape. He watched distant traffic lights changing colour and the white and red vehicle lights weaving patterns through brightly-lit streets. Suddenly, his attention was drawn to three vehicles stopping on the road outside the tower block. Although this in itself was not unusual, the sight of nine people getting out of these vehicles and running towards the entrance to the tower block did set off alarm bells in his head.

The watcher flicked his half-smoked cigarette over the parapet and turned towards the door to flat 510.

The approaching tracksuited officer reached for the watcher's exposed arm, taking a firm grip of his wrist and, in one swift, flowing motion, spun the man around, raising his arm up the centre of his back. The watcher opened his mouth to express the pain he was being subject to, but one of the robed officers swiftly placed his hand over his mouth. The two officers manoeuvred the struggling watcher away from 510 and down the walkway, three flats away. The third officer waited close to 510, pressing his body up against the wall beside the front door. It was his job to maintain cover on the flat and deal with anyone coming out of flat 510. He reached into his backpack and removed a Sig SG 516 assault rifle, taking aim on the door.

Once the watcher was away from the flat and restrained in handcuffs, the tracksuited officer spoke into his radio.

"Zulu control from Alpha One. That's the white aspect of five-one-zero secure, over."

"Zulu control, roger, out." Strong acknowledged that Alpha team had secured the front area of flat 510 ready for phase two of the operation to commence.

As he sent his report, the first of nine covert CT-FSU officers poked his head around the door leading onto the balcony, seeking out the Alpha team. He caught sight of the robed officer positioned outside of 510 and gave him a thumbs-up sign. The gesture was reciprocated.

"Bravo team from Alpha Two, you're good to go, over."

"Bravo One, roger, over. Moving now. Out."

The nine officers in plain clothes pulled out baseball caps that had been tucked away behind their body armour, and secured them on their heads. Ballistic helmets would have been too cumbersome, so the team's only head protection was the word "police" stitched neatly on each cap. With their Sig SG 516 assault rifles ready to fire, they swiftly but stealthily moved into position around the door to 510.

The nearest officer held a battering ram, a powerful tool for smashing open door locks. He stood close to the door with his feet planted firmly on the floor and the tool raised for maximum leverage, waiting for the order to go.

Either side of the door, split equally into two groups of four officers, were the Bravo team, fingers on triggers, safety catches on single shot and ready to go. The tracksuited team leader switched places with the robed officer and took his place at the end of one line of armed officers, taking the total to ten.

"Charlie One, this is Alpha One, are you in position, over?"

The tracksuited officer waited for a reply then checked his watch.

He looked across at the officer with the battering ram, who waited with anticipation in his eyes, as he stood statuesque with the heavy tool held aloft.

From their briefing, each officer knew that at least five men were inside the flat – one imam and four students. The rest of the occupancy was an unknown quantity, so the officers would initially only deal with the rooms they had been assigned to, leaving the follow-up support team – Charlie team – standing by to deal with any loose ends.

After Abass had entered the tower block, a floor plan for the flats had been immediately sourced, and details of the generic layout passed swiftly to the two teams involved in the penetration of the flat. With four main rooms – the front room, kitchen and two bedrooms – it meant four pairs of CT-FSU officers would enter 510, leaving two more to cover the bathroom at the end of the passageway from the front door.

Alpha One's earpiece crackled with static once more. He nodded towards the officer nearest the door. Charlie team had reached the fifth floor; time to act.

The officer, using every sinew of muscle and power in his arms, swung the heavy tool towards the door lock.

SIXTY-TWO

Luay Abass finished his video message and stood up, before placing his prayer beads away into his pocket. He left the kitchen and headed for the living room, passing another young man coming out of a bedroom, who had also had his explosive vest fitted.

Abass avoided eye contact; instead, he was thinking about the GPS. *Had it activated? Had the signal been received?* He now wanted to get to his jacket and operate that button. With little suggestion that al Dulhaimi was going to make an appearance, Abass just wanted to be out of this situation, especially as explosives now surrounded him.

As Abass stepped through the doorway into the living room, the front door came crashing in. The lock bounced menacingly down the passageway and small panes of glass at the top of the door shattered, as it slammed into a wall.

Abass heard loud, urgent shouts of "POLICE!"

His heart pounded as he hurried into the living room and dropped to his knees. With his hands on his head, he felt his heart thumping against his ribcage, pounding to break free.

The imam stood by the curtained window, looking down at Abass and then at the two dark-clothed figures barging into the living room. They both held guns, which were now trained on the imam. He looked on at the officers with disdain, as he slowly raised his arms in surrender.

"Zulu control from Bravo One, room one secure, over," reported one of the officers.

A further two pairs of CT-FSOs moved swiftly into the flat. One pair burst into the first bedroom and confronted a young man, wearing an evening suit, sitting on the bed. On seeing the officers, he raised his arms in surrender.

"Move away from the bed! On the floor! Get down on the floor!" shouted one of the officers.

The man obliged, without taking his eyes from the weapon trained on him. With his focus taken up by the gaping muzzle, the man flinched with surprise when the second officer approached from his side and placed him in handcuffs. The two CT-FSOs remained in the bedroom with their prisoner.

"Zulu control from Bravo Two, room two secure, over."

Strong responded, "Zulu control, roger, out."

Passing by the officers securing room two, the third pair of CT-FSOs headed forward, towards the kitchen. As they neared the doorway, a man came rushing towards them. In his outstretched right hand, he brandished a large kitchen knife; the blade gleamed menacingly in the light. The two officers stopped in their tracks. With one of the CT-FSOs dropping his head slightly, until his eye was level with the Sig SG 516's holographic sight, he squeezed off two shots.

The two rounds slammed into the man's chest. His T-shirt appeared to ripple from the force generated by the bullets striking their target. His legs buckled and he crumpled into a heap on the floor, as his pulverised heart stopped instantly. Stepping over the dead man, the two officers continued into the kitchen.

Inside the kitchen were two men. One was positioned to the side of a video camera and the other was seated on the chair in front of two flags. Both men raised their arms. One officer remained by the door, keeping his rifle trained on the two men, whilst his partner secured his rifle close to his chest with the weapon's sling. After this, he went over to the men, one at a time, and cuffed both prisoners.

"Zulu control from Bravo Three, room four secure, over,"

Again, Strong acknowledged the message.

Like the officers in the bedroom, they remained in their designated room with their secured prisoners. This tactic minimised movement and allowed other officers to carry out their tasks with minimal impairment.

The final pair of CT-FSOs diverted towards the second bedroom. They smashed into the room, one after the other, only to be confronted by three men, stood close to a single bed. Behind the men was a dark-coloured wardrobe, with one door ajar. What at first appeared to be an item of clothing, was hanging from the door. It quickly dawned on the CT-FSOs that it was in fact a suicide vest, and even though there was a gap of five feet between the men and the vest, it now became the major factor in the room.

One of the officers shouted commands at the trio.

"Get down on the floor!"

Nothing.

He repeated the command, only louder. "Get down on the floor! NOW!"

Slowly, the men started to lower themselves onto their knees. The officers kept their weapons trained on the men; only their eyes moved, scanning the men for signs of non-compliance or suggestion that one of them might try something.

One of the men glanced fleetingly at the suicide vest. He was on the end of the group and the one nearest the open door. There were no obstacles between him and the door, just the five-foot gap. The command button was clipped to the front of the vest with the safety pin still in place, but the young man knew that the police couldn't know that.

His shoulder dropped as he turned and grabbed for the vest. The two rounds that struck him opened one side of his head. Bone fragments, dark, crimson blood and globules of brain exploded across the back bedroom wall and wardrobe doors. Rivulets of blood formed, as the sticky mess oozed towards the floor. The man stumbled forward, slamming into the corner of the wardrobe, causing the vest to fall to the floor. His momentum allowed him to collapse at the foot of the wardrobe, with blood now flowing freely from his collapsed skull.

The other two men remained kneeling, not daring to look around. The room soon filled with the stench of blood and cordite.

Once the situation was under their control, with the two men handcuffed, one of the officers spoke into his radio. "Zero control from Bravo Four, room three secure. One x-ray down, over."

Strong responded once more, acknowledging the room status and the dead suspect.

Slowly, the bathroom door opened a fraction. An eye appeared at the gap, scanning what little could be seen of the passageway.

The door opened a little further and then wide enough for the man dressed in an evening suit to squeeze his way through.

"Police! Put your hands up!" echoed the voice from the tracksuited officer by the front door.

The man edged his way fully out of the bathroom. His arms were raised but not in an act of surrender. The well-dressed man wanted whoever had shouted at him to see his hands, particularly the clenched one.

The officer shouted once more.

"Stay where you are and put your hands up!"

The suited man stared straight at the police officer, showing scant regard to the weapon pointing at him. He continued to inch forward, as beads of sweat rolled down his forehead.

"Stand still!" shouted the officer.

The suited man approached the living room door; he glanced quickly to his right. He saw shadows across the walls, but no one came into view. Sweat was now forming across his top lip. The saltiness seeped down to the corner of his mouth, but he resisted the urge to wipe it away.

"Stand still! Put your hands up!" ordered the officer, fighting to keep his nerves at bay.

Thankfully, the suited man chose to heed the command to stop. He remained statuesque by the living room door, still keeping his arms raised slightly and one hand clenched tightly closed.

The officer opened his mouth to speak once more, only this time, he saw the clenched fist and the object protruding from it. He saw part of the black tube emerging, fractionally, from the suited man's hand, and his thumb resting over the top. From the bottom of his hand, the officer saw a twin-flexed wire disappear up the shirt cuff. The officer recognised the detonator switch.

He suddenly found himself racing through his orders for dealing with a suicide bomber. He recalled the numerous times he had spent on the firing range, honing his marksman skills, hitting a small circle placed around the throat of the target figure. The officer took aim with his holographic sight. He kept his left eye open so he could see the red dot projected on the suited man's throat. Blocking out all ambient noise, the officer focused on the imaginary circle.

Sever the spinal column was the best solution, according to a panel of highly-qualified senior firearms instructors. On the firing range, the instructions were simple; keep your grouping tight and inside the circle. But they came with a warning, a very specific warning: "*You only get one chance and it has to count. Anything other than perfect will have fatal consequences.*"

A voice from behind the officer shouted another command; he was deaf to the words, only the noise got through.

The CT-FSO switched focus briefly from the suited man to the doorway behind him. The door seemed to be miles away, as his eyes only saw the target, but the briefest of glimpses had registered that the background was clear.

The suited man continued looking towards the officer; his thumb twitched fractionally as his grip around the switch tightened. He paid no attention to the other figure behind the officer, the one speaking. Instead, he rolled his eyes upwards and praised his God. The suited man moved his thumb.

The officer squeezed the Sig SG 516's trigger.

One of the CT-FSOs in the kitchen heard a dull thud on the wall nearest the sink, just before the explosive retort from a discharged firearm echoed along the confines of the passageway. He turned to see a hole, the size of a 10-pence piece, in the wall above the sink taps.

In the passageway stood an officer with his weapon pointing towards a heap on the floor. The suited heap bled profusely from a gaping wound through his throat. Blood and dark-coloured spinal fluid oozed out onto the floor. The suited man lay motionless. No final spasms as life escaped his corpse; his nerve system had been obliterated. One perfect shot.

SIXTY-THREE

A week had passed since Adam Lewis had last spoken with Fullerton. He was now feeling strong enough to return to London to confront the two-faced backstabber. Only, he had to get out of Northern Ireland first.

Danny Kelly had purchased two ferry tickets for the Belfast to Liverpool crossing. After printing out their boarding cards, Kelly had driven them both to the port. As they waited in line to board the ferry, Kelly glanced over at his travelling companion. Lewis had one arm bandaged and held across his chest in a sling with a padded dressing covered his left eye and a portion of his face. Lewis had also insisted on removing his casts, despite the discomfort that he blocked with constant stream of painkillers.

Kelly inched his car forward until he drew level with the customs official. He pressed a door button that lowered his window and handed over the two boarding cards to the officer for inspection. Kelly also passed across a sheet of paper. The customs official took the sheet, carefully reading the contents. After folding the sheet in half, he handed it back to Kelly, along with the boarding stubs. The officer then squatted down and leaned in through the open window.

"I'm sorry to hear about your mugging, Mr Roberts. I hope it doesn't put you off returning to our fair isle in the future."

Lewis just turned his head and forced a smile.

Kelly closed the window and accelerated towards the large, ramped boarding port.

The previous day, Kelly had phoned an old friend and asked for a blank crime-reporting sheet, complete with official stamp marks. Then, he'd filled out details of a fake mugging, adding in how the victim's wallet, credit cards and all other identification had been taken during the robbery. With the correct form and markings, the report looked like the genuine article, and as they were now boarding the ship, it had passed scrutiny.

Lewis said his goodbyes outside Birkenhead's Hamilton Square train station before parting company with Kelly and heading inside towards the ticket barrier. Lewis fed his ticket into the machine's slot, shuffled through and limped off towards his platform for the two o'clock train.

Kelly had been kind enough to furnish his friend with a first-class ticket to London, so Lewis climbed into the respective carriage and sought out his seat. Once the train commenced its journey, Lewis took out his newly-purchased mobile phone – another gift from Kelly – and scanned through the applications until he was able to connect to the train's Wi-Fi.

Lewis typed a question into the search engine and waited for the answer. He scrolled down the screen until he found the information he needed, before jotting down some brief details onto a folded napkin.

After finishing a cup of coffee, Lewis gathered up the phone and napkin, left his seat, and walked out to the open area between carriages. He secured a window, left open by another passenger, shutting out the cold, rushing air. A passenger excused himself, as he squeezed past Lewis on his way between carriages Once the door had swished shut, Lewis dialled a number. Standing in front of a rail map of Great Britain, Lewis followed his route to London while he waited for the call to connect. He got down as far as Rugby.

"Fullerton, it's me, Adam."

The train rumbled beneath a short road bridge.

"Take this down."

"Wait a minute, what happened to calling me back in a few days?" Fullerton asked.

"Things fucking change. Now, take this down." Lewis read from the held-up napkin. "Meet me at the Royale Leisure Park, just off Western Avenue in Wembley. Have you got that?"

"Yes. In Wembley."

"Good. Drive past the bowling alley and park up in the corner by the rigging place. Be there for 1900 hours tomorrow," instructed Lewis.

“Is that it?” Fullerton asked, just as the train rattled under another bridge

“That’s it. Just remember this, turn up alone. If I get a sniff of any other fucker, you won’t see me ever again,” warned Lewis. “But your bosses will receive a nice package the very next day.”

“Wait a minute, Adam, aren’t you forgetting . . .”

Lewis ended the call. He swiftly dismantled the phone, opened the side window, and dropped the phone out, piece by piece, at short intervals. After slamming the window shut, he returned to his seat.

Fullerton stared at his phone.

Blood pumped through a vein, close to the scar by his right eye, causing his eyelid to twitch erratically. Resisting the urge to throw his phone down in anger, Fullerton redialled a new number.

“Hello Stan. A meeting has been arranged and I now have a venue for you.”

Fullerton was sat opposite his muted television as he waited for Stan Norman to retrieve a pen. He waited patiently, staring at an envelope that had arrived moments earlier by courier. He recognised the franking as that of his governmental department.

Norman returned.

Fullerton gave out the details of the meeting place, plus his own instructions.

“I want you to go there today and find yourself a good hiding place, and then, once you’re happy, go home. But be back tomorrow at four o’clock and wait.

Fullerton listened as his instructions were questioned.

“I don’t trust this man one iota, he’s a sneaky . . .” Fullerton paused, “which is why I need you to be there early. Hide and wait. I’ll be driving a silver Mondeo.” Fullerton gave out his car registration as Norman jotted down every detail.

Fullerton stood up and walked through to his kitchen. Taking the letter with him, he dropped it onto the kitchen table.

"When he turns up, I want at least 15 minutes with him then you can come over and do what needs doing."

With his free hand, Fullerton filled the kettle from the tap.

"You'll get the rest of your money once the job is done. I'll have it with me in the car."

Fullerton opened the envelope as the call ended. He took out the MI5-headed letter and began reading the contents. The single paragraph informed him that due to recent events, his hearing was postponed for one week. He would be contacted with a new date in due course.

Fullerton balled up the letter and dropped it into the waste bin beside the sink. He looked through the kitchen window, out across the dark evening cityscape. The first droplets of rain were already drizzling down the windowpane.

SIXTY-FOUR

After his visit the previous day, Stan Norman guided his car into the Royale Leisure Park. Taking a slow drive around the network of white-painted parking bays, he pulled up at the spot he'd chosen during his recce.

He switched the car stereo off just as the four o'clock news started, but left the engine running for a while longer. He reached across to the glove box and removed a black, plastic box. He placed this across his lap and opened it up. Inside, nestled snuggly between thick foam cut-outs, was a CZ 75 pistol and silencer. Norman removed them both, before carefully threading the silencer onto the extended barrel. Once done, he cocked the weapon in one fluid motion then placed it inside a small satchel.

After switching off the engine, Norman climbed out of the car and secured the locks with an electronic key fob, before setting off on a stroll around to his hiding place. He watched as shoppers packed bags into the boots of cars and small groups of people headed into the various leisure facilities on offer around the park. Carefully checking he wasn't being watched, he slipped out of the car park and through a series of bushes, until a cluster of trees safely hid him. He took up his place by one particular tree, commencing his vigil on the rigging outlet, with one hand subconsciously resting on the satchel.

Colin Fullerton strummed his fingers against the steering wheel, impatiently waiting for the traffic lights to change. He stared on intensely, willing them to change from red to green. On the side of one set of traffic lights, a green man illuminated, even though Fullerton could see no one waiting to cross the road; this only enraged him more. He wrapped his fingers around the steering wheel and squeezed until the blood drained from his knuckles. Finally, the lights changed. His tyres screeched as he accelerated away.

Fullerton arrived at the leisure park at 6:50p.m., 10 minutes before his meeting with Lewis. Having already checked the layout of the area on Google Maps, Fullerton knew exactly where he wanted to be. He drove straight to his chosen space. Thankfully, the area was both badly lit and empty. Fullerton parked up, switching off the headlights and engine. He sat in complete silence and darkness.

Norman switched from a standing to a kneeling position, as he observed a car approaching the corner of the car park. He watched as the driver swung the car around into a parking bay then switched off the vehicle and its lights.

The car had a familiar registration plate, and even in the diminished lighting, he could see it was a silver Mondeo. The vehicle was facing away from him, which would allow him to approach stealthily from the rear, which was ideal for him.

Norman rested against the tree and waited.

***

James Strong rubbed the bridge of his nose, and he took a break from his report writing. He reached for his coffee mug; seeing the milky-white film floating on the surface, he decided to make a fresh one.

He was almost at his office door when his desk telephone rang. Any other time, he would happily let the call go straight to the answering machine, but tonight, he was the duty officer. The message could be important. Strong padded back to his desk.

"Good evening, duty officer," he said, stretching across his desk for the telephone.

"Good evening, sir. I've just received a message from the team assigned to reporting on Colin Fullerton's movements."

Strong tightened his grip on the handset.

The caller continued.

"The team have reported him entering a car park in Wembley, and they are now watching him. He's parked in a secluded spot, waiting inside his car. Do you want them to continue . . ."

Strong cut in. "Tell the team they are to maintain surveillance and report anything at all to my direct number. Oh, and get a driver to collect me from the front of the building right now."

Strong hung up. Something inside was telling him this was not right. *What's Fullerton up to?* It was then that Strong realised he was still holding his coffee mug. He put it down, grabbed his mobile phone and jacket, and left his office.

Avoiding the lift, Strong headed straight for the stairs. Thoughts raced through his mind as he pushed through the fire door. *What was he doing? Was he meeting with someone? Lewis? Was he plotting something? Was he just carrying out anti-surveillance drills? Was he aware he was being watched?*

As Strong took the steps two at a time, he realised there was only one way he was going to get answers. He stepped outside of the warmth offered by the building and into the chilled night air.

A BMW 5 Series was parked up, waiting for him.

SIXTY-FIVE

Colin Fullerton checked his watch, 7:28p.m. *What's Lewis playing at?*
Another car entered the car park, but unlike previous vehicles, this one headed towards Fullerton. Even from over 200 yards away, the car's headlights illuminated Fullerton's parked Mondeo.
He sat back in his seat and watched.

Adam Lewis had deliberately chosen not to arrive on time in order to satisfy himself that Fullerton was indeed alone. He had arrived at the leisure park at five o'clock, and parked amongst other vehicles outside the bowling alley. Dressed in a thick jacket and baseball cap, Lewis had meandered around the general area, watching all the comings and goings. Nothing had stood out as unusual to him, but then, on his own, he'd not been able to cover every square inch of the leisure park. Despite this, the location suited him for what he had in mind for Fullerton. The fact that the old spook had chosen a nice, dark corner of the car park to wait definitely worked in Lewis' favour.
Lewis had returned to his car, drove back out of the car park to do one more quick loop around the outer roads, before returning to confront Fullerton.
Lewis drove around Fullerton's car before parking up on the passenger side. Checking he had everything he needed, Lewis then climbed out of his car and walked around to confront Fullerton, who was seated on the driver's side. Lewis tapped on the side window. Fullerton pressed the operating button, allowing the window to sink down into the door recess.
"Hello Colin, is the back door open?"
Fullerton looked puzzled. "Yes, it is."
Lewis opened the door and slipped effortlessly into the car, seating himself directly behind Fullerton.
"I'm surprised you're not locked up yet," said Lewis.

Fullerton just shrugged his shoulders. "I probably would be if they weren't all off chasing mad mullahs."

"You mean the bombers caught in the tower block? I saw that on the news."

Fullerton just shrugged his shoulders. "Probably," he said.

"Well then, I'm glad you're not up for small talk," said Lewis, taking a handful of cable ties from his jacket pocket. "Let's get down to business."

Strong was thankful the roads had been relatively quiet this evening as he approached the leisure park.

Taking out his mobile phone, he called the surveillance team.

"Hello, it's Strong. Any change?"

"Yes, sir, another man has arrived and now they are both sat in the car."

"Okay, we've just arrived. Whereabouts are you parked?"

Norman checked his watch. Ten minutes had passed since his target had gotten into Fullerton's car. Standing up, he opened the flap on his satchel. While the circulation returned to his lower limbs, Norman reached into the satchel and jostled the pistol so that it was in an easy to reach position.

Feeling the numbness leaving his toes, Norman held out a hand in front of his face and carefully stepped through the undergrowth. Before too long, he was stepping out onto the car park. Once clear of the foliage, Norman reached a hand back into the satchel and gripped the pistol. Confident he could pull the pistol free in an instant, Norman set off for the parked cars.

Strong climbed out of his car and hurried across to the one containing a young couple embracing each other. He slipped in behind the front seats.

"Do we know who this other man is?" Strong asked.

The lady broke off the embrace and turned to face Strong.

"We can't be 100% sure," she said, speaking directly to Strong. "But we do think its Adam Lewis."

Strong sunk back into his seat and took a moment to think, then leaned forward, resting his arms on the two front seats.

"Are you armed?" he asked the two agents.

The male answered. "Not with side arms, sir, but we do have two MP5s locked away in the strongbox in the boot."

"Right then," said Strong, "get the guns and follow me."

Stan Norman neared the two cars, when he caught sight of a man stepping out from the shadows into the orange hue cast from a nearby lamppost. He instinctively gripped the pistol tighter and started to lift it from his satchel.

Norman was less than ten feet from the two cars, still focusing on the man approaching from the far side. Suddenly, another two people breached the shadows and were moving swiftly towards the first man.

Norman dropped the pistol back into the satchel, immediately altering his route to a new path that veered away from the cars. He prided himself on his knowledge of firearms, and as he'd watched the appearance of the couple moving towards the first man, he'd recognised the distinct shape of two MP5s. Two MP5K-MPS with a muzzle velocity of 1,230 feet per second, and an effective range of 328 feet, to be exact. He smiled to himself. His CZ 75 was no match for these two weapons, even with the element of surprise. Plus, he did not know who else was hiding out in the shadows, and he wasn't prepared to hang around to find out.

Norman headed away from the cars, disappearing into the night.

As Strong closed in on Fullerton's car, he could see him sitting in the front seat, staring out across the car park, oblivious to his approach. Whomever was with Fullerton was sat in the rear of the car, obscured by the shadows.

"Cover me," said Strong, as he neared the Mondeo.

SIXTY-SIX

"Good evening," the voice came from the back-seat passenger. James Strong was perplexed by how calm the unknown man was. He lowered himself into the passenger seat.

"I hope you don't mind?"

"How could I, with your two armed goons standing watch?" said the voice from the shadows.

"Adam Lewis, I presume?" Strong asked, now puzzled by Fullerton's silence and lack of movement. His chest was rising and falling, but only slightly."

"Yes. And you are?"

"James Strong. We met in Northern Ireland, around 1994."

Lewis leaned forward.

"Nice to meet you again, James."

"I wasn't expecting to see you out here tonight, Adam," said Strong. "And you're awfully quiet, Colin."

"I'm afraid you won't get much conversation from him tonight, James. He's taken a vow of silence."

"I can see he's not dead; what's wrong with him?"

Lewis sat back in the shadows. "That's right, he's not dead, he's not worth it."

Strong turned towards Fullerton and waved a hand in front of his face; he got no response.

"What have you done, Adam?"

"Who's saying I didn't find him like this? You're making a big assumption here, James."

"My guys followed him here, and up until the moment you got in the car, Fullerton was fine."

"Ahh," said Lewis, leaning forward once more. "Here, take this." Lewis passed Strong a thin, steel rod. "Just an old trick I picked during my service days."

"Would you care to elaborate for me?"

Lewis paused a moment as Strong examined the steel rod. He noticed dark flecks along its length.

"I suppose it can't do any harm. What you do is take a rod like that one and carefully insert it just below the base of your victim's ribcage, around the point of the solar plexus."

Strong rested the steel rod across his lap as he listened to Lewis' explanation.

"As you insert the rod, you very carefully guide it up behind the centre of the ribcage. On its way up, it severs most of the nerves attached to this part of the ribcage."

Strong felt himself wince at the thought of a steel rod scrapping up the inside of his sternum, destroying nerve endings along its destructive path.

"It leaves the victim in a stroke-like, catatonic state, and the hole is almost undetectable, due to the lack of blood loss."

"Jesus Christ, Adam, what have you done? You know I can't turn a blind eye to this, you know I'll have to take you in."

Lewis passed a padded envelope forward to Strong.

"Here, take this."

"What is it?" Strong asked, as he accepted the package.

"It's the evidence you need for your case against Fullerton."

"What evidence?"

"It's a tape recording of Fullerton explaining why that informer was killed."

Strong couldn't believe his luck.

"There's also an empty casing with Fullerton's thumbprint on it. It may have deteriorated over the years but I'm sure your lab boys will get what they need. And, if the slugs that were removed from the body are still around, one of them will fit the casing."

Even without listening to the tape, Strong was confident he had all the evidence he needed to gain a conviction against Fullerton.

"Thanks, Adam," said Strong. "but you know I can't just let you go."

Lewis sighed deeply.

“I thought you’d say that. Here,” Lewis said, as he pushed what felt like a rubber ball into Strong’s hand. “You should have put some gloves on before you took that rod off me, sorry.”

The gravity of the situation soon dawned on Strong.

“It’s really down to your word against mine on what happened in the car. And as it stands, all the evidence points to you, I’m afraid.”

Strong squeezed the balled-up gloves in his hand.

“You do know that . . .”

“Hey, James, before you start going all CSI on me, hear me out.”

“What do you want from me?” Strong asked, reluctantly.

“I’ve done nothing wrong, apart from getting mixed up with this lunatic’s power trips. I once asked for his help to catch the guy responsible for the death of my daughter, but he even used that against me. I just want my life back.”

Strong listened to Lewis’ request with earnest.

“Fullerton has fitted me up for two deaths in the south of Ireland. I need the whole sorry mess cleared up. I’ll give a statement to go with the evidence, but I need the mess in Ireland sorting.”

Strong turned and looked Lewis straight in the face.

“I’ll do my best, Adam, that’s all I can do. Have you got a contact number?”

Lewis’ brow furrowed. “What for?”

“When I’ve let you go, I’ll need to call you to sort out a statement.”

Lewis’ eyes widened. “Have you got a pen?”

Strong reached into his jacket and removed a pen, along with a number of business cards. Turning one over, he wrote down the number recited to him.

“Thanks for these, Adam,” said Strong, holding up the padded envelope. Before climbing out of the car, Strong handed Lewis a business card.

“What’s this for?”

“Keep it, just in case, you never know.”

Strong got out of the car.

“Can one of you call for an ambulance? I think Fullerton has suffered some sort of seizure.”

“Okay. And what about the other man?”

"Don't worry about him. He works for me."
Strong leaned back into the car.
"You're free to go, Adam, but I'll be in touch."

EPILOGUE

The mosque had long since emptied of all those who had attended evening prayers. Al Dulhaimi was locking up a storeroom as the last imam came to bid him goodnight.

A robed figure slipped back into the mosque as the imam headed towards the large entrance hall.

"Is he alone?" the muffled voice asked.

The imam stared into a pair of dark-brown eyes. He wasn't able to make out any other features, due to the face covering the stranger was wearing. The imam lowered his gaze, as he was used to unknown strangers arriving, after prayers, to meet with al Dulhaimi.

"Yes, he is, he should be in his office."

As he walked away from the figure, the imam fell to his knees. A white-hot pain washed over his head, threatening to explode his skull with the sudden, forceful build-up of pressure. Fortunately, the intolerable, numbing pain was short-lived, as it was quickly replaced by the dark oblivion of unconsciousness.

The robed figure moved the unconscious imam into the cleansing room. He positioned him up against a pillar, opposite the sinks. He wasn't expecting the imam to remain unconscious for long, so he had to act fast.

Al Dulhaimi switched off the lights to the main hall. The fire exit signs were the only source of lighting for the large room. He headed for his office, just as the robed figure merged into the shadows around one side of the hall. The figure moved stealthily around the hall, carefully avoiding the odd stack of chairs piled against the wall. He reached the far side and watched al Dulhaimi locking a door before going into his office.

Al Dulhaimi stopped on the threshold of his office, and turned back towards the prayer hall. Was his mind playing tricks on him or did he hear a sound? He stared into the darkness for a moment, before turning and dismissing the noise as the old building settling down after a busy evening. Leaving the office door ajar, he crossed over to a filing cabinet. Outside his window, the evening traffic settled to a steady hum, as the main rush of homebound vehicles was over for another day.

The robed figure crept silently from the darkened hall and down the short corridor towards the crack of light, glowing invitingly from the gap in al Dulhaimi's office door. The rattling sound of metal drawers echoed in the stillness.

Inside the office, al Dulhaimi was now removing a picture from the wall behind the filing cabinet. It revealed a hidden wall safe. He deftly manipulated the dial until the door clicked open. After placing the storeroom key into the safe, al Dulhaimi secured the door.

The robed figure watched as al Dulhaimi replaced the picture. With barely a whisper of movement, the figure glided into the office.

"*As-salamu alaykum*," the figure spoke.

Al Dulhaimi spun around to be confronted by the mysterious, robed figure.

"*Alaikum as-salam*," he replied, not sure if he should be surprised or worried.

"Sit down," ordered the figure.

Al Dulhaimi remained standing. "Who are you?" he asked, with a strong sense of defiance in his voice.

The figure reached into his robe and produced a ceremonial dagger. The blade reflected the light from the ceiling with a menacing glint.

"Sit down!" said the man, with more authority in his voice, and using the dagger to point towards the empty chair behind the desk.

This time, al Dulhaimi followed the order. Slowly moving towards his desk, he lowered himself into the chair. As he did, he moved his right hand down towards the partly-opened bottom drawer.

The robed figure remained standing by the office door. His dark eyes stared menacingly from behind the shemagh that covered most of his face.

Al Dulhaimi's fingers rested on the lip of the drawer, slowly and silently, he worked it open, until the pistol nestled inside was fully exposed.

The robed figure pushed the office door shut then moved across the office towards al Dulhaimi. The seated holy man watched on, with his hand poised over the open drawer. The stranger reached the desk. The dagger he held in one hand reflected the overhead light once more.

***

James Strong's wife handed him a glass of red wine. It was almost 10 o'clock, and having only been home half an hour, Strong wanted nothing more than to unwind after spending another day waiting, inside the Old Bailey courthouse, to give evidence in the on-going trial of a previous operation.

"Is there anything you fancy watching tonight, darling?" Strong asked, taking his usual seat on the corner suite.

"I recorded that new detective series for you, if you want to put that on," his wife replied, curling up on the suite beside her husband.

Strong retrieved the satellite television remote control and scanned through the stored programmes until he found the one he wanted.

His mobile phone started ringing, closely followed by the house phone. Strong sighed, before getting up from his seat and padding over to the sideboard to collect his phone. His wife got up and went to answer the house phone.

"It's for you, James," said his wife, holding out the cordless phone. "It's your office."

"Can you hold on a second?" said Strong into his mobile, as he crossed the room to take the other phone from his wife.

"Hello, Strong?"

"Hello James, it's Hassan. You're not going to believe this."

Strong cut in. "Just give me a moment, I've another caller on my mobile. I'll just get rid of them."

Strong swapped phones. "Hello again, can I help you?"

"It's Adam, I won't keep you long. I just want to thank you for clearing up the Fullerton mess."

"That's okay, Adam, it wasn't too difficult. When someone carelessly gets caught on a security camera on the same day as the shooting, in a place they shouldn't be, and not helping their case by assaulting a police officer, it was easy joining the dots. Look, can I call you back? I have someone on the other line and I really need to take the call."

"That's okay, James, there's no need. I just want to tell you that you won't be hearing from me again. I don't like owing favours; it causes too many problems. Goodbye James, and thanks again for your help," said Lewis.

The line went dead, leaving Strong standing, looking at his mobile, with an expression of puzzlement etched on his face. He put the mobile phone away in his pocket.

"Sorry about that, Hassan. Now, what were you saying?"

"You'll never believe what's happened tonight," he started. "The fire brigade were called to a fire at a mosque in Islington, just after half-past eight tonight. It only turns out to be al Dulhaimi's mosque. Anyway, after extinguishing the fire, they find al Dulhaimi in his office . . ."

Strong interrupted. "He's not dead, is he?"

"No, he's not, but I bet he wishes he was."

"Why, what happened?"

"Well, first off, he's found unconscious in his office, holding a pistol, and second, this is the big one," Falah fought to contain his excitement. "The fire had started in a storeroom. Once it's out, a fireman noticed damage to a back wall. Well, it turns out that the back wall is actually a false wall, hiding a secret room."

"Go on then, what did they find?"

"The department was called by the police and I rushed out to the mosque. It turns out that the secret room was where al Dulhaimi was keeping all his contraband. It's an Aladdin's cave of replica weapons, explosive devices and vest bombs, probably used as training aids, and piles of fundamentalist propaganda paperwork. And that's before we start checking the computer equipment."

"Jesus Christ, are you still at the mosque?"

"Yes, but I'm heading back to the office. I've asked a couple of the techies to take a look at some of the laptops and tablets I'm bringing back. I checked one over at the mosque; the encryption was basic, so it was easy getting into it. What I found is plans linking al Dulhaimi to a number of attacks already carried out, in various countries, and more attacks, also, being planned for some time in the future."

Strong looked across at his wife, who had returned to her seat on the corner suite. His face was beaming.

"Right, Hassan, I'll meet you at the office as soon as I can. Where's al Dulhaimi now?"

"He's under armed police guard in our medical centre. We're not taking any chances."

"Good. Good. I'll see you soon."

"You look pleased with yourself," said Strong's wife, as he returned the cordless phone to its cradle.

"I am, darling, I've just received some fantastic news," said Strong, bowing down to kiss his wife. "I just need to pop back to the office."

As Strong started his car, he thought back to Lewis and his earlier phone call. *What was it he had said about favours?* Something about not wanting to owe anyone again. Surely, he could not be responsible, thought Strong, shaking his head.

He accelerated away from his home with a thin smile forming across his lips.

It matters not how strait the gate,
How charged with punishments the scroll,
I am the master of my fate,
I am the captain of my soul.

William Ernest Henley

18952897R00146

Printed in Great Britain
by Amazon